Sue Minix is a member of Sisters in Crime, and when she isn't writing or working, you can find her reading, watching old movies, or hiking the New Mexico desert with her furry best friend.

Murder *at the* Bookstore

SUE MINIX

avon.

Published by AVON
A division of HarperCollins*Publishers*
1 London Bridge Street
London SE1 9GF

www.harpercollins.co.uk

HarperCollins*Publishers*
Macken House,
39/40 Mayor Street Upper,
Dublin 1
D01 C9W8
Ireland

A Paperback Original 2023

5

First published in Great Britain by HarperCollins*Publishers* 2023

A catalogue copy of this book is available from the British Library.

ISBN: 978-0-00-858462-7

This novel is entirely a work of fiction. The names, characters and incidents
portrayed in it are the work of the author's imagination. Any resemblance to
actual persons, living or dead, events or localities is entirely coincidental.

Typeset in Sabon Lt Std by Palimpsest Book Production Limited,
Falkirk, Stirlingshire

Printed and bound in the UK using 100% Renewable Electricity
at CPI Group (UK) Ltd

This book is produced from independently certified FSC™ paper
to ensure responsible forest management.

For more information visit: www.harpercollins.co.uk/green

*To the one who never left my side
and never lost faith.*

CHAPTER ONE

People watching is a necessary activity for a writer. I gazed out the bookstore's window and studied the passersby. Their movements, their interactions. The expressions on their faces. Are they potential characters? Victims, perhaps? Better yet, killers.

Either way, after two hours plastered to the chair, I squirmed like a kindergartener ready for a nap. Pins and needles, brought on by immobility, constituted cruel and unusual punishment, an appropriate sacrifice to the writing gods. Too bad they weren't appeased today. Or yesterday, for that matter.

The letters on my laptop screen merged, separated, and merged again. The cursor at the end of the last sentence flashed and mocked. Elusive words disappeared into my swampy brain as quickly as will-o'-the-wisps.

The grandfather clock chimed twelve while the Davenport twins stared at the twisted limbs and oddly angled head of their father, splayed face down on the living-room Oriental rug.

Everyone loved the twins in *Double Trouble*, and now I had to come up with a sequel to the smash hit. No point in a successful first novel if you couldn't write a second. However, unlike this one, that book wrote itself. A volcano of words erupted whenever my fingertips touched the keyboard. Turning points and plot twists flowed like lava down a mountainside. Characters swirled through the air like ash and settled in perfect proportions. All of which left me with an agent and a contract for a second book that refused to allow me to write it.

So, what now? How would each of my teenaged detectives react? Dana, strong and reticent, and Daniel, the resourceful social butterfly, often traveled in opposite emotional directions. Shock for both, certainly. Perhaps anger for Dana and tears for Daniel? Perhaps not. Too clichéd. What if Daniel called for help while Dana checked for a pulse? Only, Victor wore the blank stare of death. Okay, call the police, skip the pulse check. Done. Next?

"Jennifer Marie Dawson!"

I snapped my head toward the voice. Aletha's unblemished, dark brown skin highlighted her flawless white smile. "What? Jeez, you scared me. Furthermore, I told you my middle name because you asked, not so you could use it, Aletha Looo-eeez Cunningham."

In a display of coordination I'd never even experienced in my dreams, she settled with a dancer's poise into the seat opposite me and placed a cardboard cup of coffee on the table. "Here's another round. Cream, two sugars, the way you like it."

I hefted it toward my lips, and the picture that always made me smile caught my eye. Aletha in an oversized wingback chair with a tiger-striped kitten asleep in her lap and an open copy of *To Kill a Mockingbird* in her hands. *Ravenous Readers* in cloud letters floated above her head and below: *Books Make the Best Friends.*

"Thank you. You're a lifesaver." Steam tickled my nose, and just one small sip instantly warmed me all the way down. Perfect.

Aletha motioned toward my laptop. "How's it coming?"

"It's not. Mental-pause has commandeered my brain."

"Oh, please, Jen. You're only twenty-eight."

"Maybe, but they're dog years." I waggled my eyebrows, along with an imaginary cigar.

"What's that supposed to be?"

I dropped my jaw. "Don't tell me you've never seen the Marx Brothers."

She took a sip from her cup. "Were they a boy band?"

"They were comedy actors in the thirties. Every time one of their movies came on TCM, Gary made me watch with him."

Aletha wrinkled her nose. "Sounds awful. I'm ten years older than you and never heard of them. Your stepfather was mean."

"It wasn't so bad. Nothing like a little *Monkey Business.* After a while, the old shows he loved grew on me. Besides, the positive time we spent together made it worthwhile."

Her ever-vigilant hazel eyes flicked around the store, then back to me. "No progress?"

"What else is new? Three whole sentences today. It might be a record."

"Hmmm. Three sentences in two hours. It's possible."

I stuck out my tongue, stood, and stretched my arms

overhead. The soft concerto, which emanated from the ceiling speakers, flowed over me. Russell Jeffcoat—friendly and clever with a hint of darkness underneath—poured coffee into the community urn. The bouquet of fresh brew tantalized me the way his mahogany eyes did. My fingers itched to run through his wavy brown hair. I looked away.

A fortyish woman decked out in a pink, orchid-covered sack dress flipped through a book in the Writing section.

Don't do it. Run before it sucks you in!

Aletha had named her new bookstore Ravenous Readers with the hope Riddleton actually had some. She'd lined the walls with hand-hewn cherry bookcases, giving the place the feel of some rich guy's private library. Carved wooden plaques identified genres in alphabetical order from Art to Writing. A nice idea, but maybe she should've left writing out altogether. Only a sadist would encourage someone to put themselves through that kind of torture. Aletha bore no resemblance to a sadist.

Up the middle of the store, she'd arranged tables, surrounded by tufted armchairs, which led to a coffee bar near the back stocked with complimentary regular brew, along with a variety of cappuccinos and espressos priced for regular people. I ogled the pastry case stocked with fresh cookies, muffins, and croissants, courtesy of Bob's Bakery across the street. Nope, not today. Only as a reward for progress. In the front of the store, more tables, and a comfy couch with a couple of wingback chairs covered in a low-key brown-and-gold-striped fabric tempted folks to settle in for a good, long read.

"I love this place." Circulation restored, my bottom

reunited with my well-padded seat. "You've made it personal, not like one of those chain stores." I twirled my not-so-lucky monogrammed pen on the table. "You have a gift for atmosphere, and I can't imagine writing anyplace else. Except, maybe, at home, in my pajamas."

"Thanks, Jen. I hope more people will feel the same way someday."

The Writing woman wandered on, empty-handed, to the Romance section.

Aletha's gaze followed her. "This was always a dream of mine. My old neighborhood didn't even have a library. If even one kid gets hooked on reading, I'll consider it a success. Story Time's getting some attention. We had four children this morning. The most yet."

"Three more than when I fill in for you." I checked out the empty children's section. Child-sized tables and activity zones, along with hundreds of titles selected to satisfy each level of reader, created a safe haven for imaginations to run wild. All nestled under the protective eyes of a pair of life-sized giraffes, which bookended the heading Ravenous Kids painted on the wall in rainbow colors. If I'd had this place to go to as a child, I'd have my tenth book completed by now. "They'll come once word gets around. People in small towns can be weird. It takes them a while to warm up to new things, but once they do, you can't get rid of 'em. That's one of the reasons I left."

Aletha relaxed into her chair. Her fingers massaged the pearl choker around her neck. "Maybe, but you've only been back six months. Things might've changed over the ten years you lived in Blackburn. Sometimes I wonder if I made a mistake."

"I don't think so."

"You're only saying that because you're my friend. I picked this town because I thought, out here in the boonies, people would appreciate one of the advantages of urban life without the hassles of the city. Maybe it was foolish to believe they still love books." She cradled her coffee cup with both hands. "Growing up poor the way I did, reading gave me a way to escape. And hope for a better future. I have my mother to thank for that. We read together every night when I was little." Her eyes glistened.

"You're not foolish at all." I reached across the table and patted her hand. "Business will pick up. Just give it time."

She offered a half-smile and examined her impeccable manicure. "I'm not sure how much time I have. We might not make it until next year's payment."

Next year's payment. "I wouldn't mind winning a writing contest that pays that much." Enough to open a bookstore from scratch and maintain it for five years until it could support itself. I took a large swallow from my cup. With luck, the caffeine would travel straight to my brain.

"The Your Life contest wasn't a real writing competition. Not the kind you might enter. It was an essay contest."

Resting my forearms on either side of my laptop, I inched my untouched how-to-write-something-people-want-to-read book away.

"They make a selection based on what you want to do with the money if you win. I never would've won if they'd judged my writing skills." She took a dainty sip of coffee. "Those people changed my life. Years of running businesses for others, and now here I am, finally doing what I was meant to do. No way that happens without the contest."

"Maybe, but don't be so fast to give up on your dream. You convinced the contest judges how much this meant to you, you'll convince Riddleton." I sent her a crooked smile. "You hooked me, didn't you?"

She jutted her chin toward my laptop. "Good advice. Perhaps you should listen to yourself once in a while. I'm counting on your book signing to bring them here in droves."

"Sorry, I don't have that many friends or relatives. Or the money to bribe them."

"The signings you did for *Double Trouble* brought lots of people in."

"True. I made ten whole dollars off those sales. It paid for lunch, remember? Well, mine, anyway." I flashed my best grin.

With a wink, she stood, and her gray skirt swished at her knees. "You have more friends than you think."

Doubtful. Couldn't worry about it right now, though. A book needed writing.

My latest attempt to memorialize Daniel's reaction to his father's death had fallen prey to my delete key when the bells over the door jangled. Eric O'Malley materialized, resplendent in his navy-blue Riddleton Police Department uniform. He waved to Aletha, sauntered to the coffee urn, and filled a cup.

Eric, a couple of years older than me, had red hair, combined with freckles sprinkled across his pallid cheeks. He reminded me of a third-grader. Take away his standard-issue protective vest, which gave him a chest, and he resembled Opie Taylor in a Barney Fife suit. Hard to believe elementary-school Opie managed to become a police officer. Nevertheless, Eric had graduated the police academy, so either the academy functioned as a Montessori school or he hid his strength well.

I hadn't trusted law enforcement since the FAA investigators determined my father's plane crash had resulted from "pilot error." My mother always said Jack Dawson could fly a bumble bee if its wings were big enough to carry him. No way did he make a mistake. Something else had to have happened, and someday, I would find out what.

Eric was hailed as one of the good guys, though. We became buddies the day he stopped me because my car's muffler roared like a bull moose during mating season. He gave me a warning. Even helped me fix it the next day. "Have duct tape, will travel," he said when he showed up at my door, unexpected, with the large, gray roll.

I held my breath and scrunched in my chair behind my laptop to avoid a rehash of our last conversation: fifteen minutes of Eric determined to convince me running could solve my writer's block problem. Just once, I'd love to meet a man who didn't assume he knew what I needed.

Eric sipped his coffee and his gaze fastened on me. No doubt his calculations included how to restrain me while he shoved running shoes on my feet, without using a Taser.

The back of my neck prickled. I tried to concentrate on my work, while actually listening to Russell's mellifluous voice—smooth, rich, and soothing as honey—entertaining someone in the background.

Who was the person at the counter? I couldn't quite

see from where I was sitting. Not that it was any of my business. My relationship with Russell so far had consisted of a few casual chats, a collision of hands when we both reached for a stirrer at the same time, and lots of covert appraisals by me.

When Eric dropped his empty cup in the trashcan by the door, waved, and went back on patrol, my lungs resumed their function. Mental forehead wipe. Whew! Dodged that conversation for today.

I refocused on Russell, but Aletha's lithe frame appeared between us.

"He's sweet on you."

"What?"

She angled her head toward the door. "You heard me."

I crinkled my nose. "Eric? No way. We're just friends."

Aletha arched one eyebrow.

"Besides, he only wants me to go running with him. With his group, anyway. He says it'll help my writing."

Eric had invited me to join the Riddleton Runners, the three of whom trained for the town 10K next year. He even believed he would win. Possibly, if his cop buddies stopped everyone ahead of him in the race for speeding.

"And?"

"And I'm not going. I'm not a runner." Last time I ran anywhere I'd had too much coffee on an empty stomach. It took two days for my legs to recover. Even worse, Eric wanted me to do it at eight on Saturday morning. Maybe if a psychopath chased me. Then I might break into a trot.

Her eyes sparkled. "Your lack of interest wouldn't

have anything to do with a certain coffee guy we both know, would it?"

Russell passed a ham and cheese croissant to a twenty-something blonde whose shiny hair fell halfway down her back. His smile reached all the way to his visible-from-a-mile-away eyelashes while she giggled at whatever he'd said.

"Perhaps." I pursed my lips. If pressed, I'd describe Russell as a witty charmer, oblivious to the effect he had on people around him. His good looks—more longshoreman than barista—and mischievous smile reminded me of what I'd neglected since my ex-boyfriend Scott had discarded me to take a job in Paris. Loneliness seemed an odd sensation for someone like me, who'd spent most of my life either alone or wishing I was. "Why bother, though? He's not interested."

"You sure about that? Besides, maybe if you go out with him, he'll give up on me."

I lifted my eyebrows. "What do you mean?"

"Forget it. I'm sure it's only my imagination." Aletha picked my pen up off the table. "I might get my husband one of these for Christmas. Where did you get it?"

"Scott gave it to me when *Double Trouble* was published. To bring me luck with the second book." Leave it to my ex-boyfriend to give me a defective lucky charm. He should've just bought me a box of cereal instead. At least, the marshmallows would give me a little enjoyment.

She handed it back to me. "You mind if I take a picture of it? Maybe I can find it online."

"Sure. Go for it." I centered the pen on the table.

Aletha took out her phone and snapped the photo. The bells jingled again. She turned to greet a gray-haired man who held hands with a pigtailed girl, around six or seven years old.

As Aletha squatted to chat with the child, I clipped my pen to the front cover of my how-to book. The cursor on my laptop screen summoned me back to work.

What would Daniel say? Maybe Dana should start. It might work out better.

The grandfather clock chimed twelve while the Davenport twins stared at the twisted limbs and oddly angled head of their father, splayed face down on the living-room Oriental rug.

"Oh my gosh, Daniel, it's Father! What's happened to him?"

Ugh. Highlight, delete. Time to give it a rest.
Add me to the list of one-hit wonders.

Chin in hand, I stared out the window. There were never many people on the street on a Friday afternoon. Riddleton—the best-kept secret on the shore of Lake Dester—had become a bedroom community as more young people relocated from the city to the country. Ironically, the young people who grew up here and then departed for college vowing they'd never return came back when they had kids of their own. Regardless of how big the former stagecoach rest stop in the middle of nowhere grew, though, the small-minded, one-horse-town mentality still suffocated me. I had to get back to the city, where I could fly, without concerns about the naysayers' judgment.

The place wasn't all bad, though. The one-horse-town mentality also included the belief that someone in need was everyone's responsibility. So, while it challenged my

11

sanity when everyone knew everything about my business, if I needed something, help was never more than an outstretched arm away. They had to stay that close so they could hear all the gossip.

I slid my laptop into my messenger bag and gathered the empty cups lined across the table. Shot glasses on a bar for losers. My usual goal consisted of one written page per cup. But today? It was more like one word per cup.

I waved to Aletha, disposed of my trash, and stepped out into the inferno known as a South Carolina autumn, the bag hanging from my shoulder, a weighty reminder of another wasted day.

A shout from behind stopped me in front of the police station, next door to the bookstore.

"Jen! Wait up!"

I swiveled around as my lungs worked overtime to suck in the water-weighted air.

Russell trotted toward me with a book. His biceps strained against his polo shirt sleeves, riveting my attention. "You left this."

My how-to book. *Way to make a good impression, Jen.*

"Thanks, I forgot about it."

His crooked grin glistened in the sun. "No problem."

Heat crept into my cheeks. Why did I turn into a twelve-year-old every time he came into view? With a reply stuck in my throat, I nodded and headed for home, the sidewalk hot enough to melt the rubber soles of my sneakers. Perfect day to spend at the lake. Or wandering around the shopping malls of Blackburn or Sutton, the two cities closest to Riddleton, collecting characters. And expensive things I didn't really need.

I quickly covered the three blocks and climbed the stairs to the second floor of my building. My apartment brought to mind the pictures of the aftermath of Hurricane Hugo, just the way I'd left it. I flung my messenger bag on the couch and dropped the worthless advice book on the coffee table. It rebounded off the clutter onto the carpet. A piece of paper fell out.

Meet me at Antonio's at 8:15 tonight.
Russell

Huh. I might have a reason to stay here after all.

CHAPTER TWO

The scrap of paper quivered between my fingers. Did Russell just ask me out? My mouth went dry. Why didn't he ask me in person? He was a shrinking violet now? He flirted with every female under sixty. Some older if they didn't look it. Was his suave, debonair façade just an act for the public? Maybe, deep down, we had more in common than I thought.

However, visions of my arrival at the restaurant, a perfect meal with conversation that snapped and sparkled, then Russell ghosting me, appeared in quick succession. A silent movie in my head. That did it. No way did I want a handsome, witty distraction from my writing. Yup, I'd tell him that. He didn't need to know about the dread that wrapped itself around my heart whenever I found myself in the same room with him.

Actually, why tell him anything? Maybe the note fell out on my way home. Or, I didn't see it.

Nope, not going.

The crumpled note hit the trash on the first shot. Problem solved. No man would ever hurt me the way Scott had, again.

Although, I had to consider Russell's cheeky grin

when he handed me the book. Those crinkles on either side of his eyes, and the way they reflected the sunlight. The bowling ball in the pit of my stomach when he spoke to another woman.

Who am I kidding? Of course, I'd go.

Or not.

My shoulders sagged, eyelids heavy. A nap might help. My overburdened brain needed a rest.

I stretched out on the couch, and my thoughts wafted like feathers on a breeze. I tossed and turned, too hot or too cold, yet managed to drift into a fitful, dream-filled sleep. My eyes exploded open amid a tirade by my mother, but her words evaporated into the mid-September living-room twilight. A good thing. She never said anything worthwhile in my sleep.

Six thirty. Time to get ready for my date. It seemed I'd decided I was going after all. A straightforward dinner with someone new might reconnect me with the social world, which could bring me back to life. Bring my work back to life.

Or, Russell could shatter my heart into a billion pieces.

In the shower, hot water poured over my shoulders to sluice away my folly. An involvement with Russell would amount to the act of an emotional kamikaze. Still, we'd share a meal, not plan our wedding. What did I have to lose? Besides my favorite place to write?

Nonsense. I wouldn't give up my sanctuary or my friendship with Aletha just because I had a bad date with Russell. Perhaps I could convince Aletha to fire him instead. After she finished laughing at the concept.

Teeth brushed, I tussled with my straight black hair, which declined to cooperate. Even my cowlicks had cowlicks. *Just call me Alfalfa*. My blue-eyed, thin-nosed, pink-cheeked reflection in the mirror stared back at me for three whole seconds. A personal best. Dr Margolis, my shrink, insisted I look myself in the eye to recognize and validate the person inside. My mother taught me about the vanity of such contemplation and to only look in the mirror when necessary. Twenty-eight years of indoctrination had the lead so far. *Thanks, Mom.*

Now, what about clothes? Russell had on khakis and a polo shirt at work, except, since the store closed at eight, he'd have time to change. But the invitation seemed spur of the moment. Would he have anything with him to change into? Probably not. So, something casual. For a date at a nice restaurant? No, he'd expect more. Although, he'd seen me in jeans or shorts and T-shirts pretty much every day and had still asked me out. Perhaps he assumed I'd dress casually. Perhaps not.

Enough. I should look the part. Tonight called for a little black dress. Add pumps and a black patent-leather handbag, which held a smidgen more than my keys, and consider the ensemble complete. If only I could put myself together as well on the inside.

It took three tries to lock the door behind me. My heart raced in a constricted chest.

Forget this.

A mantra Dr Margolis had taught me dropped into my mind. *Deep breath in, slow breath out.*

The influx of oxygen steadied my nerves. A few more deep breaths had me downstairs, ready to hike the three blocks through the finally-beginning-to-cool moist air to Antonio's.

The hardware store, bakery, and drugstore had already closed for the night, which left Main Street near

16

deserted. Only the Piggly Wiggly and Antonio's displayed signs of life. The stores across the street rested in darkness, except for Ravenous Readers, which stayed open late on Friday and had just closed.

Although alone on a nighttime street, I had no apprehension. My experience writing mysteries had taught me people had the capacity to do just about anything, but Riddleton's crime rate neared zero, bolstered only by bored teenaged vandals or shoplifters. Kind of surprising, though, given the town's location. When the engineers built the dam to create Lake Dester, the population grew much less than expected, and Riddleton remained a relatively sleepy little town. Plus, Blackburn and Sutton were just far enough away to keep most of their trouble to themselves.

There was one exception, however. A guy whacked his neighbor with a baseball bat three years ago because the neighbor's dog pooped in his yard. They settled out of court with a handshake and an agreement by the bat-wielder to pay the medical bills. The dog, however, ended up sentenced to life imprisonment within a newly fenced backyard, with no possibility of parole.

As I arrived at the restaurant, Russell, on his way out of the bookstore, held the door for a tall, thin man to enter. Russell nodded to him, stuck his hands into the front pockets of his khakis, and sauntered toward me.

My heart trip-hammered, and I squeezed dents into the almost purse.

The cocky grin he flashed when he stepped onto the curb proved he knew how desirable he appeared.

He scanned me from head to toe. "You clean up pretty good."

"Thank you. Nice jacket."

He'd donned a chocolate-brown sport coat over his Ravenous Readers polo shirt. He brushed imaginary lint off his shoulder. "This old thing? I've had it forever."

"I'll bet." We'd officially had our longest conversation to date. Now what?

After a silent moment, he said, "I see you found my note."

"What note?" He broke into a smile, which made my heart do backflips. I might survive this evening, after all.

I pointed across the street. "Was that Tim who went into the bookstore?"

He peeked back over his shoulder. "Yeah, which is a big surprise."

"True. I've only met him twice, neither time at the store. He doesn't come in very often as far as I can tell. Not his thing, I guess." We strolled the few feet to the door. "Did he tell you about the surprise party, yet?"

"What surprise party?"

Oops. "He's throwing a party for Aletha's birthday next month. I guess he's waiting until we get all the details ironed out before he invites people. He seems like a good guy. I know he loves Aletha, without question."

Russell held the door open for me. "He's all right. A little tiresome, though. All he ever talks about is his sailboat."

We passed into the dining room of Antonio's, and the aroma of fresh bread carried me back to the bakery my father often took me to before he died. The last time I enjoyed a black and white cookie. I choked back the lump in my throat and immersed myself in the gentle murmur of couples, families, and Nana's ninetieth birthday party, as displayed on a banner draped across the back of the room.

Italian dinner music played as a hostess in a black vest with Antonio's embroidered on it in red led us through the romantic glow of Tiffany ceiling lights to a table for two. Good thing I went with the LBD.

I rested my purse on a real tablecloth—no red and white checkerboard plastic in Tony Scavuto's place—and we settled into our seats. A crystal vase filled with fresh snapdragons rested between us, flanked by two glasses of water. I hadn't dined in an upscale restaurant since Scott and I had celebrated the fifth anniversary of our first date—a month before he accepted the job in Paris.

The hostess supplied us with leather-bound menus and disappeared to retrieve the bottle of wine Russell ordered. The menu shook in my hands, so I propped it against the table.

A woman whose skin-tight sequined dress screamed more Monte Carlo than Riddleton stopped at our table. "Hi, Jen. I loved your book."

Heat rose into my cheeks. Would I ever get used to this? "Thank you."

"Can't wait to read the next one. Those twins are marvelous. How much longer do you think it'll be?"

Sometime between next week and never. "It's coming along. You can't rush the process, you know."

"I know, but hurry, okay?" She showed me every one of her thirty-two pearly whites and shimmied away.

I smiled at Russell and locked my teeth together so tension wouldn't twist it into a grimace. What had he said? Oh yeah, something about Tim and his sailboat. I opened my mouth and my jaw cracked. "I take it you have no interest in sailing?"

"It's not that. Tim's obsessed with it. One afternoon, he spent an hour telling me about the properties of new rope and how it stretches when it gets wet, if it's not synthetic. I wanted to hang myself. He never noticed my eyes rolling back into my head." Russell sipped his water. "At the very least, he should've given me a merit badge for sitting through the whole lecture."

"I agree." It had to be a bad scene if Russell complained about it; he loved conversations with people. Tim had never seemed self-absorbed to me. The night I had dinner with them, he doted on Aletha, supporting her ideas about the bookstore and ensuring her wineglass never emptied. Then the day we'd discussed Aletha's party at the diner, he'd focused entirely on her happiness. Clearly, Russell didn't share Tim's interests, though. "How about two badges. One for boat safety and one for knot tying."

His smile made his eyes twinkle in the lamplight. "Definitely! Did you know Tim insisted on using some of Aletha's prize money to buy the sailboat and the house? The payment was supposed to go into the store. When I asked her if she enjoyed sailing, her eyes bulged like a Pekingese puppy's. I changed the subject before they popped out."

Aletha kept her secrets well. Guess it was safe to assume Russell wouldn't be escorting Tim to the prom this year. And Tim wouldn't be taking Russell sailing anytime soon. I couldn't fault Russell for being protective of Aletha, though. However, which one of us was wrong about Tim?

"She never told me."

A waiter poured our wine and we placed our orders: chicken parmesan and spaghetti for me, linguini with clam sauce for him. I sipped the white Moscato, which I'd never tasted before. An excellent choice. Sweet enough and it didn't come in a box. I lifted my glass in a silent toast to my new favorite wine. The alcohol reduced the tremor in my hands from six point eight to four point three on the Richter scale.

Russell tasted his drink. "Aletha told me, in Tim's mind, the contest was about wishes, so he wanted his fulfilled, too. She tried to make him understand the hundred-and-fifty-thousand-dollar-a-year prize money payout had to go into the business. He pouted like a three-year-old and she relented. They made down payments on both the house and boat so she'd have enough left to open the store."

I took another sip from my glass. Apparently, Aletha wasn't as forthcoming with me as I was with her. "What a shame. Aletha never said a word to me about any of this."

"She broke down and told me one day after they'd had a big fight. Otherwise, I wouldn't know either." He grinned. "On the bright side, if he hadn't bought a boat, I wouldn't have my merit badges."

"Very true. Were you a Boy Scout?"

He pinched his lips into a line. "No. My father didn't believe in stuff like that. And, we moved around a lot while he climbed the corporate ladder."

Scott had also moved around a lot as a military brat. Consequently, commitments weren't his thing. A hard lesson for me to learn. My next mouthful of wine didn't taste quite as sweet. "How did you end up here?"

He rearranged the napkin in his lap and clenched his jaw. "I needed to get away from my father. Live my own life without him trying to control every aspect of it."

Russell refilled my wineglass and I took another gulp, which sledgehammered my gullet. Some food had better show up soon. I reached for my water, caught the lip of the tumbler, and almost knocked it over.

He studied me over the rim of his own glass. Perhaps calculating how much difficulty he'd have if he had to carry a sozzled me to his car. Poor guy, I'd gained some weight in the last few months.

Luckily, the waiter returned with our salads and rolls.

Bread buttered, greens slathered in vinaigrette, we ate in silence until Russell considered me with his last forkful of lettuce halfway to his mouth. "I've been doing all the talking so far. Let's talk about you for a while."

Let's not. "There isn't much to tell."

"I'll start with something easy. How did you become a writer?"

My water went down the wrong way, and I coughed. Deep, racking coughs.

The waiter brought our dinner and held the plates until I regained control.

My cheeks blazed, as did my ears. Slinking under the table into a little ball crossed my mind. I took another sip of water and nodded to our server.

He set the food down. "Are you all right?"

"Yes, thank you." I'd bet Russell would never want to see me again, and nobody would blame him. I was surprised he hadn't walked out, yet. Scott might have toward the end of our relationship, when he'd become so irritable. He'd given up on us months before he left. Nice of him to tell me.

"Good," the waiter said. "I couldn't remember a

single thing from the Heimlich poster we have hanging in the kitchen."

Alcohol-induced laughter made my ribs hurt, and my breath hitched into hiccups. Russell stared for a moment, then joined in until tears streamed down his face. The waiter smiled, red-faced, and backed away. People at tables around us, including the chief of police, Tobias Vick, and his wife Anne-Marie, chuckled too, although they couldn't have known why. *Hope he doesn't call the men in white coats to take me away.* Even some of the kitchen staff peeked through the swinging doors to check out the fuss.

The merriment tapered off the same way it began: table by table. I stared at my food and willed the warmth in my face to subside. Russell sat back in his chair, arms crossed, and a half-smile creased his full lips.

What do I do now? Make some lame excuse? Pretend nothing happened? Could work. "So, what were we talking about?"

"I believe we were talking about you."

Not the response I'd expected. Scott would've had something nasty to say about my behavior. Maybe a relationship with Russell could turn out better, after all. Not that I was ready to even think about that, yet.

I took a gigantic swig of wine and recounted my father's death and my mother's subsequent remarriage. Then, a little about my years with stepfather Gary, which Russell punctuated with comments and questions that I sidestepped like a running back streaking toward the end zone. We'd have plenty of time later for all of that.

We ate and drank and laughed. Two hours seemed to have passed in about fifteen minutes. I had way too much wine, and Russell matched me glass for glass. But, unlike me, he showed no ill effects. The Tiffany lamps whirled above my head, and I ordered my queasy stomach to maintain control. It worked, for the moment. No way to know what five more minutes might bring.

When the restaurant emptied, busboys put the chairs on tables. Russell paid the check, and we stepped into the moonlit chill. He insisted he'd escort me home, and I rested my hand in the crook of his arm. He leaned in to kiss me. I jerked back and thrust him away.

Russell stumbled but maintained his footing. He flushed. "I'm sorry. It's too soon. I just—"

"It's okay, I'm sorry. I don't know what came over me." Not true. The wreckage Scott had left behind had more than a little to do with it.

He ran his fingers through his wavy hair. "It's my fault."

"No, really. I shouldn't have pushed you." I turned away to avoid his gaze.

Over Russell's shoulder, lights still blazed in Ravenous Readers. Inside, Aletha and Tim sat at a window table. The store had closed hours ago; why were they still there?

Russell turned to see what had seized my attention. Aletha frowned and pointed her finger at Tim. When he reached for her hand, she yanked it away and stood, knocked her chair over, and stormed into her office. It seemed I was the one wrong about Tim.

CHAPTER THREE

A bladder call woke me at six on Saturday morning, my tongue stuck to the roof of my mouth. Nothing compared to the hailstorm in my head. How much did I drink last night? Enough that my memory failed me. A hot ball in my gut suggested I root for the amnesia. The last time I drank that much, I dumped a pitcher of beer on myself at a frat party and won a wet T-shirt contest nobody else participated in. Or so I'd heard. It took months to live it down.

I stumbled to the bathroom with a bottle of Tylenol in one hand and a tube of Crest in the other. Tidbits of dinner with Russell surfaced. Splashes of Tim, Scott, Aletha, and lots of wine. And laughter? Aletha had argued with Tim. What was that about? Should I ask her? Nah, she'd never tell me.

The rest hovered out of reach, snagged in the mire coating my brain. I vacillated between a need to know what I'd done and relief I had no idea. For now, relief led by a nose.

I swallowed a few capsules of pain reliever with a bottle of water, which knocked my headache back to a tolerable level. I loaded the coffee maker and fired up my laptop for another round of writing roulette, although the odds of a winning number came close to a million to one. However, the work on the fictional whodunit might take my mind off the real-life mystery of what I'd done, or hadn't done, last night.

By the time the Davenport twins reappeared on-screen, optimism had become my word of the day. My writer's block would collapse under my powerful mental sledge-hammer. It had to. If I didn't break through soon, my old pattern would reassert itself. I'd come too far to get discouraged and give up now.

The grandfather clock chimed twelve while the Davenport twins stared at the twisted limbs and oddly angled head of their father, splayed face down on the living-room Oriental rug.

My fingertips hovered over the keyboard, poised, waiting for brilliance to present itself. Two minutes later... I was still waiting. Random thoughts floated through my mind like soap bubbles, which collided, then popped out of existence in an endless cycle. Why did I sign that stupid contract anyway? This second book might buy me a one-way ticket to the funny farm.

What was that noise in the kitchen? A mouse? Never mind, it was the icemaker.

Focus.

Five more minutes...

How did I get home last night? Walk? Did Russell drive me home? Did he come in? Did we...? Nah, I'd have figured that out by now. Wouldn't I?

Caffeine.

The wait for coffee struck me like having to stand

in line for the bathroom with a Big Gulp-filled bladder. I poured the piping-hot brew into my "Creativity Begins with Coffee" mug and returned to my desk to stare at the screen some more.

Where's my lucky pen? That would fix it.

I searched the desk, the coffee table, the floor, and my messenger bag. No luck. The pen had disappeared. Just like the guy who gave it to me.

Forget it. It hadn't helped much, anyway.

Back to work.

Was that a fly by the window? No, it was a mosquito. The new guy moved in downstairs yesterday. I'd have to go introduce myself later. Brittany said he was a banker or a lawyer or something.

FOCUS!

An hour and three cups later, I glared at the screen while my right leg bounced nonstop. Obviously, creativity *didn't* begin with coffee. Not today, anyway. Time to concede defeat. Almost seven thirty, and any progress I'd made involved my headache, which, after another bottle of water, had all but disappeared. However, what to do with all this excess energy?

I could clean my apartment.

Nope. Not gonna happen.

I paced from living room to bedroom and back. Deep breaths forced oxygen into my brain, and the mental fog thinned into a haze.

More deep breaths…

What if Eric had a point about exercise?

No way. I didn't run. Would never run. My two left feet were all thumbs. I'd fall and hurt something. Or someone. What a crazy idea.

Crazier than staring at a computer screen all morning?

Yes, well… maybe. *For Pete's sake!*

I'd need an EpiPen for my exercise allergy. However, my current writing plan didn't work.

Oh, what the hell. It couldn't get any worse—could it?

At a quarter to eight, my feet dragged me downstairs for the two-block walk to meet Eric, along with the rest of his cult. I'd lost my ever-lovin' mind.

A couple peered in the window of Bob's Bakery, known for its egg and cheese croissants and overfilled donuts. They were the only people on Main Street while the sun burned off the morning mist. The temperature remained tolerable, but humidity added ten degrees, so sweat blossomed on my forehead. An impulse to turn left toward the bookstore grabbed me. To turn toward Russell.

Russell. His half-closed eyes.

Oh my gosh, I'd pushed him! He'd tried to kiss me, and I'd shoved him away. My best first date ever, now maybe the last.

When would I learn? Maybe I had a worse allergy to relationships than exercise.

Concentrate on something else.

My stomach dropped as I passed the 1940s A-frame houses on either side of Park Street. My childhood had been spent in a similar neighborhood on the other side of town.

I thrust away the memory. I'd escaped and would never go back.

About a hundred yards past Second Street stood a wrought-iron arch. Riddleton Park. Two people jogged in place beside a fence.

Last chance to turn around.

Eric waved. "Hey, Jen! I didn't expect to see you here."

Too late.

"I didn't expect to be here."

His baggy green running shorts and red Riddleton Jackrabbits tank top hung from his reedy frame. Maybe he'd grow into them one day.

Eric gestured to a short, rotund man beside him, in gray sweatpants with a matching sweatshirt long enough to double as an evening dress. "Do you know Angus?"

"I've seen you in the diner." I stuck out my hand. "Jen Dawson."

Rather than shake my hand, he just held it in his warm, moist one. "Our resident writer. I loved your book so much, I read it three times." He bowed.

My cheeks flushed. For a second, I'd expected him to kiss my hand. Or ring. Good thing I hadn't worn one.

"Angus Halliburton, proprietor of the Dandy Diner, at your service, ma'am."

A snicker bubbled up, but his earnest gaze made me bite my lip and try for a curtsy, except I caught my foot on my opposite calf. My leg buckled. I grabbed for his sweatshirt, missed, and hit Angus in the belly. He doubled over, and knocked me sideways into a stone bench. Air expelled from my lungs in a grunt Porky Pig would be proud of, and pain shot through my ribs. *Smooth move, Jen.*

Eric leaped to help me back to my feet. A knight in baggy gym shorts. I took a tentative breath and massaged my side.

Sir Eric peered at me. "Are you okay?"

I nodded, desperate to avoid his concerned expression. "Sorry, I'm such a klutz. It's pretty typical, though."

Angus straightened, chuckling, and the red drained out of his face. "I'm glad you came. What made you change your mind?"

"I figured I had nothing to lose but my dignity, and I took care of that, so check it off the list. However, it doesn't mean I'm going to stay."

Eric flashed his Opie smile. "Sure you will, you'll see. You're gonna love it."

Like a trip to the dentist. "I'll be happy just to survive it."

Angus chuckled. "I felt the exact same way when I started." He patted his ample midsection. "Look at me now. Don't I remind you of Usain Bolt?"

He reminded me more of a Weeble than an Olympic sprinter. I tugged at the neck of my black T-shirt.

"What on earth do you have on your feet?" Eric galloped in to save the day. Again.

I glanced at my beloved, well-worn Nikes. "What do you mean?"

"Those things are going to kill you. You have to get some decent running shoes."

He lifted one of his spindly, yet muscular, legs to showcase a red and white sneaker. No flashy logo, but I'd bet he'd invested a ton of money in them. "You see these? They're top-of-the-line running shoes. Reebok Floatride Run Fast, designed for speed."

I angled my foot to the side. "You see these? Nike, I have no idea what model, designed for comfort."

"You should let him pick you out some shoes." Angus pointed to his own feet. "He recommended these for me, and I love them."

Nike, same as mine. "What's so special about yours? That's what I'm wearing."

"Not quite," Eric said. "His are running shoes. Yours are... well, I don't know what yours are. Or, used to be."

Okay, so he was a pompous knight. Maybe this idea should've landed on the scrap heap. My fragile ego had taken two hits already, with more to come no doubt. Besides, why did I need new shoes for a one-time event?

Angus knelt to retie his shoe. "Was that you I saw in Antonio's last night with Russell from the bookstore?"

I looked away and smoothed my hair down at the sides. "It was. Nice place."

He stood and lowered his voice. "You should be careful with that guy."

"Why?"

"He's not what he seems to be."

I edged away from him. "What are you talking about?"

"He's filthy rich. At least, his father is, and he wanted Russell to marry his business partner's daughter. Russell refused, so Daddy cut him off without a cent. That's why he's working in the bookstore."

Eric cocked his head. "What's wrong with that?"

"Nothing. However, I don't want to see Jen get hurt when Daddy changes his mind and Russell scampers back to him."

Funny he never mentioned any of that last night. "Thanks for your concern, Angus," I said. "But we've only had one date. I don't think there's anything to worry about."

Angus pulled at his earlobe. "Maybe you're right. After all, he did save little Jimmy Peterson's puppy from

31

getting run over the other day. The silly beagle ran to greet Jimmy getting off the school bus, and Russell snatched it out from under the tire as the bus was pulling away. A selfish rich guy wouldn't have done that."

Eric clapped his hands together. The last breeze I would encounter all day. "We ready to get this party started?"

"What about Lacey?" Angus asked.

"She has to work."

I propped my foot on the bench to retie my sneaker. Loose laces would add to the likelihood I'd end up on the ground at some point. And a great way to delay the inevitable. "Who's Lacey?"

Angus jiggled his legs and rotated his arms. "Lacey Stanley, our third musketeer. You must've seen her at the bookstore. She helps out there once in a while."

The one who rivaled Aletha in her knowledge of books. Good thing she took the day off. She might've asked me about my progress with mine. Plus, she'd be the one Riddleton Runner I could still look in the eye come Monday.

Eric pointed toward the park. "C'mon, let's get warmed up."

We gathered inside the gate and stretched. Well, they did, anyway. My legs proved as flexible as the pine trees dropping cones on the ground. I breathed in pine-scented air, absorbed the serenity, and ignored the squeals from my lower body.

Angus and I set off together down the mile-long asphalt track around the park's perimeter, while Eric ran circles around us like a vulture waiting for one of us to die. It took all my willpower to not stick my foot out to trip him when he orbited us for the fifth time.

With my lungs filled to the brim, I turned to Angus. "Does he always do this?"

He rocked his head back and forth. His combover flopped like a mouse caught in a trap. "He's trying to stay with us and still get some exercise. He runs with Lacey. She was a track star in high school and started running again after her second kid. They're pretty well matched."

I focused on the accumulation of enough oxygen to stay conscious.

"It's nice to have someone to run with," Angus puffed. "Especially somebody famous."

Not for long. "Thanks, but that's an exaggeration."

"Oh, no. I know lots of people who've read your book. They all loved it."

"That's nice to hear. Thank you." Somebody stabbed a knife into my ribs, and I became a victim in someone else's mystery. Doubled over, hands on my knees, I panted. "You go... I'm resting... for a minute."

Eric stopped mid-circle and placed his hand on my back. "It's a stitch. You've overstretched your ligaments." He stuck his fingers below my ribs and pushed against the pain. "Breathe evenly. In and out, nice and slow."

I followed orders as if he'd given me a breathalyzer test.

He breathed with me. His sweat dripped off his forehead onto my shoulder for about a minute. Gross, but effective.

The pain subsided. "Thanks."

"My pleasure."

My instincts encouraged me to quit while behind,

but I had to continue. I'd once claimed I'd try anything to break my writer's block. Not quite what I had in mind at the time, but this needed to work because my writing career depended on it. Although, ten years stuck behind a desk so I'd one day *have* a writing career may have contributed to my difficulties to begin with.

The stitch struck two more times, but thanks to lessons learned from Eric's invasion of my personal space the first time it happened, I jabbed my hand into my belly fat each time to ease it. Despite many pit stops, I managed to get all the way around the track. Once. A whole mile. Time to stop or risk permanent damage to my body. Too late for my self-esteem.

Eric and Angus jogged in place and waved.

I mustered enough energy to flap my hand in their direction.

Escape through the arch was almost within reach when Angus called, "Hey, Jen! When's the new book coming out?"

I plastered a smile on my face, gave him a double thumbs-up, and shuffled out of the park. My leg muscles ached. And my feet, but I'd never tell Eric my shoes had failed me. My mind coasted along and random pictures flew willy-nilly through my brain. Russell smiled at me over his wineglass. Aletha teased me about my writer's block. I stared at my laptop screen for hours on end.

Staring at my laptop screen.

That's it!

Ideas, prose, and dialogue flooded in. I had to get home.

I hobbled faster, reached my building in a few minutes,

and pulled myself up the stairs, hand over hand. Pain stabbed through my thighs with each step.

Brittany Dunlop came out of her apartment on her way to work, decked out in her favorite blue librarian frock, sensible shoes, and oversized glasses. A perfect mix of intelligence and sensitivity. Luck had created a vacancy in the apartment opposite Brittany's. We'd momentarily considered living together, but Ms Neat-As-A-Pin in an apartment with me, Daisy Disaster, would end our lifelong friendship.

She raised her eyebrows. "Who did this to you?"

I collapsed on the top step. "Would you believe I did? Running in the park."

Brittany pushed several flyaways from her shoulder-length blonde hair behind her ear. It always poofed out in places as if she'd just stepped out of a wind tunnel. "Who was chasing you?"

"Nobody! Well, there was a cop trying hard not to catch me."

"I don't believe you." Her wide smile created creases beside her pale-blue eyes.

"Eric suggested it to cure my writer's block, and believe it or not, I think it worked. My laptop is calling. Gotta go."

Brittany swiped at another loose hair, which infiltrated her mouth. "I still don't believe you. I haven't seen you run since high-school gym class. Even then, you stopped every time Ms Ferguson wasn't looking."

"Aren't you going to be late for work?"

"The kids'll wait. They love me."

"Well, don't let me keep you. I have a chapter to finish." I shoved myself upright, thighs screaming, and inserted my key into the lock.

"Go while it's still fresh in your mind. I get off at noon, so I'll pick you up around twelve thirty."

I turned back to her. "Pick me up?"

"To drive out to my parents' house for lunch."

Brittany's parents lived in a small cottage on an undeveloped section of Lake Dester. Long dirt roads, pine trees, and spectacular views awaited me. No place else I'd rather be.

Except, I'd forgotten.

"Right. I'll be ready."

I closed the door and made a beeline to my desk to get the ideas out while still fresh in my mind. My laptop keys groaned under the weight of a thousand words, pouring out of me the way they had when I wrote *Double Trouble*. The twins had joined my team again.

About to type word one thousand and one, the afternoon trip reasserted itself.

Oops, forgot again.

My joints creaked when I stood. I waddled in a brilliant imitation of *Gunsmoke*'s Festus, to the bathroom for a shower. My lower extremities had stiffened into pillars, and it took two hands to lift my legs, one at a time, into the tub. *Where's Matt Dillon when you need him?*

I'd surmounted the challenge of the shoelaces seconds before Brittany knocked, right on time. I could set my watch by her, if I had one. I grabbed my keys and opened the door. "Here I am."

She'd changed into a flowered silk blouse and brown pants. My polo shirt and jeans jarred like a stick figure next to the *Mona Lisa*. Good thing that kind of stuff didn't matter to me.

Brittany tipped her head to the side. "What a nice surprise. I don't have to wait for once."

"Yup. But, you know, some things are worth waiting for."

"True, but what does that have to do with you?"

I clutched my chest. "Ouch! Brittany Dunlop, you are no longer my best friend."

"Yeah, like anyone else would have you."

True. When our kindergarten teacher's alphabetical seating chart put us next to each other, Dawson and Dunlop became friends for life. I hadn't made many more since then, introvert that I tended to be. Aletha had become one of them, though.

We strolled to the parking area, my legs stiff but usable. The airborne moisture sucked the oxygen out of my lungs. "Do you want me to drive?"

"No way. I want to live."

"Hey! I'm a great driver." I poked out my lower lip.

"If you say so. Although, the possum you almost hit last month might disagree."

"I missed him, didn't I? There's your proof of what a good driver I am." I threw an arm around her shoulders. "Besides, I'd never seen a live one before. I was startled."

We climbed into her blue Chevy Cruze and took off for the other side of the lake.

Our trip to Brittany's parents' lake house turned into a long, relaxing afternoon, which included a surprise visit by Russell. Apparently, at some point in my drunken stupor, I'd invited him. I still had no memory of it, though. He showed up with his boyish grin and a bouquet of pansies, violas, and mums, and my discomfort sailed away on the breeze. The Dunlop family was welcoming as always, simply because he was a friend of mine.

The day ended at my desk in front of my laptop.

I'd pounded out a couple thousand words when a knock on the door broke my concentration. Someone here in the middle of the night?

Wait. Sunlight peeked through the gap between the balcony door curtains. The clock at the bottom of my laptop screen read 8:02 a.m. *Holy crap.*

I pried myself out of my chair and staggered to the door on stilts. Brittany had better have coffee with her to show up this early.

I took a habitual glance through the peephole. A dark-haired man in dark-rimmed glasses raised a gold badge. A real one, from what I could tell through the wrong end of a telescope. A cop here on a Sunday morning? Wrong apartment, unless they sent detectives to collect on unpaid parking tickets.

I rubbed my bleary eyes, opened the door, and not one, but two stone-faced cops stared back at me.

My voice cracked. "Stan Olinski? I didn't think I'd ever see you at my door, again." My high-school boyfriend hated me because I'd moved to Blackburn for college instead of staying here to play Little Jenny Homemaker married to him. I couldn't blame him for being upset at the time, we'd dated all four years, but it had been ten years since graduation, and he still held a grudge. Not cool.

A younger woman—so starched and pressed she resembled a human ironing board—stood two feet behind Olinski, whose rumpled clothes proved he'd never heard of one. No surprise there.

Olinski slid his glasses up. "Police business. We need to talk to you, Jen."

My muscles tensed beneath my Pat Benatar T-shirt. "What's going on?"

He gestured toward the ironing board. "This is Detective Havermayer. We want to ask you a few questions. May we come in?"

Someone's hurt. Icy fingers marched down my spine. I shivered despite the warm air drifting through the doorway.

"Questions about what?" My voice wavered, and I blinked my gritty eyes way too much. A deep breath brought back my normal tone. "What's going on?"

"It'll only take a few minutes of your time."

Okay, he's in professional cop mode. No point in asking any more questions. I stepped aside.

Havermayer patrolled the partitioned box, otherwise known as my home. She observed everything and touched nothing, like a visitor at the Guggenheim. Tiny jackhammers went to work on my stomach. I tried to follow both detectives, but they traveled in opposite directions.

"We need to talk to you about Aletha Cunningham." Olinski fixed his gaze on me.

My brain froze. "Aletha?" That was the last thing I expected. My neighbor Charlie, sure. He could've done anything. Vandalism, shoplifting, even public nudity. Aletha on the other hand... I rubbed a stress tic under my left eye. "Is she all right?"

I relocated a pile of clean towels to the coffee table to make room for Olinski on the floral-print couch saved from death by suffocation in my mother's basement. He continued to stand. I opened the curtains over the balcony doors.

Havermayer cleared her throat, which pierced the silence like fingernails on a chalkboard inside a cement mixer. She leaned against my bedroom doorjamb with her arms folded across her chest, dark eyebrows raised, not a sandy-blonde hair out of place.

What's with this woman?

My glance ping-ponged between the two detectives. "Is Aletha in trouble?" Stupid question. No way Aletha had legal problems.

Olinski spoke first. "I think you should sit down, Jen."

I clenched my fists. "I don't want to sit down. Tell me what's happening."

"I regret to inform you Mrs Cunningham has died."

CHAPTER FOUR

It felt like a mule had kicked me in the chest. "No."

Olinski's voice softened, gaze steady on my face. "I'm sorry for your loss."

"You must be mistaken." I lowered myself into the cracked leather recliner purchased from the Goodwill down the street. "I saw her Friday night. She was fine."

He shifted his feet, arms loose by his sides.

I dug my fingers into the chair's arms, which drove all the blood out of my knuckles. "What happened?"

"There was an explosion on her husband's sailboat yesterday afternoon."

"The boat exploded?" A dense fog rolled through my head. Aletha had died. Killed on a boat I'd heard she'd never step foot on. Not alone, that's for sure. "What about her husband?"

"He was in the house."

The kitchen offered an escape from the scenario that couldn't possibly be true. My thigh muscles vibrated from knees that struggled to hold me upright. An old Ravenous Readers cup sat on the counter and the image of Aletha smiled at me. Her flecked eyes danced in amusement.

My heart bounced off my breastbone. A sharp pain spread to my neck.

Deep breath in, slow breath out.

I spoke over the half-wall, which separated the two rooms. "Do you want some coffee?"

Olinski slid his hands into his pants pockets. "No, thank you. Are you okay?"

Since when did he care?

Deep breath in, slow breath out.

"Fine." Anything but fine.

My heart rate slowed, and the pain dulled to an ache. I reached for the coffeepot, but I'd left it on overnight. Auto shut-off had failed again and burned sludge coated the bottom. I took a Mountain Dew out of the refrigerator instead and wiped the condensation off the can onto my gray sweatpants, which made me shudder. Whether from the cold or the news, I couldn't tell.

Deep breath in, slow breath out.

Olinski broke my concentration. "Jen?" He pulled a tattered notebook from his creased jacket and perched on the edge of the couch as if he might catch a disease from the thing. "Let's get started."

I staggered back into the living room. My legs buckled, and I collapsed into the recliner.

His words echoed in my ears, but didn't quite drown out the sounds of Havermayer, who puttered around in my bathroom.

Why was she searching my apartment? "Can I help you with something, Detective Havermayer?" I asked.

No response.

"Do you need a minute?" Olinski asked, to draw my attention back to him. Or maybe to distract me from Detective Starchy.

Havermayer migrated to the kitchen, where she started to rummage around. Open cabinet, close cabinet. Open cabinet, close cabinet.

Could she search those without a warrant? Whatever. I had nothing to hide.

"No, I'm okay."

"All right, then." He scribbled something in his book.

I focused on the sunlit treetops, visible through the balcony door, to help me hide the pools of tears in my eyes. *Big girls don't cry.*

Olinski scrutinized me. His furrowed brow matched his wrinkled suit. "Tell me about your relationship with Aletha Cunningham."

"Um... we met when she opened Ravenous Readers." My voice crumbled.

He waited.

With a wobbly hand, I sipped my drink and spilled a drop on Pat Benatar's nose. "I went to the bookstore to write. Sometimes we'd drink coffee and talk. We became friends."

Deep breath in, slow breath out.

Detective Havermayer abandoned her search and shook her head once. Olinski nodded.

Whatever she was looking for, I could've told her she wouldn't find it.Olinski cleared his throat. "What kinds of things did you talk about?"

I kneaded the back of my neck and pressed the tension down into my shoulders. What didn't we talk about? She moved me to reveal thoughts I'd never told anyone. I trusted her. "Books mostly. Nothing significant." Even with my past relationship with him, I didn't trust Olinski, or Havermayer. He'd changed, and she made my skin feel a size too small.

Havermayer jumped in. "You were in there more or less every day. She must've shared a personal story once in a while."

How did she know I was in there every day?

"We talked about the usual stuff. Our childhoods, our families. The weather. The contest. Whatever came to mind."

"What about the contest?"

"Family and friends showed up after she won. An ex-boyfriend resurfaced. That's all." Was that what she wanted to hear? I didn't know anything about Aletha's death.

"That would be..." Olinski flipped through several pages in his notebook. "Marcus Jones?"

"I don't know. Aletha never mentioned his name, only said an old boyfriend texted her out of the blue after he saw her on TV."

"How would you describe her marriage?" Olinski asked.

I crossed my arms. "She said Tim was the best thing that ever happened to her." Although, Russell had made it clear the other night he didn't share that opinion.

Olinski lifted his lips in a half-grin. "Sometimes money transforms relationships. Not necessarily for the better."

What a jerk. He *had* changed.

"Aletha came from nothing. She understood there were more important things than money."

"Did he?" He studied a point over my head. "Did Mrs Cunningham ever indicate she might be afraid of someone?"

"No, and I'd remember that." I squirmed in my seat. "You don't think it could've been an accident?"

"We don't have enough information yet, but the circumstances surrounding her death are concerning."

Concerning? What did that mean?

Deep breath in, slow breath out.

I pulled my legs underneath me. "Who would want to kill Aletha?"

"That's why we're talking to everyone who knew her. Maybe you can help us." Olinski pulled his phone out of his pocket and swiped a couple of screens. He turned it toward me. "Can you explain this?"

The screen displayed a picture of an inscribed title page of *Double Trouble*.

Three things I'd kill for:
love, money, and a bestselling novel.
Love, Jen

"It's what I wrote in Aletha's copy of my book. We were brainstorming the second one. Talking about what it might take to turn us into killers. It doesn't mean anything."

He stared at me. "Did Mrs Cunningham ever mention any marital problems?"

"Not to me. I heard she was unhappy about the sailboat. Also, they might've had a disagreement the other night, but I can't be sure."

Actually, I'd never seen Aletha so angry. Before their fight, I'd had the impression she had a perfect home life, her husband the savior of an otherwise humdrum existence. Before she won the contest, of course. The interaction I'd observed bore no resemblance to a conversation between savior and saved. Perhaps Tim wanted to buy something else they couldn't afford.

45

Havermayer crossed her ankles. "What makes you believe that?"

"I saw them in the bookstore Friday evening, when I left Antonio's. They appeared to be arguing." How did I remember that when I'd forgotten almost everything else?

Olinski crossed his arms. "What made you think so?"

I rubbed a hand over my face. "They were sitting by the window and Tim tried to take her hand, but she pulled away. Then she got up and marched into her office."

Havermayer rested her elbows on her thighs. "Did they fight a lot?"

Late to the party as usual, my inner mystery writer joined the conversation. "You think Tim killed his wife?" The husband was always the first suspect.

"Why do you say that?"

"It's how things work on every cop show I've seen."

Olinski slid his glasses back up on his nose, again. "Answer the question, please. Did they fight a lot?"

My antenna went up. Did they think I'd help them railroad Aletha's husband? It had to be an accident. Why would Tim want to kill Aletha? "She never mentioned it, if they did. I assumed it was just a marital spat. Look, I've told you everything. I have no idea about their relationship behind closed doors."

Sunlight streamed through the balcony straight into my head. The ache in my chest relocated to a spot behind my eyes. I wanted to close the curtains, but nausea changed my mind.

"How well do you know Tim Cunningham?" Olinski asked.

"Not well. We've met a few times, but that's all."

Havermayer gawked at me as if I embodied a species of slug she'd never seen before. "You sure?"

"Yes, I'm sure."

She leaned forward. "Would it surprise you to learn we've heard you and Mr Cunningham were closer than you're letting on?"

I dropped my jaw. "That's ridiculous. I've seen him at the store and met him once at the diner to talk about a surprise party for Aletha's birthday next month. Oh, and I had dinner at their house one time. He was there."

She pulled a plastic evidence bag from her pocket and held it up. "Do you recognize this?"

A mangled piece of metal lay in the bottom of the container. I identified the clip with the initials JMD engraved on it. Acid bubbled into my throat. "I think it's my pen. Where did you find it?"

"In the grass at the crime scene. Care to explain how it got there?"

Was someone trying to frame me? "I have no idea. I thought I'd lost it."

Havermayer tucked the bag back into her pocket. "Can anyone corroborate that?"

"I doubt it. Except maybe whoever found it and left it on the boat. But I have no idea who that might be." I leaned toward her. "Do I need a lawyer?"

"What makes you think you need a lawyer?"

"Your attitude." I met her gaze, thumped my feet to the floor and reached for my Mountain Dew. Courage in a can.

Olinski inspected his craggy cop shoes with a hint of a smile. He stood. "All right, Jen, that'll do for now. We'll have more questions for you later." He pulled a business card out of his jacket pocket and handed it to me. "If you think of anything else, give us a call. Thank you for your time. We'll be in touch."

Havermayer opened the front door and Olinski turned back to me.

"And, by the way, I know how you think. You're not the sit on your hands and wait for everyone else to do the work type. I won't tolerate any interference in this investigation. Don't even try it. You wanted to be a hotshot writer, so write. Leave this alone."

"What are you talking about?"

He shook his head and strode out the door.

I rested my cheek against the cool, painted wood.

What just happened?

This had all the earmarks of a nightmare, or my subconscious mind offering a plot for my next novel. It couldn't be real. It just couldn't.

Tears welled behind my closed eyelids. I brushed them away, stepped to my paper-covered desk and rested my fingers on the copy of *Double Trouble* kept there for inspiration. In that book, the brilliant Davenport twins overcame each obstacle, solved each problem. Me? Not so much.

I paced a track around my four-hundred-square-foot apartment for the next hour. Random emotions competed for attention but settled into their own compartments in the end. Someone had stolen my friend from me. My kind, caring, helpful friend. The loss was all-encompassing.

A hard swallow loosened my esophagus. Why did this happen to her? Nobody would want to hurt Aletha. Tim loved her. Why would he go through all the trouble of planning a surprise party for someone he expected to be dead before the first noisemaker sounded? To deflect suspicion? Ridiculous. The explosion had to be an accident. I couldn't even contemplate it being anything else.

Hoping something mundane might help organize my thoughts, I gathered my wardrobe from the floor and dropped everything that would fit into my prehistoric washing machine. Doing laundry, like vacuuming, was one of those mindless occupations I enjoyed simply because they were mindless. I'd solved problems, written thousands of words, even struggled through painful self-analysis while my underwear tumbled in the hot air. Today, I had to find a way to cope with Aletha's death, and even the mother of all dryers wouldn't bring peace to my mind.

A call to Russell went to voicemail. I sighed and left a message. If the police had found me, they must've already spoken to him. He spent every day at the book-store. They should've already interviewed him, so why hadn't he called me? Maybe the shock had overwhelmed him and he didn't want to talk to anyone.

In the shower, I massaged shampoo into my hair while pictures flooded in. Aletha, upbeat, energetic, ready to take on the world. Her smile when I came through the door, her wink to show she had my back, her attentiveness when I needed to talk. If this could happen to someone of her caliber, it could happen to anyone. My tears mingled with the water.

Deep breath in, slow breath out.

When my skin turned an angry red, I shut the shower off and buried my face in a steam-warmed towel, savoring its spring-garden fragrance. A momentary respite. My shoulders tensed again, so I reached for my baby-blue robe to trap warmth and give me the illusion of being safe and snug.

The rumble of the dryer in the laundry closet stopped. I removed a sweatshirt and a pair of Wranglers, dressed in a hurry to stay warm, and almost branded myself with the heated zipper of my jeans.

My hunger added to the wicked ache in my head, and the cupboards were empty, as usual. No wonder Havermayer didn't find anything. I'd better go get something to eat since I already had more than enough reasons to move to Migraine City. And, somebody out there might know what happened to Aletha. Except Olinski had told me to stay out of it. Still, the diner was blabbermouth central, and I had as much right to second-hand news as anyone else in town. Besides, as my grandmother used to say, what he didn't know wouldn't hurt him.

At Angus's Dandy Diner, I had to overcome the challenge of the almost nonexistent open seat on a busy Sunday. Locals gathered after church to reconnect with family and friends, or subdue a hangover left from a Saturday night spent at Bannisters Bar and Grill.

Angus stood behind the service counter, waving his hands to direct waitresses, cooks, and busboys like the conductor of the New York Philharmonic. His abdomen protruded over a once-white apron, now stained with reds, browns, and yellows. Modern art, restaurant style.

Padded orange booths lined the old-timey advertisement-covered walls, which pulled me back into what had always seemed to me a much simpler world. Black was black and white was white. Today, my realm seemed shrouded in gray.

Two large church groups had shoved the Formica-topped tables together in the middle, so I slid into a vacant booth in the corner, with crumbs still on the table. I took a menu under the watchful eyes of a fedora-clad man who leaned against a De Soto with a Lucky Strike pinched between two fingers. The place buzzed with the news of Aletha's death, the town gossips delighted with the unexpected bumper crop.

"You know that bookstore lady…"

"Oh yeah, I heard she was trying to kill her husband and—"

"He jumped off the boat at the last minute. I heard that too!"

Murder presented a momentous opportunity for this tiny town's scandalmongers. In the six months since I'd returned to Riddleton, the most significant headlines had come when three teenagers got caught shoplifting in the Piggly Wiggly. That fueled the chin-waggers for two weeks. This story could power them for months.

Angus, the chinwagger-in-chief, squeezed into the seat opposite me, and his belly drove the table several inches in my direction. "How are you, Jen?"

"Well as can be expected, I guess."

"I know how close the two of you were."

Were. Past tense.

I breathed through the tightness in my chest, nodded, and squeezed his hand in place of an answer.

"Well, you came to the right guy. I know just what you need."

Another one? First Eric, now Angus. If one more man said that to me, I would scream. In my head, anyway. Maybe out loud.

I examined the cracks in the Formica tabletop, waiting for him to grace me with his wisdom.

My frown must have given him pause because he released my hand. "I know what you need to eat. Something soothing." He escaped from the booth with remarkable agility. Maybe Usain Bolt had something to worry about after all.

I scrolled through my phone, hunting for news about Aletha and I'd searched every news site I knew of by the time Angus set a tray on the table. Not much to find, other than a couple of paragraphs on the *Sutton Chronicle* website. He shoulder-surfed, and I held the phone up so he could see better.

He finished the article. "You know what I think?"

"What?"

"I think it had something to do with the contest she won."

I unloaded the tray. A grilled cheese sandwich and a bowl of tomato soup. Seriously? How about a hot fudge brownie sundae? Whatever. My stomach would take it, either way. "Why?"

"Any time there's free money involved, bad things happen."

I dipped a corner of the hot sandwich into the soup and took a bite. The flavors mingled on my tongue and my muscles loosened a tiny bit. He *did* know what I needed.

Angus kept me company while I ate. He chattered about anything other than Aletha's death. I chewed and slurped and listened to stories about Mrs Wilson's lumbago, and Charlie Stevenson's new job, and the skinned knee Eric got showing off yesterday. By the time I scraped the last of the soup from the bottom of the bowl, my outlook had improved and I'd accumulated a whole lot more information about my neighbors than I needed or wanted.

Angus lifted his arm and called to Eric, who'd slipped in unnoticed.

Maybe Eric could tell me something about the explosion. My heart hammered. I needed to find out what he knew.

I pointed at the empty seat next to Angus. "Join us?"

He ambled over to our table. "For a minute, sure. I stopped in for a cup of coffee."

"I'll take care of it," Angus said.

Eric replaced him in the booth. "How are you feeling? Did you hear about Aletha?"

I grimaced. "Olinski and Havermayer questioned me this morning."

"I'm sorry."

"Thank you." Although, he couldn't possibly know how much she meant to me.

"Have your legs recovered from your run?"

"Sort of. At least I can walk today."

"It'll be better next time."

Next time? Fat chance.

"I heard you had a little dust-up after I left."

His reddened face quarreled with his orange hair. "Yeah, something like that."

Enough small talk. I inhaled and feigned an only passing interest in how Aletha died. "Have you heard anything about the explosion?"

He squeezed his eyebrows together. "That was a terrible thing."

No help.

How would Daniel Davenport handle this? He'd use tact—a skill not found in my normal repertoire.

"Yes. I imagine the investigation will be challenging."

"The detectives are working on it. They're talking to everyone who knew her, trying to find someone with a motive."

"What happened?" Did I want to know?

"All I can say is there was an explosion and she died. I'm sorry. I know you two were friends."

Nothing I couldn't have read online or learned eavesdropping on the conversation at the next table. The guy had to have some information.

One more breath, one more try. "Aletha died. I thought she... was your friend, too."

He picked a few crumbs off the tabletop and dropped them on my empty plate. "She was, but I still can't do anything about it. I'm a patrol officer, not a detective."

I leaned closer. "It must be difficult for you to deal with such things."

He winced. "We're trained to handle it."

Angus returned with a to-go cup of coffee. Steam rose out of the tiny opening in the lid. He handed it to Eric, who stood.

"Thanks. Well, I'd better get going." He nodded at me and turned toward the exit.

Angus followed him, and they chatted at the door while I held my breath. Sandwich and soup jockeyed for position in my stomach.

The moment Angus returned, I asked, "Anything interesting?"

"He isn't allowed to talk about it."

I fell back against my padded seat. "Really?"

He shrugged. "Even Eric has to follow the rules."

"I figured he'd talk to you. You're the daytime bartender around here. Everyone tells you their troubles."

"Yeah, they do, don't they?" He grinned. "I'm sorry, but all he would tell me is they're sure the husband did it. They just can't prove it yet."

CHAPTER FIVE

On Monday, rain and malaise ruled my world. Ditto Tuesday and Wednesday. I'd spent the last three days in old sweats and useless activities. I'd paced, watched TV, and ate whatever I could find. Anything to relegate Aletha's death to an inconspicuous shelf in my mind. I'd ignored my phone and the Davenport twins lay dormant on my desk, untouched and unthought-of. From the look of it, today wouldn't shape up any better.

Within minutes of getting out of bed, I collapsed on the couch and slipped into my comfortable semi-vegetative state, prepared for an instant replay of yesterday. A knock on the door pulled my eyelids back open.

Before I could get there, Brittany opened the door and handed me a cup of coffee, breezing past me into the living room. "You ready to talk yet?" She flopped into the space I'd just vacated on the couch.

I sat beside her, and the dormant volcano erupted.

She held me while I sobbed into her shoulder. An upside-down, Italy-shaped patch took shape on her pink blouse. My breath steadied and I squeezed my eyelids shut. Finally, I pulled away and wiped my face. I cleared the misery out of my throat. "Aletha's dead."

"I heard. I've been giving you space to deal with it. Since you wouldn't answer the phone, I knew you were doing what you always do, hiding from the world."

I sipped my coffee. "Her husband's sailboat exploded while she was on it."

Brittany took the cup from me and cradled my head against her chest. "I know she meant a lot to you."

Her heartbeat reassured me as if I were an anxious puppy. "It doesn't make sense, Britt. Russell told me the boat terrified her. Why was she on it? And why was her husband in the house?"

"I don't know. Perhaps she was trying to face her fear."

"Anything's possible, I guess." Was that a pig flying by the window?

She forced me into an upright position. "So, what are you going to do now?"

"What do you mean?"

"If I know you, you've been hiding in here for days. It's time to rejoin the human race."

"Aletha was my friend. I'm allowed to grieve."

She took my hand. "Yes, you are. But there's a difference between grieving and falling apart. You have a tendency to do the latter."

"I'm fine, and I was there for you when Frankie disappeared in Afghanistan."

Tears pooled in Brittany's eyes. "Aletha was your friend, and you cared for her, but I don't see the comparison. Frankie was going to be my husband. He disappeared two weeks before he was due to come home. Three weeks before the wedding." She stood. "I'll be here whenever you need me."

I'd stepped over the line. *What's wrong with me?* "Britt, I'm so sorry. Please forgive me. I'm an—"

"Ass. Yes, I know." She opened the door. "I'll stop by when I get off work."

The door clicked shut behind her. I covered my face with my hands.

The phone rang.

My mother. She'd called six times yesterday. Not going through that again. I swiped the screen.

"It's about time. I've been calling you for two days."

And, we're off! "I know, Mother. I haven't been feeling well, I'm sorry." Why did I apologize?

"Oh." Her tone softened to conciliatory, but she regrouped for another attack instead.

I held my breath.

"Running around drinking and partying, I suppose. I know that's why you moved out."

I moved out to get away from her. "My friend died on Saturday."

Deep breath in, slow breath out.

"Mmmph. Who, Brittany?" Her pitch lowered an octave.

"No, someone I met here after I came back."

"Oh, so you didn't know them very long."

I sighed and shifted my phone from right ear to left, in the hope the ringing in the right one would subside.

"Still, I suppose it's upsetting. I'm sorry."

Wow, two words my mother never said. She must be on vacation from herself. The only possible explanation.

"So, how's the job hunting going?"

And, she's back.

Deep breath in, slow breath out.

"I have a job, Mother. I'm a published author working

58

on my second book." Which I'd get back to as soon as I could tear my mind away from Aletha's death.

"Sure, but when was the last time you got a paycheck?"

I switched ears again and massaged the ache in my forehead. "What exactly did you want to talk to me about?"

"I wanted to know if you're coming to my birthday party next Saturday, but now I don't care if you come or not."

If only that proved true. I ignored her snide tone. "I'll be there. What time?"

"Don't worry about it. I'll be gone soon enough. Then you won't have to think about me at all."

"Give me a break. You're turning forty-seven, not eighty-seven. You'll outlive us all just for spite."

"When did you get to be so mean?"

Mean? Me?

"I will do my very best to make it, so tell me." I removed my fingernails from my palm. "What... Time... Does... It... Start?"

"Lunch is at one. Don't be late. You know everyone hates to be kept waiting."

Everyone, which meant my stepfather. Easy for Gary to be on time. He never went anywhere.

"I'll do my best."

"Your father will be pleased to see you. It's been a long time since you've been home."

"My father's dead, remember? He died in a plane crash when I was six." *Oh God, I'm on a roll today.* If only my words were on a hook so I could reel them back in. The only fish I'd caught today so far was crappie.

Her voice climbed into the screech zone. "Gary has

been a father to you since you were eight, and you've done nothing but reject him. Jack Dawson wasn't a good father. He had no discipline. Gary treats you like one of his own."

His own what? Emotional punching bag?

"How would you know? You were never there."

"You know I had to work. You have a blind spot when it comes to him. Maybe someday you'll forgive him for not being the superhero you always imagined your father to be."

My nails engraved half-moons in my palm again. "He didn't have to be a superhero. I would've been happy with a human being."

Silence.

Did she not understand how he treated me those years after he couldn't work anymore? How could she not know? He crushed my spirit, my soul. What about the time he backhanded me because I said "Yeah" instead of "Yes, sir" and he knocked out my loose tooth? She didn't say a word. Not even when I crawled around on the floor to find the incisor for the tooth fairy. What made her believe he treated me any better when he had no supervision at all? She didn't want to know. She chose not to know. I hated her for that.

Still, she's my mother…

I rubbed the back of my neck. "Let's call a truce, okay? We never get anywhere when we do this."

Icicles hung in the air. "I'll tell your father you're coming. He'll be happy to hear it."

I dropped my phone in my lap, settled back, and closed my eyes. Maybe I'd wake up to find a nightmare had trapped me in it.

My eyelids popped back open, and my body quivered.

Adrenaline rush. Fight or flight. I could do neither, but had to find a way to burn off the unexpected burst of energy. I could clean out my desk. Hadn't done it since my freshman year of college. When I moved, all I did was take the drawers out and carry them. Cleaning would give me something constructive to do.

I found the top left drawer stuffed full of scribbled first draft notes, pens, and old receipts. I sifted through a large handful, which included two gas receipts, various first lines for my novel, and a note from Brittany to call her. How long ago? Then, Scott's face stared at me. He'd left behind his *Sutton Chronicle* ID badge. Just what I needed, another kick in the guts.

I swept the pile back into the drawer and slammed it shut, almost smashing my thumb.

Okay, so what now? Go for a run? Huh. A new and unusual concept. I laughed out loud for the first time since Saturday afternoon at the lake. Five days ago.

A walk would do. And, maybe a decent meal.

The sun seared my scalp as I strolled down Main Street to the diner for a late breakfast. An old Remington manual typewriter in the window of the Goodwill caught my eye. Perhaps I should buy it. Then I'd have a good excuse for writing three sentences in two hours. Better still, a feather quill and ink. Perfect.

"Miss Jen! Miss Jen!"

I turned around. Old Mrs Washington, ninety-four on the outside and sixty-five on the inside, stood in front of the Piggly Wiggly across the street, waiting for the bus to Sutton to visit her husband in the nursing home. Same time every day, rain or shine.

"Miss Jen, come see what I'm bringing my Harry today."

"Why don't you let me give you a ride, Mrs W.? It's hot," I said when I reached the opposite curb.

"Oh no, honey. I couldn't let you do that. You're way too busy writing that book of yours. I'll be fine. Don't you worry."

Same answer as usual, and no argument would convince her otherwise.

"So, what's on the menu today?"

She opened the oversized shopping bag she carried each day. "I got roast chicken, collard greens, and home-made corn bread. Nothing like a home-cooked meal to raise his spirits and beat off that cancer. He'll be home any day now, I'm sure of it."

Harry had stage four pancreatic cancer. "Yes, ma'am. I believe you're right. Any day now, for sure."

Her smile deepened the pruney wrinkles which covered her face.

The bus pulled up to the curb, and I helped her to her seat. "You tell Harry I said hi, okay?"

"I sure will, honey."

I retraced my steps, and cars parked in front of Ravenous Readers brought me to a standstill in the middle of Main Street. Specifically, Russell's green Honda. An opportunity to find out why we'd had no contact since Aletha's death, but my gut lurched at the idea of the bookstore. Too many memories of Aletha and the godawful jokes she made, like the one about the horse and the bartender who says, "Why the long face?" Not to mention the way she coaxed me to share things I'd never revealed to anyone and the warmth in my chest whenever I found myself in the same room with her.

However, I needed to know why Russell hadn't returned any of my calls. I opened the unlocked door, stood on the threshold, and allowed my eyes to adjust to the dim light. A hint of coffee mixed with ink filled each breath. Even in semi-darkness, Aletha lived everywhere. She dusted shelves, restocked books, read to kids. Her essence infused the air, which forced its way into my lungs.

Raised voices came from the stockroom. I made my way along the wall and tapped on the open doorframe. Russell, snappy in his faded jeans with a striped button-down shirt, turned mid-sentence and froze.

"Am I interrupting?"

Russell cleared his throat and inspected the clutter on the floor.

I turned to Tim. "I'm sorry for your loss."

"Thank you." Tim's face appeared drained of all color under his summer tan, his cinnamon hair unkempt. His khaki slacks and white shirt seemed clean, but rumpled. The indigo circles under his green eyes, along with his sunken cheeks, underscored the strain of the past few days. A husband drowned in grief, or a guilty conscience keeping him awake at night? "Russell stopped by to express his condolences. Wasn't that nice of him?" He pressed his lips into a thin line.

The tension skulked like a stalker between them.

"Yes, very," I said.

Russell evaded my gaze. "I wish I could do more." He addressed the floor, hands clenched at his sides.

Tim glowered, his eyes flinty. "You've done more than enough already. Thanks for stopping by." He grabbed a broom and started sweeping.

Russell maneuvered past me and strode through the store.

My brain shifted into gear, and I couldn't let him go. "Hey, Russell, wait up."

He halted outside the front door.

"How've you been?" I squinted against the sun.

"Fine. Busy."

He seemed more upset about Aletha's death than I'd expected. He admired her, but I never got the impression they had a close relationship. Of course, unexpected unemployment could have an effect on his reaction as well. "The police came to see me Sunday."

"Yeah, me too. Saturday night."

"What did they say?"

"I don't want to talk about it." He rubbed a spotless white sneaker on the back of his calf.

"I understand you're sad. I am too. Can I help?"

"Not really. I just need to process things in my own way."

"I know what you mean." However, I needed to discuss the scene on Friday night which haunted me. The pantomime argument we'd witnessed through the bookstore window. "I've been thinking about what we saw when we came out of Antonio's. How about we grab some breakfast? I was headed to the diner when I noticed your car."

"I can't." He stared straight ahead. "There's something I have to do." He turned to me, frowning. "Look, I'll call you later, if I can. Okay?"

Did I have a choice? "See you later."

A deep breath didn't quite fill the new hollow behind my breastbone as I headed back to the stockroom.

CHAPTER SIX

Boxes and books covered the floor, as if a cyclone had passed through, somehow leaving walls and roof intact. Tim picked up a full carton and placed it on an empty shelf. "Can I help you?" He ran his fingers through his collar-length hair.

I massaged my stress tic. "I'm very sorry about Aletha."

He nodded, lips trembling. Then a twinkle flashed through his eyes. "She told me about the time she dumped a full cup of coffee in your lap. And, the way you jumped up, spilling the cup you had on the table. She felt terrible, but it was so funny. We laughed so hard, I..." He pinched the bridge of his nose, grin fading.

"That was an interesting day. At least she missed my laptop." I half-smiled. "Anyway, I just stopped by to see if you needed anything."

"Thank you, but I'm okay." He knit his brow and hoisted up another full carton. A display of physical strength, which belied his fragile demeanor. "Hope you don't mind if I keep working. I have to clean up."

I selected a book from the pile on the floor. *Gone*

With the Wind. One of my favorites. "What happened here?"

"The police searched the store. Looking for clues."

"I'm sorry." They had discarded paraphernalia everywhere, without the consideration to put any of it back. Aletha would've erupted in outrage even though, or maybe because, they had created the mess on her behalf.

"Thank you." He wiped his hands on his pants, which added streaks of grime.

He behaved like an innocent man. Or perhaps he deserved an Academy Award. Would I ever know which? My face burned as I studied the creases in the leather uppers of my Nikes. Unshed tears stung my eyes, again.

"Do you want some help?" I placed the novel in an empty carton while Tim composed himself.

His expression crumpled into half-gratitude, half-agony. "No help necessarily, but I wouldn't mind some company. Being here is tougher than I anticipated."

My chest ached for him, and me, but I had to maintain my focus. This man still could've killed his wife.

"I keep expecting Aletha to come running out with a book catalog she wants to show me. Or some new gadget she wants to get."

He gave me a sad smile. "She loved her gadgets. Always asked for them. I thought she'd never give up that fidget spinner."

"I remember. She played with that thing for weeks."

Tim collected several volumes, wiped them with a towel he kept in his back pocket, and loaded them into a box. "I have to keep busy. Otherwise, all I do is think."

"Keeping busy sounds good to me, too. Where should I start?"

He surveyed the ruin and tossed me a towel. "Anywhere you want."

We worked in silence, each lost in our thoughts. Mine? How much Aletha had enriched my life. How much I already missed her. How much I needed to understand what had happened to her and why.

Despite what he'd said in our interview, Olinski believed someone had murdered Aletha. The determined set of his mouth gave him away. The same look he'd had the day I told him I'd received a scholarship to college, and I'd live on campus instead of commuting. The day he'd asked me to marry him.

Still, I'd held onto the possibility a tragic accident had taken my friend from me. My brain refused to accept that someone Aletha knew, someone she loved, could have killed her. Perhaps someone I knew too.

Who did I know capable of murder?

I hoisted a full carton of books onto an empty shelf and glanced at Tim. He held a copy of *To Kill a Mockingbird* in his hands and turned the pages with care, a tear working its way down his cheek. "Are you okay?"

He snapped the book shut and held it to his chest. "Aletha loved this book. She said it showed the world for what it really was. I always told her she was wrong. Things had changed." He placed it in the box at his feet. "She would smile at me like I was a wayward child and say, 'Have they? You sure about that?' I thought I was, but not anymore." He turned to me, torment etched into his face. "Who could have done this to her?" Tears dripped into his open-necked shirt and grief emanated from him like heat waves off a radiator.

"Have the police learned anything about what caused the explosion? Could it have been an accident?"

He held his breath, then continued in a rush, as if to get words out before they self-destructed. Or he did. "They haven't told me much. I know there was nothing on board that would ignite without help. Not on that scale, anyway."

My insides liquefied and the accident theory sloshed away. "I'm so sorry, Tim. I wish there was something I could do to make it easier for you." And, myself.

"I know. Thank you." He studied me through narrowed eyelids. "You loved her too, didn't you?"

I nodded with furrowed brows.

He slid to the floor and buried his face in his hands. "Then you should hate me as much as I hate myself."

My eyebrows shot up. "What do you mean?"

"She wouldn't have been on the boat if it weren't for me."

His words mimicked helium balloons in my head, which declined to settle into anything that made sense. "What are you talking about?"

Tim spoke to his hands as if they had life apart from his body. "We had a fight on Friday. Bigger than usual, a real blowout. I thought she was going to ask me to leave, and later she did. It was so stupid. She wanted me to show more interest in the store. To spend more time here. I wanted to go sailing before the weather changed. She accused me of not supporting her. Not being there for her." He stared at the ceiling. "She was right."

He hesitated.

Should I say something? I had no idea what, though. My social skills had mummified in my teenaged bedroom. What would social butterfly Daniel do? Prompt Tim into explaining? No, Daniel would wait and listen. Tim had something he needed to say.

"When she packed my clothes, I realized how much I'd screwed up," Tim said in a low voice. "I begged her to change her mind. I convinced her if she went sailing with me, we could talk, undisturbed, the way we used to when we first got married. When we spent every Sunday morning sitting on the porch, drinking coffee, and swapping sections of the newspaper. Talking about anything and everything."

He brushed his hand across his eyes, but rivulets produced clean stripes through the dirt on his left cheek.

I dug a crumpled tissue out of my pocket and handed it to him. He stared at it as if he'd never seen one before.

"I convinced her to let Lacey run the store while we went out on the boat Saturday afternoon. Maybe we could put our relationship back together." His hands shook. "We made a deal. I'd spend more time at the store with her, and she'd spend more time on the boat with me."

The words flew, unbidden, past my lips. "But she hated that boat." I slapped a hand over my mouth. "I'm sorry, I shouldn't have said that."

He twisted his lips. "Why not? It's true."

"Still..."

"She wasn't always afraid of the water, you know. That was my fault." He tore little pieces off the tissue and they floated to the floor as he spoke.

"How so?" Dammit, I wasn't supposed to ask any questions. Too much Dana in me, not enough Daniel.

Tim's voice dropped. "When we first started dating,

we went out on a friend's powerboat, just the two of us. I wanted to prove... Hell, I don't know what I wanted to prove. Trying to get her attention, I guess. I revved the boat up to full speed and did figure-eights in the middle of the lake. Aletha screamed and begged me to slow down. I thought it was funny.

"I cut a circle too close and she fell over the side. She wore a life jacket because she didn't swim well. I knew, and I did it anyway. She wasn't hurt, but it took twelve years for her to even consider getting out on the water again."

Poor guy. He tortured himself over something he did as a stupid kid. "It was an accident. Could've happened to anyone."

His voice fell to a whisper. I leaned closer. "I was supposed to be off work by one, Saturday. We planned to leave by two, two fifteen at the latest." He rubbed his right cheek and left a matching dirt streak behind. Now, he resembled a tall, thin football player prepared for an afternoon game. "I'm a control room operator at the power plant. My replacement was late. I didn't get home until two thirty." Tim rested his elbows on his knees. "When I got home, Aletha had our lunch packed and drinks ready to go. It was close to three by the time I'd changed clothes and loaded everything. Then it took a few minutes to get Aletha aboard. Her fear paralyzed her at the last minute. I was about to untie from the dock when she remembered the cooler sitting on the kitchen counter. I went back for it."

My throat tightened. "You don't have to do this." *Please don't do this.*

"I was in the house and there was a boom, like thunder, except the floor vibrated and the windows rattled." He covered his face and spoke into his hands. "When I ran outside, the flames had engulfed the boat. Black smoke burned my eyes, choked me. And the heat. I couldn't get near it." He massaged his temples. "There are so many things I wish I'd told her."

His words brought home the truth in a way I couldn't ignore. Aletha had died. My close-to-empty stomach retched. I covered my mouth and jumped to my feet, but the nausea passed.

Tim stood and brushed off the back of his khakis. "Thanks for letting me get all that off my chest. Let's get this done, shall we?"

"You bet."

It took us about an hour to put everything back in its place, working predominantly in silence. By the time we had straightened the last chair, my empty belly could take no more. "How about some lunch?"

"I don't have much of an appetite."

"I can understand that, but you need to eat." Something Aletha would say. Or Angus.

"Thanks, but I'm a mess, and I don't think I'm up to facing the madding crowds."

"What do you mean?"

Anger flashed in his eyes. "The whole town thinks I killed my wife."

Probably, if I know them.

I arranged my face into the picture of sincerity. "No, they don't."

"You sure about that? We've been here for hours and not one person has come in to offer condolences. I've received no calls except from family, no cards, not even a casserole. They've already convicted me without a trial."

I couldn't argue with him. I'd holed myself up in my apartment since Sunday, grieving the loss of my friend. The rumor mill had probably been grinding away at full force, though. "I'll tell you what. Come with me to the diner. If anyone bothers you, we can leave. Though, I'm betting Angus won't let that happen."

Tim looked down, then back at me. "All right, I'll give it a shot."

We trudged out onto the street. His long, lean, six-foot-plus frame carried his grief like a sack of rocks thrown over each shoulder. Under the now cloud-covered sky, we traversed the block to the Dandy Diner in silence. The few people on the sidewalk averted their eyes. Disappointing, though not unexpected in a town the size of Riddleton. One man tripped over an uneven section of walkway and almost fell. Also disappointing. He should've landed on his disapproving face.

Angus greeted us with an ear-to-ear smile. Three other diners were enjoying a meal. A man in a western-style shirt and white cowboy hat sat alone at a table, while the mayor, Teresa Benedict, chatted with Chief Vick in a booth near the back door. Perfect for my lunch date with a suspected murderer.

Ever the politician, Teresa spotted us and came over to our table, her striped dress fluttering at her knees. She briefly touched Tim's shoulder. "I'm so sorry for your loss, Tim. Aletha was an important member of our community and she'll be missed."

He nodded. "Thank you."

She turned to me. "Hi, Jen. Are you okay?"

"I'm all right."

"Glad to hear it. How's the book coming along?"

Good grief, not now. "Fine, thanks."

72

"I hope so. The town sure could use all the traffic you're going to bring in." She gave me a thumbs-up and turned back to the chief.

Angus led us to a corner booth, away from the curious. "I'm sorry about what happened to Aletha."

"Thank you," Tim said.

"Are you feeling better?" Angus asked me.

"I am, thanks to your magic cure." I gestured toward Tim. "You think you can whip up another one for my friend here?"

Angus arched one eyebrow.

"I'm not hungry," Tim said. "Just some coffee, please."

"Nonsense. I'll fix you right up."

"I'll have the same, Angus. With coffee, please."

"You got it."

Tim studied his fingertips like he had an upcoming test on cuticles. The very pores in his skin exuded abject misery. Yet, the police had decided he'd killed his wife.

He broke into my reverie. "You don't think I did it, do you?"

Oh, boy. The million-dollar question. "Honestly, I haven't considered it not being an accident, yet."

"Really?" He stared into my eyes. "You must be the only one, then." His words hung, acrid, in the air. "Frankly, I don't see how it could have been an accident. I only had a trolling motor with a twelve-volt battery. And I'd never used it. Have you ever heard of a brand-new battery in a car just exploding while it's parked in the driveway?"

I shook my head.

"Well, it would be essentially the same thing if that boat battery exploded. An old corroded battery maybe, but not a brand-new one."

Way to destroy my fantasy, Tim. No choice but to admit to myself that someone murdered my friend. With a bomb. Could it have been him? Not sure why, but I just didn't think so.

I picked up a paper napkin and covered my lap with it. "I don't know you very well, but I believe you loved your wife. I know you have a lot to gain, the money and bookstore, but you had that, anyway. You didn't need to kill her." Always the possibility he wanted to, though.

"I'm glad you understand, but what if Aletha wasn't the one supposed to die? What if that part was an accident?"

My mouth fell open. "Meaning what?"

"Everyone knew Aletha would never get on the boat. It would be a stupid way to try to kill her. But, when the sun was out and I was off work, I was always out on the lake."

He had a point. Russell had made it clear Aletha never tried to hide her fear of water. "An interesting idea. Have you mentioned it to the police?"

"I tried, but they wouldn't listen. Accused me of trying to deflect attention away from myself. Someone could've wanted to get rid of me to get my wife and her money. When Aletha won the contest, people appeared out of nowhere. Everyone wanted a piece of her. A piece of the money, anyway."

Yet, according to Russell, he was the one who insisted on using the contest money to buy a sailboat. "Aletha mentioned something along those lines, but she never seemed afraid. Then again, if she wasn't the target, she wouldn't have anything to be afraid of, would she?"

"No, I guess not."

Angus arrived with our lunch, and as he set down the tray, Tim's face crept into a sad smile. "Tomato soup. That's what Aletha always gave me when I felt down."

"Nature's medicine." Angus placed a bowl of soup and a sandwich in front of each of us. "There's nothing better to chase your blues away."

Tim pressed his lips together. "That's what she used to say."

"Great minds think alike." Angus smiled.

"And, she was right." I dipped a corner of my grilled cheese sandwich into the soup and chewed a bite slowly.

Olinski and Havermayer thought Tim killed Aletha for her money. With his wife gone, he could buy whatever he wanted. Nothing I'd seen in him led me to agree.

I waited for Tim to swallow his bite, then asked, "Are you going to be all right?"

Tears filled his eyes, again. I had no idea how to console him. Too young to help my mother with her sorrow when my father died, I'd buried myself in my own. Since then, I'd learned about distraction, otherwise known as the best trick in writing.

"Who knew you were going to be out on the boat Saturday afternoon?"

He cleared his throat. "I didn't tell anyone, but Aletha might have."

Who could she have told that wanted her dead?

I looked him in the eye. "For what it's worth, I don't think you had anything to do with it. You couldn't have placed the bomb on that boat."

"What would I know about bombs, anyway? I didn't do this."

And I would help him prove it, despite Olinski's

warning. Or maybe, because of it. I never did like being told what to do. I had to put up with it from Gary. I didn't have to put up with it from Olinski. Another reason our marriage would've been doomed from the start.

CHAPTER SEVEN

My toe caught a tree root, which had forced its way through the sidewalk in front of my apartment building, at the exact moment Detectives Olinski and Havermayer pulled up in their black Suburban. I hopped twice and twirled my arms like windmills engaged in an effort to generate enough electricity to power Blackburn. Havermayer watched me from the passenger seat, her face chiseled in granite. I bowed. She rolled her eyes and opened her door. Killjoy.

Olinski jumped out and trapped his wrinkled jacket in the door as it closed. Red-faced, he freed his blazer and slammed the door shut again.

I leaned against the building and forced myself to relax while the windmills relocated from my arms to my stomach.

The stairs beckoned, the safety of home one flight away. No point though, the detectives would stick to my shoe like toilet paper.

"Hey, Jen, do you have a minute for a few more questions?" Olinski asked as Havermayer stepped out in a crisp white blouse under a spotless black suit. Did she sleep in a mangle iron?

"It's been a tough day."

Olinski nodded and drew his eyebrows together. "We'll be quick. Shall we go inside?"

If I didn't know better, I'd almost think he cared.

"I'm fine here." *Havermayer's not getting another crack at my underwear drawer.*

Havermayer shrugged. "All right. Where were you Saturday afternoon?"

My breath wedged in my throat. "I'm a suspect?"

She dropped her hands onto her substantial hips. "We're trying to get a picture of everyone's whereabouts."

I swallowed against the pulse that pounded in my neck. "With Brittany Dunlop at her parents' lake house."

Olinski inched his glasses back up his nose. "Was anyone else there?"

"Her parents, and Russell Jeffcoat showed up later."

"Showed up?" Havermayer asked.

"Yes. We weren't expecting him."

Olinski raised one thick eyebrow, barely discernible over the black rims of his glasses.

Havermayer laser focused on me. "He showed up uninvited?"

"Maybe. He said I invited him, but I don't remember doing it." Heat flowed from my neck to my ears.

"Has he been there before?"

"No, not that I know of."

"How did he know where to find you?" Havermayer folded her arms across her chest.

In my excitement, I hadn't questioned how Russell had found us. My head buzzed like the occupants of a shattered beehive. Random thoughts everywhere and some of them stung. "I... I don't know. I'd told him where I'd be. He probably used GPS."

"Did you give him the address?"

"Not that I remember. Look, I was really drunk. If he says I invited him, I must have. And I must've told him how to find us. How else would he know?"

The detectives exchanged glances.

Where's the Rosetta Stone for cop facial expressions?

Olinski slid his hands into his trouser pockets, jingling about two washes worth of quarters. "All right, that's all we have for now."

"Does this mean you're not focused on Tim anymore?"

Olinski frowned. "We never said we suspected him, but we're not ruling anyone out."

Yes, you did. Eric admitted as much. "Tim told me he was working Saturday. A solid alibi. So, now you're looking elsewhere for the bomber, right?"

Havermayer broke in. "You said you knew nothing about him."

"I stopped by the store to pay my respects this morning, and we talked while I helped him clean up the mess you left."

She created a slash across her face with her lips.

Olinski fingered the lapel of his jacket. "Why do you assume it was a bomb?"

"What else could it have been? A drone strike?"

He sealed his face against a smile. "I think we can rule out military action. As far as Mr Cunningham's alibi is concerned—"

Wait a minute. "Did the device have a timer?"

"Thank you for your time, Jen." Olinski stepped toward his car.

Anger flashed through my body out of my mouth. "Tim works in a power plant, not a coal mine. He doesn't know anything about explosives."

Olinski turned back to me. "If you say so." His laughter came from deep in his belly.

A warning flag went up, and a petulant whine crept into my voice. "What's so funny?"

"Nothing. Have a good day." Halfway to his car, Olinski turned around. "And, Jen, I'm asking you for the last time. Stay out of this investigation. This is real life, not some book you're writing."

Pissant.

After Olinski and Havermayer got into the car, the Suburban eased away from the curb.

I sank onto the steps and rested my head in my hands. Why did Olinski laugh at me? *If you say so.* It didn't make any sense. Unless Tim had omitted some details from his story.

A car pulled in next to mine. Charlie Nichols jumped out to showcase five thousand dollars' worth of dental work his parents would get little return on. "Hey, sweetheart."

"Hi, Charlie." I clambered to my feet and started upstairs, eyes averted to ignore his black leather pants topped with a pink, satin, balloon-sleeved shirt, orchestrated to blend in with a crowd.

"What's the rush, doll?" He followed me, hopping onto the first step. Zorro minus the cape, the mask, and thankfully, the sword.

On any other day, I'd have laughed at him. A thirty-five-year-old computer geek who behaved like a teenager at the nerd table in the cafeteria. "I'm tired and want to put my feet up."

"How about dinner at my place tonight? I'll rub your feet afterward."

"No, thanks. I'm not up for it."

"Okay, we'll go out. I know a great steak place."

I continued to climb. He trailed behind and touched my arm.

"Hey!" I pulled away, resisting an urge to push him down the stairs. The spot where he'd made contact tingled and soapy water and scrub brushes flitted before my eyes. "What do you want, Charlie?"

"You've been promising to go out with me for six months."

"No, I've turned you down every time you've asked." My words escaped through gritted teeth.

"Come on, you're gonna give in sooner or later."

Normally, I played along. Not today. I refused to look back as I forced my leaden legs inside and closed the door behind me. As I rested against it, my breathing slowed, but my mind churned.

Had Tim misled me about what he knew about bombs? If so, why? What made me so important? My friendship with Aletha? If he could convince me of his innocence, perhaps others would fall in line. However, the opinions which mattered belonged to the police. I had zero sway with them. What did he hope to accomplish?

Then, there was Russell. On Saturday he'd followed me to Brittany's as if attached by a rubber band. It must've snapped since he now seemed reluctant to speak to me. Like Scott's flip of his wrist and promise to call—broken almost before he even made it—as he boarded the plane to Paris. I would've married Scott, had kids with him. Grown old and sat on a porch swing with him.

Nope. The rubber band always snaps.

I kicked off my shoes, changed into my house-only sweats on my way to the kitchen, and deposited a trail of discarded clothing in my wake. Balanced on the open refrigerator door with my chin, I pulled my pants up, grabbing the last can of Mountain Dew at the same time. A rare talent achieved through years of practice.

Since the real murder fell under Olinski's purview, as he seemed to remind me every chance he got, I'd better get to work on my fictional one. I fired up my laptop, settled into my chair, and braced for another battle of the book. Like the Battle of the Bulge without the snow.

Dana studied the typed note they'd found in the secret compartment of their father's desk.

PAY UP OR ELSE!

What did it mean?

"Daniel, did Father owe someone money?"

"I don't think so, but he didn't talk about those kinds of things." His eyes widened. "What if he was being blackmailed?"

"Obviously. Still, it doesn't make sense to kill him. They'd have no chance of getting their money. Besides, Father didn't have any secrets, anyway."

"Would we know?"

"I guess not."

Daniel furrowed his brow. "What if it wasn't only Father's secret to keep? The other person involved might have killed him to protect himself. Or herself."

Dana studied the paper while a single tear blazed a trail of black mascara down her cheek.

And, my brain shut down.

I coaxed and cajoled. No luck. The running magic had drifted away while I'd been hiding from the world. Only one way to recover it. Ugh.

Maybe I could do something for Aletha, instead. Olinski had treated me like I belonged in the nearest dumpster. His go-to stance in an effort to break the world record for holding a grudge. Still, why had he laughed at me? Only one possible reason. He knew something I didn't.

An internet search produced nothing but promo pics for the contest. Somehow, Tim Cunningham had no history before his wife wrote the winning essay. Maybe he was in witness protection. In Riddleton, South Carolina? No way. This place is where they'd send the person he helped convict. Besides, how would Olinski find out about Tim's past? His badge didn't have US Marshal stamped on it.

Brittany might have an idea. Her librarian skills led her to bunches of information I couldn't find. I pressed the icon next to her college graduation picture on my phone, and relayed my odd encounter with the detectives.

"Puzzling," she said.

"I know, right? Looking Tim up didn't help, but I don't have access to those fancy databases you use."

"I don't have access to anything you don't. I just know where to look. Let me see what I can find out. I'll call you back."

"Thanks."

Not much I could do now but wait for her call. Might as well see if I could get the magic back. No matter how painful the process might be. I had to finish this book.

I donned shorts, paired with a Motor Supply Company T-shirt, and my beat-up Nikes, and skipped down the stairs with manufactured enthusiasm. A twinge in my left foot when I hit the sidewalk reminded me of Eric's advice. Should I invest in new shoes as he suggested? Nah. This definitely wasn't going to become a regular thing.

In the shade of the ancient oak tree, I struggled through the little of the stretching routine my memory had retained, then started down Park Street full of good intentions. A run to the park, one lap around, and run back home.

Halfway there, my side reminded me about the road to hell. Fingers under ribs, even breaths, pain gone. Lather, rinse, repeat.

The park gate loomed over me the fourth time the stitch struck. My legs shook and lungs screamed. I shambled home with a brain even more muddled than before. Except for the knowledge I hadn't even made it all the way to the park. *Way to strut your stuff, Jen.*

Running alone didn't do it for me. Perhaps, I needed someone to push me past my limits. I needed the group. Saturday morning at eight, I'd stand at the gate and wait for everybody else.

Unbelievable. *Who are you, and what have you done with Jen?*

Home again, my couch broke my fall. Time for a nap.

I'd begun to doze when Brittany called.

I snatched the phone off the coffee table. "What did you find in your secret database?"

"You mean Google?"

"Ha, ha. What did you find?"

"Tim Cunningham used to be an army demolitions expert."

Swear words crashed on my tongue. "Thanks, Britt."

"Any time. I'll send you my bill."

I laid the phone on the coffee table so I wouldn't fling it against the wall. No insurance on it. Tim had lied. Well, left out some pretty significant information, anyway. He'd convinced me he had nothing to do with Aletha's death. Now I didn't know what to believe. Our next conversation would be quite interesting, but at the moment, my hands trembled too much to handle the phone. My mind needed to clear first. I settled back on the couch.

Half an hour later, hunger woke me up. A quick, fruitful search of my lightly stocked refrigerator, and a few minutes with a frying pan produced a fluffy, colorful, western omelet. I cooked because restaurants cost too much, and I ate out because I could screw up a bowl of cereal. Every so often, though, one of my creations surprised me. Like today.

As the last bit of yellow connected with the last bite of toast, my phone rang. I recognized the number Aletha had given me in case of emergency. Tim. Did I want to talk to him? No, but he could want to confess. Nah, too easy.

I thrust my irritation aside and swiped my phone's screen.

Tim blurted out, "I know why Aletha ended her relationship with Marcus. I found a letter he wrote. He went to jail for armed robbery."

Why was he talking about Marcus? I carried my

empty plate to the sink to be washed on a later date. "Okay, what about it?"

"His cellmate's nickname was Billy the Bomber."

"You're joking, right?"

"That's what Marcus wrote. What if he wanted money, or worse, Aletha back, and she wouldn't cooperate, so he got a bomb from this guy Billy, or learned how to make one while they were in prison?"

An onion-flavored belch rose in my throat. I held my phone away so Tim couldn't hear. "Yeah, and maybe Elvis is working at the convenience store on the corner. Besides, you can find detailed instructions for bombmaking online. He wouldn't need to go to all that trouble. What would he gain by killing Aletha, anyway?"

"I told you, I was the target, not Aletha. If he killed me, he might be able to rekindle her feelings for him." His voice cracked. "It's worth looking into. I'm serious."

He can't believe I'm this gullible. "That's what worries me, but if you think you should look into it, go for it."

"I tried. Marcus won't talk to me. When I told him who I was, he hung up. Someone else has to do it."

Someone like me? No way he's sending me off on some wild goose chase. "Why don't you give it to the police?"

"They'll think I'm trying to deflect attention away from me."

"You mean deflect away from the fact you used to be a demolitions expert?"

The silence lasted so long I checked for a dropped call.

Tim released a hard breath. "I guess you've heard."

"Why didn't you tell me?"

"I thought you might believe I killed Aletha."

I clenched my free hand into a fist, then forced it to relax. "I'm not sure I can believe anything you say at this point."

He breathed into the phone. "I know, and I don't blame you."

"What do you want from me, Tim?"

"I… I guess I need to know there's somebody in this town on my side. Somebody who doesn't think I killed my wife for her money."

"Look, just because you learned how to blow things up in the army, doesn't mean you blew up your wife." A lump formed in my throat. I cleared it away, wishing he'd been honest from the beginning. "Give me a little credit."

His voice broke. "I'm desperate. I don't have anyone else I can trust."

"What makes you so sure you can trust me?"

"Aletha trusted you, and I trust… trusted her. Besides, you told me earlier you didn't think I had anything to do with my wife's death. Did you mean it, or did you just tell me what you thought I wanted to hear?"

What could I say?

"Please, I need your help. Everyone else thinks I did it. I need you to call Marcus. Find out if he had anything to do with the bombing."

I closed my eyes. Dana would jump on this opportunity, and Daniel would do it just because Tim asked him to. I fell somewhere in between. "Fine. What's his number?"

I wrote it down.

Tim cleared his throat. "Would you consider coming

by the house tomorrow? I found something I think Aletha would want you to have."

My belly fluttered. "What is it?"

"I'd like to surprise you, if you don't mind."

I loved a good surprise, along with a chance to look at the crime scene. I might find something the police missed. And, I'd have something to remember Aletha by. "All right, I can do that. I'll call you tomorrow morning."

I dropped onto the couch once again. Billy the Bomber? *Please.* Either Tim made it up, or he read it in a bad novel.

Aletha once talked about old friends who'd materialized after she'd won the contest: *I even had an old boyfriend turn up. Hadn't heard from him in ten years. Imagine that! Money is the honey that draws buzzards and flies. My mama used to say that.* She had laughed. No fear of Marcus, no evidence he'd tried to contact her.

Who else had showed up? She hadn't said, but if one of them had asked for a handout, and she'd turned him or her down... If only I had a clue.

Okay, so how do I get a clue? What would Dana and Daniel do? Investigate. They couldn't find clues they didn't look for. A mystery writer could figure this out.

Consider Tim's theory that Aletha died when someone tried to kill him. That would make Marcus a threat, if he wanted Aletha back. Did Aletha want him back? Had she ignored the text Marcus sent her, as Tim said? Why had she kept the letter he wrote her from prison? Unless the letter functioned as a red herring in Aletha's mystery. After all, Tim's the only one who's seen it. It might not

88

exist at all. He might just be trying to deflect attention away from himself.

Maybe the detectives had the right idea. Tim had a solid motive. Money. However, a boat explosion only worked if Aletha stayed aboard and he didn't. No way he could make that happen with any certainty. Unless he drugged her. Plus, if there was a timer, the killer had set the time so they would both be out on the water, in Tim's version of events. No delay at work, or no cooler forgotten on the counter, and Tim's dead too. Unless he left the cooler behind on purpose.

Unless, unless, unless...

Circular logic. The puzzle pieces lay there on the table for me to put together.

With luck, I'd learn something useful tomorrow. I'd go to Tim's house. Aletha's house.

What if Tim had killed Aletha? What if he'd invited me over to get rid of me because he imagined I knew something?

Silly idea. *Paranoia is not my friend.*

I called Brittany. He wouldn't try anything in front of a witness, and four eyes noticed more than two. If nothing else, she could distract him while I investigated.

"Hey, you want to play bodyguard tomorrow?"

"What are you talking about?"

"Tim Cunningham invited me to his house tomorrow. To give me something of Aletha's."

"So, what do you want me to do, protect you from the big, bad wolf?"

"Yup. I'll even wear my hooded red cloak, if you want."

"Oh, brother! Pick me up when I get off."

That settled, I surrendered to fatigue and slid into

bed. Enveloped in the cool sheets, my muscles let go, one by one. To relax my mind, however, remained the greater challenge. Thoughts swirled like debris in a tornado.

Toto, I've a feeling we're not in Kansas anymore.

CHAPTER EIGHT

Dana studied the paper; a single tear blazed a trail of black mascara down her cheek.

Okay, new chapter. Where should we go from here? Their father was dead, plus they found the note. Now what? How about they commiserate over breakfast the next morning.

After a long night, during which sleep danced out of their grasp, the twins pushed scrambled eggs across their plates. Mrs Barlow, wearing a black armband around her uniform sleeve, had prepared a breakfast of their favorites: bacon and eggs, blueberry muffins, and pancakes. But the food soured in their mouths.

Dana laid her fork on the plate and held her head in her hands, elbows resting on the table.

Daniel leaned over to put an arm around her shoulders. "It's going to be all right, Sis."

Easy for Daniel to say. However, Dana can't say that to him.

Why not?

Because she's not snarky like me.

So, what does she say?

I leaned back in my chair; the 10:48 a.m. in the lower right corner of my laptop screen taunted me. Twelve more minutes to work, then I had to get ready to pick up Brittany for the trip to Tim's house.

Why did I agree to this? To get a look at the crime scene. The spot where my friend had died. Might not have been the best decision, though. Too late to change my mind now.

On my way to the bathroom, I listened to my voicemail. Maybe something from Russell? Nope. I got my mother. Twice in one week. Should I call her back? She'd give me a headache. Still, I tapped the icon. Long-distance guilt.

She answered on the first ring.

I braced for the inevitable. "Hi, Mom, what's up?"

"What do you mean, what's up? I need an excuse to call my daughter? I can't pick up the phone if I want?"

I threw up my left hand and let it fall back to my side. "You can call me whenever you feel the urge."

"You can call me once in a while, too, you know."

"Yes, I know. I've been a little busy lately. Besides, I did talk to you the other day."

She huffed. "Well, excuse me! I didn't realize it was such a hardship for you to talk to me twice in one month."

What's going on here? "Is there something in particular you wanted or is this supposed to be a friendly chat?"

"Actually..."

I tapped my fingers on my leg.

"I... um..."

My mother at a loss for words? Somebody must've died. She must've died. "Mom, what is it?"

She mumbled in a low voice. "Nothing. I wanted to say I'm sorry for the way I acted last time we spoke."

I stared at my phone. Now, *I'd* lost my words. "It's fine, don't worry about it."

"I wish things were different between us." She hesitated. "I love you, you know."

I did, but couldn't believe she'd said it. My mother had told me she loved me a half-dozen times, at most, in my entire life. "Are you sure nothing's wrong?"

Her voice climbed an octave. "I hear your father calling me. I'll talk to you later."

My response traveled into a dead phone while my brain spun like a top. As much as I hated to admit it, though, I loved her too.

After my shower, I followed the trail of clothing I'd left on the floor last night to my jeans. A quick sniff test gave me the go-ahead to wear them one more time. A plain red polo shirt and my Nikes and I declared myself ready to go.

The deserted parking lot meant my neighbors had gone to work. Something I should do, but instead I had to go to the lake. I stepped out into a balmy, cloudless day and imagined lying on a towel, soaking up the rays. Then reality—my year-round pasty legs combined with the knowledge my trip had little chance of being a picnic—obliterated the fantasy.

Some kid had written: "Wash Me Please" across the back window of my white, '07 Nissan Sentra. Forget it. The dirt held the car together. Under the scribble, I wrote: "Test Dirt. Do Not Remove."

The Sentra had burgundy leatherette—a fancy word for plastic—interior and seats in perfect condition, although a while had passed since I'd seen the floorboard carpet. The distinctive bouquet of stale Fritos, or dirty socks, permeated everything, but my car started right up. One of the few reliable things in my life.

I traversed the two blocks and pulled into one of the four empty spaces, which constituted the library public parking area. The Riddleton Public Library inhabited a sun-bleached, brick building on Pine Street, tucked between the Piggly Wiggly and Circle K, and across from the cubbyhole called the Riddleton Post Office. An aged pine dropped cones from thirty feet up onto a weather-beaten picnic table, which listed in the grass. Someone should tack a sign to the tree above the table:

SPLINTERS
FREE TO A GOOD HOME

Brittany locked up and settled into the car, every bit a librarian in her white blouse, black skirt, and flat shoes.

For once, she didn't comment on my driving or clutter under her feet.

When we reached the turn, a brick mailbox marked a hardwood-lined dirt road, which doubled as a driveway. The trees' branches overlapped, creating a leafy tunnel around the car. Aletha had invited me to visit when the reds, oranges, and yellows of autumn exploded into existence. Of course, she'd intended to enjoy them with me.

The tunnel opened into a clearing, which revealed a

white, Victorian-style house about a hundred yards from the lake. I followed a circular driveway past a meadowy lawn.

Brittany craned her neck for a better view out the window as I drove. "This is beautiful. A splash of color would make it perfect."

"Aletha had planned to add flowerbeds next year. She loved to tell me her ideas for the house." The weight of memory sat on my chest like a thousand-page manuscript.

In the distance, yellow plastic crime scene tape cordoned off where the dock once stood.

Police Line Do Not Cross

My breath hitched. Brittany squeezed my hand.

I nodded and opened the car door.

Tim came out onto a wraparound porch in jeans and a plain, blue T-shirt. I introduced them.

"It's nice to meet you, although I wish it was under better circumstances," Brittany said.

Tim scanned the yard.

She continued, "I'm sorry about your wife. She was always nice to me."

"Thank you." He swallowed hard, his Adam's apple riding up his throat. "Do you want some coffee?"

I flashed my best fake smile. "Always."

He led us through the house to the kitchen. Soft yellows and pastel greens brightened the walls and countertops, and, in an instant, Aletha filled the room. If Tim experienced the same phenomenon, I couldn't imagine his misery. His hands shook as he fumbled with coffee filters. Brittany took over.

While they made coffee, I meandered into the living room, decorated in subdued browns accented with harvest golds. The fireplace in one wall seemed intended more for romance than warmth. Simple and earthy, like Aletha herself. Her presence pervaded it all. How could Tim stand it?

Photographs framed in ornate wood lined a chestnut mantel. Aletha and her family on the left, Tim and his on the right. Pictures of them together dominated the center, presided over by a large photo of the bride and groom on their wedding day. I picked up the picture of Tim, beaming in his black tuxedo with tails, and Aletha, radiant in a simple, white dress, which accentuated her dark brown skin. A tear fell on the forehead of my reflection in the glass. I wiped it away.

Tim and Brittany hadn't yet appeared, so I stepped through the patio doors into the yard. The life-giving rays of the sun on my face offered a welcome change from the death that had shadowed me for most of the week. Moist grass clippings adhered to my Nikes as I stumbled to the yellow tape stretched across pine trees near the lakeshore.

Police Line Do Not Cross

I fingered the soft plastic strip. Safe to assume the police didn't want the area disturbed, but they'd found pieces of my pen out there and considered it evidence against me. I ducked under the barrier and inspected the grass all the way to the water's edge, where the pylons that once supported the dock poked out of the water like sea turtles as they came up for air. Speedboat-induced waves lapped at the toes of my shoes, rinsing away the grass.

Lake Dester stretched for miles in each direction, so big we hadn't heard the explosion from Brittany's parents' house on the other side. The sun glistened on the water, and blue, white, and yellow sails dotted the horizon. Motorboats towed orange-vested skiers, balanced against swells created by jet skis crisscrossing behind them, the peaceful scene a bitter contrast to the turbulence which roiled within.

How different the place must've appeared before Aletha died. Before a brand-new sailboat, which had bobbed against a brand-new dock, exploded into a billion pieces. Taking the pier, and my friend, with it.

My legs crumpled and I collapsed more than sat.

Deep breath in, slow breath out.

I poked at pebbles with a twig, in search of something, anything, investigators might've missed. Dana Davenport would've dived into the lake, but I emulated Daniel instead, and settled for what remained on solid ground or just offshore. Small bits of blue and white wood floated nearby. Tim told me the police had collected everything, but these must've drifted closer to the shore after they had finished. When I picked one up and threw it back into the water, it left wet flecks of paint on my palm. I wiped my hand on my jeans.

The sodden wood traveled farther than I expected and created several rings when it disappeared below the surface and popped back up. I selected a larger chunk and drew back. A metallic glint caught my eye, and something cool and wet hit my forearm. A tennis racket on a thin gold chain dangled off the wood chip. Electricity surged through my head. Did this belong to Aletha? I pictured it around her neck when the sailboat exploded. My shaking hand lost its grip. I searched for the chain, but it had disappeared. A sob escaped my throat while tears burned my cheeks. Where did it go?

I raked my fingers through the grass and collected sandy soil under my fingernails until my thumb hooked the charm. I scrambled to my feet, hugging the necklace to my chest while my tear-stained face dried in the breeze. Once composed, I carried the necklace back to the house, trudging through the grass as if the jewelry weighed a ton.

Tim watched through the open glass doors. I laid my find in his palm. My muscles tightened around the emptiness I'd carried in my chest along with the necklace in my hand.

He frowned. "What's this?"

My shoulders slumped. "I assumed you would know. It was caught on a piece of floating wood."

Tim held the chain up to eye level to study the charm. "I've never seen it before. Aletha never played tennis." He blinked several times in succession. "You know, one of her friends lost a necklace a few weeks ago. This could be it."

"Do you want me to return it for you?"

"No, I can't hide from everyone forever."

"Tim, the police found a damaged piece of my pen out by the lake. Do you have any idea how it got there? Did Aletha mention finding it or something?"

"No, not that I remember. How did they know it was yours?"

"It had my initials on it. I lost it, and somehow it turned up here, as evidence."

"I'm sorry, I don't know anything about it."

Baffling. If Aletha found it, why would she bring it here? She could've returned it at the store. Maybe the killer found it and brought it here to throw suspicion onto me. That would mean the murderer knew me well enough to recognize my pen. A scary thought.

Tim settled onto the couch beside Brittany. When he dropped the chain on the mahogany coffee table, the pendant dulled in the artificial light. Similar to our mood as we tried to talk about anything other than the one thing on our minds.

He asked us to attend a memorial service planned for Aletha on Tuesday morning at the bookstore. We agreed, and the conversation trailed off into an extended silence.

Brittany salvaged the moment. "This is a beautiful house, Tim. How long have you lived here?"

A grin broke out on his face, then faded. "Five months. We moved in right before Ravenous Readers opened. Do you want to see it?"

"Absolutely."

Tim escorted us down the hall to a formal dining room. An enclosed space with an entrance at both ends. Aletha had decorated it in burgundy and beige, with a twelve-seat table and a china cabinet centered on the far wall. A touch of elegance in Aletha's down-to-earth life.

Brittany ran her hand over the top of a cherry chair. "What a wonderful room."

Tim rubbed his chest. "Aletha special-ordered every piece. The china cabinet came in last week. She never even got to see it."

He stepped back into the hall. We followed in silence.

To the right of the kitchen doorway, he showed us into a utility room with a door that led to a finished basement with a stocked bar, two overstuffed couches, and a pool table. Several rectangular windows along the top of one wall revealed ground outside. Tim wilted in the middle of the room, hands in his pockets.

Brittany squeezed his arm. "Let's check out the upstairs, shall we?"

We trooped up to the second floor and down the hall. On the left: a master bedroom with its own bathroom attached to a dressing room, and a walk-in closet large enough for another guest room.

Brittany smiled at Tim. "This is amazing. Your closet is bigger than my high-school bedroom."

Tears filled his eyes. He swiped them away. "This was our dream house. Everything we ever wanted. Now, I feel lost in it and don't know what to do with myself."

On the right side of the hall, he showed us the real guest room, a bathroom, and his office. Tim stepped inside and pulled a book off a shelf.

"This is what I wanted to give you."

A signed first edition of Stephen King's *On Writing*.

"Thank you, Tim. I don't know what to say." I gently riffled through the pages once handled by Aletha.

"You don't have to say anything. I know Aletha would've wanted you to have it."

I blinked against the tears, knowing he was right.

Our awkward chit-chat continued downstairs for a few more minutes, then Brittany and I drove back to Riddleton. I hadn't managed to discover much new information about Aletha's death, but Tim's gratitude for the company turned it into a productive afternoon. And my gift would hold a place in my heart. Aletha would always be with me.

The necklace nagged at me. I shouldn't have given it to Tim; it didn't belong to Aletha and, while Aletha's friend may have lost the chain, it also might've belonged to the killer. I resolved to encourage him to turn it over to the police.

As we reached the outskirts of town, my phone rang. The screen showed an unfamiliar South Carolina number. A robocall, I'd bet. I put it on speaker.

"Ms Dawson, my name is Jason Fiero and I'm an attorney with Fiero and Coleman. Your name has been mentioned in Aletha Cunningham's will."

Aletha's will? Despite the AC blasting from the vents, I broke into a sweat. I glanced at Brittany.

She shrugged.

"Okay. What do you mean, Mr...?"

"Fiero." He cleared his throat. "Ms Dawson, this is a matter best discussed in person. Your presence is requested for the reading, Tuesday afternoon after the memorial."

CHAPTER NINE

I gave up the effort to sleep around four Saturday morning. I'd spent the night flipping from one side to the other and back again, once or twice asleep long enough to dream. Bizarre nightmares, which starred Aletha and Tim, Olinski and Havermayer, and, of course, my mother. If my imagination when awake possessed half as much creativity as my asleep one, I'd have a string of bestsellers on my bookshelf.

How did I end up in this mess? Someone had killed Aletha, and because I'd spent time in her bookstore, lost a pen and written a silly inscription in a book I'd given her, I'd become a person of interest. And, if someone had told the police I'd had an affair with Tim, they did it to redirect attention. With the assumption it wasn't Havermayer trying to bait me into a confession with the old, "What would you say if...?" trick.

The real trick, however, would be to figure out what had happened to Aletha.

If I wanted to write this story, what would I do? First, I'd create the victim and method. Got that. Then surround her with characters with potential motives and the means to carry out the crime with the chosen method. No problem. Plenty of those around. All I had to do now was find motives and opportunities for each of them. Yup, that's all I had to do.

I'd forgotten to call Marcus yesterday, probably because I didn't really want to. I'd given Tim my word, though. Regardless, I couldn't do it at this hour on a Saturday, so helping the twins solve Victor Davenport's murder would have to do. More a mental challenge than the emotional one I faced when I thought about Aletha.

> Daniel put an arm around her shoulders. "It's going to be all right, Sis."
>
> "I know." Dana sat straight up in her chair. "We're going to find out who did this and put him away for the rest of his life."
>
> "Agreed. What do we do now?"

Good question. They found the note in their father's desk. Other evidence existed in Victor's office. Time for them to find one thing, but not the other. The twins couldn't discover the giveaway clue too soon or readers would guess whodunit halfway through the book. Couldn't have that.

Dana should suggest another search of the office, but how would I stop them from finding both clues? I didn't want them to seem haphazard in their quest for information. An interruption coupled with a red herring could solve the problem. Which narrowed the disruption to the police or the killer. Too soon for the killer, so Detective Abernathy should ask them questions about their father's friend Peter Robinson. The follow-up investigation would keep Dana and Daniel busy for a while.

Along the same lines, if Aletha had any secrets, perhaps I'd find them in her office. The police had searched it already, but what if they had missed something? It wasn't like the detectives knew her well enough to recognize the potential significance of something that might seem innocuous.

First, I'd have to figure out how to get in. Who had a key? Tim had Aletha's key, but Russell might still have one. Or did he give his key to Lacey that Saturday she worked for Aletha? If so, I could ask to borrow it. But what reason would I give? I left something in the store and wanted it back. That might work—except why didn't I get it the other day?

Hold on. What if Tim Cunningham was the red herring in Aletha's story? What if the police had targeted the wrong person? He could be the distraction that allowed the real killer to get away. Something to ponder on my run.

My run. Two words I'd have bet anything would never enter my mind. Hard to believe one morning in the park had affected me that much.

Seven fifty-five found me sprawled on the stone bench by the park gate. Eric sauntered over from the parking lot, dressed in his Christmas colors, a white towel draped around his neck. The ninety percent humidity in the air had his face, and my underarms, already dripping.

Eric's face split into a grin. "You came back!"

"I did. Against my better judgment."

"Come on, you know you loved it. It's addictive, isn't it?"

Great. Another habit I couldn't break. Writing wasn't bad enough? "I guess we'll see."

He plopped down beside me. "How are you holding up? You were pretty upset last time I saw you."

"Better. Aletha's death hit me hard."

"Understandable."

We sat in silence for a moment, then Eric said, "The others should be along any minute. Lacey's coming today. You'll finally get to meet her."

"Sounds good." My conversation with Tim resurfaced. "Is that Aletha's friend Lacey?"

He frowned. "Probably. I haven't met anyone else in town with that name."

"She covered the store last Saturday so Aletha could go sailing with Tim."

Eric tilted his head. "Seems something she would do. She did say she had to work. Maybe that's what she meant."

"Any news on the investigation?" Might as well take advantage of having Eric all to myself.

"Not that I've heard. The detectives aren't sharing much with us peons."

I turned to face him. "Tim Cunningham told me something the other day that might be relevant."

His eyebrows arched. "What?"

"Aletha's ex-boyfriend, Marcus Jones, shared a prison cell with a guy who made bombs."

"Interesting. How did he find that out?"

"A letter the guy wrote Aletha from prison."

"You should tell the detectives."

"I'm telling you. You should check it out. If it turns out to be important, you might get some brownie points. Maybe even get you out of that uniform into a suit."

He wiped his brow with the towel. "Or get me in trouble for withholding information. I think I'll pass it along the way I'm supposed to."

"They won't take it seriously."

"They might. You never know."

I forced a laugh. "Yeah, I do. Once Olinski finds out you got it from me, he'll dismiss it as my overactive imagination. You leave me no choice."

Eric bent to retie his expensive running shoe. "About what?"

"I'll have to look into it myself. Of course, it would be a lot easier for you."

He rose and waved to Angus and Lacey, who approached us. "I'll relay the information. After that, I'm staying out of it and I suggest you do the same."

I opened my mouth to tell him what to do with his suggestion, but Angus introduced me to Lacey, a mid-thirties, soccer-mom type, with long brown hair pulled back into a ponytail.

We strolled into the park for our stretching routine. My body protested in every possible way, then we set off around the path. Eric and Lacey bounded out of sight, and Angus settled into position beside me as we raced a snail down the pavement.

The first pain split my ribs about halfway around. I stopped, hands on knees. Angus jogged in place, and Eric and Lacey caught up as I jabbed my fingers into my abdomen.

"Are you okay?" Lacey asked.

Eric and Angus took off together.

I looked up into her concerned frown. "I will be... in a minute."

"You're breathing wrong."

The agony subsided. I stood up straight. "Are you kidding? In, out. In, out. I've been doing it my whole life."

Lacey rotated her torso from side to side. "How's that working out for you?"

No matter how hard I tried, my oxygen-starved brain couldn't produce a witty comeback. "What did you have in mind?"

"Let's start with your posture." She placed one hand under my chin, the other between my shoulder blades. "Relax your shoulders and pull them down, away from your ears."

I complied, and she steered my chin.

"Keep your head up, aligned with your spine."

Shoulders down, head up. Got it.

"How does that feel?"

"Like I'm a guard at Buckingham Palace."

"Relax, you're too tense." She pinwheeled her arms and rolled her head between her shoulders. "Loosen up and try it again."

Loosen up? Simple. Like trying to unbend a horseshoe.

I mimicked her actions and eased back into position. Better, but still awkward. "You expect me to run this way?"

"Up to you."

Eric and Angus trotted by. Eric turned and ran backward for a few steps. "Attagirl, Jen. Looking good!"

I resisted an impulse to give him the one-finger salute. Lacey reclaimed my attention. "You ready to try it?"

Never. Well, eventually, but I needed to find out something first. I rotated my arms and turned my head. "In a minute. Let me loosen up a bit more."

She jogged in place. "Okay."

I did my best to sound casual. "I used to spend a lot of time at the bookstore. Didn't you help out there once in a while?"

She bobbed her head. "I remember. You sat in the corner by the window. I still can't come to grips with what happened to Aletha."

"I know what you mean. You were working for her that afternoon, right?"

"Yes. Although now, I wish I'd said no." Lacey guided a stray hair back off her forehead, and puckered her brow. "I should've known something was wrong. She sounded so strange when she called me."

"Strange?"

Her gaze locked on mine. "She seemed nervous. I assumed it was about going on the boat, but now I wonder if she was afraid of him."

"Tim? Why?"

She studied her dusty shoe tops. "Because of what happened, I guess."

The scene between Aletha and Tim in the bookstore last Friday night popped up. I couldn't see Tim's face, but Aletha's radiated fury. What if his had too?

Enough anger to kill his wife?

He didn't strike me that way, but that didn't mean anything.

Aletha's office could contain something to help me figure it out. I had to get in there. "Do you still have a key to the store?"

"Yeah, why?"

Could I trust her with the truth? What's the worst that could happen? "The police seem hell-bent on pinning Aletha's murder on Tim. And, maybe they're right, but what if they aren't? The real killer might get away with it, and I don't want to see that happen."

Lacey twisted side to side while rotating her arms at the shoulder. "Neither do I."

"Would you consider letting me borrow your key so I can get into Aletha's office to look around?"

She folded her arms across her chest. "No."

My insides sank. "I understand."

"Unless, you let me come along. I want to help."

I stuck my hand out to shake hers. "You've got a deal."

We trotted down the track. Lacey paced me while playing cheerleader. A new mantra took over: *Head up, shoulders down. Head up, shoulders down.*

About a quarter of a mile in, it became easier, but the stance would never feel natural to me. Keeping my head down had helped me survive my teen years with Gary. If he didn't notice me, he wouldn't berate me. A hard habit to break. All the more reason to do it, though. My life belonged to me, now.

Halfway around, Eric and Angus caught up again, and Angus and Lacey switched places. My shoulders relaxed and my footfalls relaxed into a familiar rhythm. We smiled at each other, and I plodded on, finding it simpler to translate Lacey's words into action.

A hot shower washed away the sweaty remnants of my morning run. My limbs remained heavy, but my mind functioned as a freshly honed razor. Which mystery should I tackle? I'd worked on Victor's this morning, so what could I do, right now, to help find Aletha's killer?

I sifted through the coffee-table clutter to unearth the scrap of paper with Marcus Jones's phone number on it. I punched it into my phone and tapped the green button. A woman answered ring number four and I asked for Marcus.

"Who is this?"

"I'm a friend of his ex-girlfriend, Aletha. I only want to talk to him."

"Aletha? Lord, I ain't heard that name for a hundred years. She still married to that fella who don't treat her right?"

Tim abusive? Even Russell didn't mention anything like that.

I equivocated. The truth might make her hang up on me. "They were still married when I saw her last week. Is there any way I can speak with Marcus?"

"You a cop or something? What do you want with my son?"

"I'm not with the police. I'm a writer and... and he might be able to help me with a story I'm writing."

I held my breath, and the phone slid in my sweaty fingers.

She remained silent for an hour-long minute, then said, "He's working at the Waffle House 'til six."

I'd be there when Marcus got off work, if for no other reason than to find out why Marcus's mother believed Tim mistreated Aletha. It seemed I might have been wrong about him after all. That still didn't mean he killed his wife, though.

Lacey already had the door open when my Sentra stopped in front of Ravenous Readers.

"You ready?" she asked.

"You bet. Let's do this." And with luck, we wouldn't get caught.

"So, what are we looking for?"

"I'm not sure. Anything that seems out of place or tells us something we didn't know before. Even if it seems irrelevant."

She contemplated the area. "Okay. How do you want to proceed? I've never done this kind of thing before."

"Neither have I, except in my head." I chewed on my upper lip and surveyed the store. "In a novel, I'd have us split up to cover more ground. Even though you have a key, we're not supposed to be in here. I want to search fast in case somebody notices us. You know, we probably should've done this later tonight."

"I agree, but we're here now. Let's get it over with. Getting arrested is not high on my list of things to do today."

"Mine either. I wouldn't want to give Havermayer the satisfaction. How about you start in the front, I'll start in back, and we'll meet in the middle."

My half included the kids' section, stockroom, and Aletha's office. I headed for the office.

Organized clutter dominated the decor. Book catalogs adorned a corner table, two file cabinets occupied the opposite corner, and a large metal desk, covered with papers except for an empty spot where her computer resided before the police confiscated it, encompassed most of the room. I worked my way through the file cabinets and most of the papers on the desktop. Nothing of any use, as far as I could tell.

I went through the desk one drawer at a time. Only the usual assortment of business-related chaos. The only personal item I found, besides the photo of Tim propped on the corner, was Aletha's fidget spinner. She'd stopped playing with it, but apparently couldn't quite manage to throw it away. I spun it between my fingers and my mind whirled along with it, an anvil taking up most of the room in my chest.

As a last resort, I checked underneath the drawers and behind the posters on the wall for hidden clues. Nothing there. Perhaps the police had already found anything useful to the investigation.

With reluctance, I moved on to the kids' section.

No answers jumped out at me there, either. Everything seemed in order, as Tim and I had left it the other day, rows of books on shelves, chairs tucked under tables, toys in proper places. Still, I inspected beneath each table, behind random books, and under toys. If only the giraffes could point me in the right direction.

While on my way to the stockroom, the front door opened. My heart took off like a rabbit being chased by a fox.

I sprinted toward the front of the building and skittered to a stop when a uniformed Eric stepped into my path. "Hi, Jen. You mind telling me what the two of you are doing in here?"

My pulse slowed a bit. Better Eric than one of the detectives.

Lacey crossed and uncrossed her arms. "We're looking for the travel cup I left here the last time I worked."

Eric knit his brows and failed to suppress a smirk. "Jen, is that true?"

I dipped my hands into my pockets. A lie to a cop could land me in jail. Well, Lacey shouldn't have to go by herself. "Yup."

His lips twitched. "Okay, what does it look like? I'll help you."

Lacey said, "It's plastic and…"

At the same time, I said, "It's metal."

Eric looked from one to the other of us and suppressed a smile.

My cheeks and ears grew hot. "Fine, that's not why we're here."

Eric chuckled. "No kidding. What's going on?"

"We wanted to see if you guys missed anything when you searched. A clue to help find Aletha's killer."

He rubbed the back of his neck. "That's our job. You should leave it to us."

I pulled at my T-shirt. "I have and what good has it done? Have you learned anything new?"

He glanced over his shoulder. His partner had remained in the patrol car, preoccupied with his phone. "Well, we've verified Cunningham's alibi for the day in question, and the bomb was on a timer, which could've run for up to twenty-four hours. New enough for you?"

"Nothing I didn't already tell you. Except maybe the timer part."

Eric checked outside again. His partner watched him through the window. "Well, I suggest you find your cup and get out of here, ASAP." He left.

Lacey and I looked at each other, and we both blew air out through pursed lips at the same time. Lacey clapped her hands. "We'd better hurry up and get out of here."

"I agree. And, would you please lock the door?"

She bowed her head. "You bet."

The stockroom remained the way it was when we finished cleaning up a few days ago. Entrenched in the routine though, I checked under and behind the racks, examined boxes, and swept the floor in case we'd missed something. I even sifted through the trash bag we'd left by the back door and found nothing.

Lacey tapped on the doorframe. "What do you make of this?" She handed me a business card.

Anderson J. Klein, Attorney-At-Law.

"Where did you find it?"

"Under the cash drawer."

The brown and orange card had embossed print and a photo of, I assumed, Anderson J. Klein. "An ambulance chaser trying to drum up business? I find business cards by the cash registers in lots of places."

"Yeah, but this one was under the drawer, not next to it. Turn it over."

On the back I found: *Mon 2:00*, in Aletha's handwriting. No date. Last Monday or last year? Wait. Aletha had taken the afternoon off a while back. "Lacey didn't you cover for Aletha a couple of Mondays ago? The Monday before...'

Lacey chewed on her lower lip. "Now that you mention it, I think I did. That must've been where she was going. I wondered why she was so secretive that day." She tapped on her phone, waited for a minute, then gawked at me with wide eyes.

"What?"

"He's a divorce attorney."

CHAPTER TEN

The question of why Aletha had contacted a divorce attorney dominated my drive to Blackburn, although Lacey volunteered to call him and find out. He probably wouldn't tell her anything. Attorney-client privilege and all that. But still, we had nothing to lose.

The occurrence of the explosion five days after the appointment troubled me. Coincidences didn't work for me when it came to murder. Was I wrong about Tim? Had he played me for a fool? I didn't want to believe Aletha could've married a man capable of killing her. Wouldn't be the first time I'd allowed someone to bamboozle me, though.

I made it to the Waffle House by five fifty-five. Five minutes early, twice in one day. Some kind of record for certain. I hadn't always had problems with punctuality. Tardiness had qualified as a capital offense in Gary's house, where each minute past due resulted in an hour of diatribe. My rebellion began in college, and I'd struggled to get it back under control ever since. Today was a good day.

A tall, muscular man stepped out of the restaurant holding a Waffle House uniform shirt in his hand, and strolled toward the street. I caught up as my target reached the sidewalk. His clipped hair had a part cut into the right side. Throw in his pencil-thin mustache, along with a well-cut six-pack suggested by the sweat-soaked Banana Republic T-shirt glued to his torso, and Tim's jealousy made sense. "Excuse me, are you Marcus Jones?"

He paused, his muscled arms and thin face a gleaming chestnut brown. Around his neck, a gold chain glinted in the sunlight, similar to the necklace I'd found at the crime scene, without the tennis racket. "Who wants to know?"

"My name is Jen Dawson. Can I talk to you about Aletha Cunningham?"

Marcus crossed his arms, biceps bulging. "What about her?"

"I'm trying to figure out who killed her and hoping you can help."

His eyes widened. "What? Somebody killed Aletha?"

Nice going, Jen. How could he not know? The police interviewed me, but not him? It made no sense. "I'm sorry, I assumed you knew. She died in an explosion last Saturday afternoon."

Clenched jaw muscles became the sole outward sign of his grief. He studied me through narrowed lids. "Where did you get my name?"

"Aletha mentioned you." A forgivable fib. I gestured toward the restaurant. "Can we talk over coffee?"

He held my gaze. "Is Aletha really dead?"

I tightened my lips and nodded.

Marcus grimaced and strode back toward the diner with an athlete's assurance. Inside, overhead lights illuminated the crowd of exhausted shoppers who'd escaped from the nearby mall. He stepped behind the counter, poured coffee for me and cold water for himself.

We slid into a booth. "Thank you for speaking with me."

Lower lip pinched between his teeth, he studied his fingernails. "How did it happen?"

"There was some kind of explosion on her husband's sailboat."

He jerked his head up but remained silent.

"I used to hang out with Aletha at her bookstore."

Marcus stared out the window, jaw working.

I clenched my fists under the table, searching for a tool to get Marcus to open up to me. I channeled Daniel again. "When I talked to your mom, I heard kids in the background. I haven't had any yet, but I think about it sometimes." Another forgivable fib.

His stony face broke into a smile. "You heard my girls. Larissa and Latoya."

Maintain the momentum. "Nice names. There's nothing like a little girl's giggle to brighten your day."

"Larissa is six, Latoya four. They giggle a lot."

"I'll bet their mother has her hands full while you're at work."

His face darkened. "Not her. She's out there somewhere, getting high. 'Bout all she does. I gave her five hundred dollars one day to leave us alone for good. We moved in with my mama, and we've been fine ever since. Mama watches the girls, and I help with the bills. 'Sides, I want my kids raised up like I was." He watched me out of the corner of his eyes.

I took the bait. "And how's that?"

"By my mama!" His perfect white teeth took over

his expression, liquid-brown eyes sparkling. Idris Elba had nothing on him, and he knew it.

"So, how did you meet Aletha?"

He fingered a scratch in the tabletop. "She was waiting tables at this dive 'cross from Arnold that I used to hang out at."

"Arnold College?" I asked, as I stirred cream and sugar into my coffee.

He sipped his drink. "Yeah, she was in school there, and I was working hard at not working, if you know what I mean."

Aletha's face hovered in my mind. Beads of sweat collected on my forehead even though the air conditioning was blowing hard.

"I started talking to her, but she kept putting me off, you know? She didn't want nothing to do with me. You know what I'm saying?"

I laid it on thick. "She must've been crazy not to go for a catch like you."

Marcus lifted his chin and puffed out his chest a little. "She was, but I didn't quit. I talked her into going out with me one time."

His powers of persuasion began with that grin. "What happened?"

He gave me a sidelong glance. "She was hooked."

"Just like that? I don't believe you."

His grin faded. "You're right. It took a while for me to trust her enough to show who I really was inside. She must've sensed I was different, though, 'cause she stuck around. She said the outside me was a product of my environment. Then she made me promise to quit slinging and get a job."

My vocabulary word for today. "Slinging?"

He spoke into his chest. "You know. Dealing dope."

Clearly, he'd changed a lot since then. "Oh. That must've been hard for you."

He nodded. "I did it. For a while, anyway. I went to work for this janitor service and things were cool, you know? Then, I lost my job 'cause some other dude stole a watch out one of the offices and told them it was me. I was afraid to tell her. Afraid she'd quit me, you know?"

I nodded and he continued.

"Every day I'd leave like I was going to work, then I'd hang out with my posse. I had to start slinging again to have money every week, to keep up the act. Then I screwed up."

My left eyebrow shot up. I was about to hear the why-I-went-to-prison story. "How?"

"I tried to hit a convenience store. I got a piece from a guy I knew and held up the night clerk. Hell, everybody was doing it, except I picked the time a cop stopped in for his free coffee. I did five years in Broad River. Aletha left me after I got sent up." Marcus glanced at the clock on the wall. "I gotta get going. The bus'll be here soon."

Not yet. I still had a million unanswered questions. And regardless of what he might have done in the past, he seemed harmless enough now. "How about I give you a ride home?"

"I don't have money for gas. Only bus fare."

"No problem. It's on my way home, anyway."

"You don't even know where I live."

"It doesn't matter. I can get home from anywhere." *And I need answers to those questions.*

"Okay, thanks."

Marcus reached the car three strides before me and ran his finger across the hood. A long white streak remained in its wake. "You ever thought about washing this thing?"

Everyone's a critic.

I unlocked the passenger door, and he folded into the seat, sliding it back to make room for his legs. His head brushed the roof of the car.

I buckled my seat belt. "So, where are we headed?"

"River Street. You know where it's at?"

"I think so. Tell me if I get too far off track."

I inched onto the traffic-infested road.

"Five years is a long time to be in prison."

"My buddy Travis helped the time pass. My cellmate. He was cool." Marcus studied his grease-stained fingertips.

So much for Billy the Bomber. Nice try, Tim. Guess I was right about the letter being a deflection. "Seems like you've gotten your life together pretty well since you got out. You should be proud of yourself."

"I'm getting by."

This guy didn't seem like a killer, but it could be a performance for my benefit. I poked the wasps' nest to see what came out. "Must've been pretty irritating to find Aletha married and rich after you ended up in prison trying to make money for her."

He scratched his neck. "Not really. I heard she got married my second year in. She deserved to be happy, and I ain't got nothing to offer a woman like that, anyway. She deserves a whole lot better than me."

I changed lanes to make my turn. "Maybe. You might not be giving yourself enough credit, though."

"I saw the thing on TV where she won the contest,

and I texted her to let her know I was happy for her, but she never answered. I left her alone after that."

No stingers on those wasps. Either Tim had it all wrong or Marcus should move to Hollywood.

I turned onto River Street. "Okay, which one is yours?"

"That one, over there." He pointed to a faded, brown two-story with a listing chain-link fence around it.

He unbuckled his seat belt as I shifted into park.

"I have one more question for you if you have a minute."

"Sure. What's up?"

"When I spoke to your mother this morning, she seemed to think Tim didn't treat Aletha the way he should. What did she mean by that?"

He looked away and shrugged. "I got no idea. Don't know what she's talking about."

Why didn't I believe him?

Marcus climbed out of the car. "Thanks for the ride."

"You're welcome. Thanks for talking to me." Strange he'd never asked any other questions about Aletha, though.

He entered the yard and two little girls dressed in matching pink blouses and denim shorts burst through the door, pigtails flying. Each tackled one of their father's legs. A hot ball flared in my chest. Had I greeted my dad the same way when he came home from one of his flights? My mother always said my world began and ended with Jack Dawson.

A full-figured woman, brown hair streaked with gray, face weatherworn as her home, stepped onto the porch. Strength radiated from her like rays of light. Her expression while she watched the children race across the yard told me she ruled her roost with an iron fist full of love. She said something to Marcus I couldn't hear and he looked back at me before replying.

I shifted the car into gear and made sure the street had cleared enough to make a U-turn.

As I rolled forward, Marcus turned and trotted in my direction, waving his arms. I stopped and lowered the window. "What's up?"

"Are you the one who wrote that mystery book? The one with the twins?"

"Yes, why?"

"My mama loved that book. She recognized you from the picture on the back. She wants to know if she can meet you."

"Sure, I'll be happy to say hello."

I followed Marcus into the yard and the girls took up their positions on his legs as soon as they could reach.

His mother called, "That's enough, girls. Let your daddy come in the house."

Marcus stepped to the porch. "Mama, this is Jen Dawson."

His mother came down a few steps. She wiped her hands on a faded blue apron. "Nice to meet you. I'm Evangelina Jones, but folks call me Vangie. I loved your book. I've about wore it out, I've read it so many times."

I grasped her proffered hand. "Thank you. I'm happy to meet you too, Vangie."

"I just took my meat loaf out of the oven. How 'bout you stay for supper tonight?"

A tempting opportunity to learn more about Marcus, with the added bonus of a real home-cooked meal. The prospect didn't sit right with me, though. It felt like false pretenses to me. "I'm sorry. I'd love to, but—"

"You have to stay," said the taller girl, Larissa. Her dark eyes gleamed while she hopped from one foot to the other. "Grandmama makes the bestest meat loaf in the whole world."

I captured a good case of her enthusiasm. "I'm sure she does. Maybe next time." *When I didn't have fake friendship on my menu.*

"But—"

Marcus's hands swallowed her shoulders. "No buts. Take your sister out back to play."

She jumped against his hands on an invisible pogo stick. "But I don't wanna play in the back. I wanna stay here."

Vangie took a step down toward her. "Child, you best take Latoya in the back before I make you sorry you didn't."

"Yes, ma'am." Larissa took her younger sister's hand and they ran into the backyard.

I smiled, warmth filling my chest. Surprising, since for the most part, I regarded children as a necessary nuisance. "They're beautiful little girls."

Vangie turned to me. "Yeah, but the hard part is keeping them that way."

"I know what you mean." Their childish wonder would soon disappear in the world they lived in. The world we all lived in. "I'd better get going so you can eat your dinner while it's still hot."

"You sure you won't stay? We've got plenty, and you're very welcome."

"Yes, ma'am, but thank you again. I have to go."

"I understand. I know how busy you must be working on your next book."

I turned toward my car to leave. Instead, a loud, high-pitched shriek summoned us to the backyard.

Marcus reached the sobbing Latoya in seconds. She lay beside a metallic-blue Grand Am. I dropped to my knees in a puddle on the other side of the distraught child. Water soaked through to my skin, but the chill that ran down my spine had more of a psychological than physical basis.

Marcus held Latoya against his chest until she calmed enough to tell us what happened. While playing hide-and-seek, Latoya hid under the car and became frightened when her cat ran over the backs of her legs. A rust-colored tabby rubbed its face against the little girl's hand as she related her horrifying tale. Another family pet gone mad. Cujo in a cat suit. I would've bet the four-year-old would take all of five minutes to recover, but it only took three.

While Marcus dried the last of Latoya's tears under Vangie's protective gaze, I pulled myself upright, dependent on the car for balance. The right fender was crumpled and bent where someone had pulled it back off the tire, and it had bits of reddish-brown debris in the space between the bumper and the headlight. Rust? Maybe mud—except I saw none splashed in the wheel well.

Marcus responded to my raised eyebrow. "I hit a deer down the country the other night when I was taking one of my boys to his mama's house. We fixed it so I could drive home, but the radiator is messed up and I couldn't do nothing with it."

I brushed at the mud on my jeans. Pointless.

"Sorry about that. Water always puddles up there. Don't know why."

Vangie seized my elbow and led me to the house. "Girl, you come with me right this minute, and let me fix those clothes. I ain't sending you home looking that way, with your pants all messed up and such. What'll your husband think?"

"I'm not married," I said to her retreating back.

The tiny pink bathroom couldn't hold both of us. Vangie tried to reach my knees with a wet washcloth, but the room closed in. I took it from her, and she squeezed out but supervised the process from the doorway. My resolute scrub at the spots proved useless. The stain adhered to the denim. I'd have to soak my jeans in detergent water and hope for a miracle. Couple that idea with a sudden yearning for real food, and the universe seemed determined to domesticate me, but I would fight to the death if necessary.

"That settles it," Vangie said. "You have to stay for dinner now. The least we can do after ruining your clothes."

The aroma of fresh-out-of-the-oven meat loaf filled my mouth with saliva, and I closed my eyes. "It's not necessary, but it smells so good, I can't say no. Thank you."

"Larissa! Set another place next to your daddy for Miss Jen to sit at."

Larissa stuck out her lower lip. "But that's where I sit."

"You can sit next to me tonight. On the stool."

Larissa's eyes lit up. "On the stool? Yay!" She pulled the three-legged seat to the square, Formica table, then placed an empty plate and silverware in front of it.

I stepped into the tidy, well-used kitchen. "Is there anything I can help with?" *No cooking, please.* I wanted to enjoy my dinner.

"Oh, no. You're the guest. The girls'll help me." Vangie gestured toward my chair. "You sit there and make yourself at home." She poured tea from a flowered pitcher into a glass and handed it to me.

"Thank you." I took a sip. Liquid gold flowed over my tongue. "Wow! Best sweet tea I've ever tasted."

Vangie beamed. "It's my mama's secret recipe. All I can say is, two different kinds of tea all mixed up with lots of sugar."

And a warning label: for best results serve with insulin.

I settled into my chair. On a corner shelf, above where the stool had stood, perched a small trophy. A person with a tennis racket. "Who's the tennis player in the family?"

Latoya presented a gap-toothed smile. "That's my daddy's trophy. From when he was little like me."

I glanced at Marcus.

"It was one summer when I was about ten," Marcus answered. "A program to give kids something to do. Everybody got a trophy."

And a necklace, too? "Were you any good?"

"Nah, I only did it that one summer."

Vangie rubbed her hand on Marcus's back. "All right, girls, dinner's ready."

Our dinnerware took up most of the table, so, one by one we passed our plates to Vangie, who filled them with juicy meat loaf, mashed potatoes, corn-on-the-cob, and fried okra. She handed a full dish to Larissa, who topped it off with a fresh, hot biscuit and carried it to the table with care. Latoya followed with butter we

126

each slathered on our potatoes, corn, and biscuits before they cooled.

We ate in silence, broken only by silverware clanging against stoneware, satisfied sighs, and the resonance of my blood vessels as they filled with cholesterol.

I drained my tea and set the empty glass on the table. "That was awesome, Vangie. I can't remember the last time I had a meal so good." My jeans cut into my overstuffed belly. I leaned back in my chair, careful not to pop the button.

"Thank you, darlin'. Kind of you to say."

"I liked it too, Grandmama." Latoya lifted a doll out of her lap. "And so did Elsa."

"Child, what you doing with that toy at the table? You know better."

"It's not a toy, it's Elsa. You know, from the movie you took us to last Sunday. Don't you remember?"

Marcus jerked his head up. "No, honey that was Saturday, not Sunday."

"Nuh-uh. It was Sunday 'cause—"

Vangie stood up. "That's enough, Latoya. Take the doll back to your room, then come help clear the table."

"Yes, ma'am."

Saturday or Sunday matinee? The difference between Marcus with an alibi and without.

I collected his dirty dishes and carried them, along with my own, to the sink.

Larissa stopped me. "I gotta do it, Miss Jen. Me and Toya, or—"

"Toya and I," Vangie corrected.

The little girl rolled her eyes, then checked to make sure her grandmother hadn't noticed. "Toya and I gotta do it or we don't get no 'llowance."

I handed her our plates. "I'm sorry, Larissa. I didn't mean to interfere with your ability to earn a living."

She tilted her head. "Huh?"

Marcus squeezed her shoulders. "Never mind, honey. She's just teasing you."

"If I'm not going to be allowed to help clean up, I guess I'd better get out of the way." I turned to Vangie, who scraped remains off plates into the trash. "Thank you for a fantastic dinner."

"You come back any time, darlin'. We'd be glad to have you."

I waved to the four of them as they watched my departure, and an empty place appeared in my chest. They represented the closest thing to a family group I'd hung out with since Brittany's. However, if Marcus had wanted to rekindle his relationship with Aletha or protect her by eliminating her abusive husband, this one might have a murderer in its midst. From what I'd seen today, I couldn't imagine him trying to murder Tim in order to get back together with Aletha. His protective instincts were another thing, though. If Marcus really did believe Tim was harming Aletha in some way, I could easily see him doing something about it. The real question, however, was where did Marcus and Vangie get that idea about Tim?

CHAPTER ELEVEN

Monday morning, the blaring clock radio yanked me into consciousness as Bob Seger ran against the wind. I slapped at the snooze button, missed, and the red 7:00 mocked me. By the time I silenced the thing, the disc jockey had generated a squall, and I wanted to blow. Hot coffee and a hot shower became the order of the day, not the moronic mania of a radio morning show.

The hot water worked its magic while the coffee brewed. I towel-dried my hair until my phone rang. Caller ID showed a familiar New York phone number tagged with my agent's name. *Uh-oh.* Nothing good could come of this call. My publisher must've run out of patience. On the other hand, maybe Hallmark had decided to make *Double Trouble* into a movie.

Deep breath in, slow breath out.

I swiped the screen. An assistant whose voice I didn't recognize said, "Ruth Silverman calling, please hold."

Great. The muscles in my shoulders tightened. Still, she might take pity on me. Ruth functioned more as counselor, teacher, and friend than agent, everything wrapped up in a four foot, ten inch, blue-haired, brown-eyed package. The one time we'd met, I towered over her like the Empire State Building, but I wouldn't count her out in a fight. She was little, but so was a stick of dynamite. I still wouldn't mess with it.

I played name that tune with the ersatz music. "Greensleeves," "California Dreamin'", and something too obscure to recognize, then Ruth's heavy accent interrupted the prerecorded drone. Although born in New York, for reasons she refused to share, she'd adopted an Eastern European inflection, even though the last of her immigrant ancestors had come through Ellis Island in the late eighteen hundreds.

The aroma wafting from the coffee pot filled me with a promise obliterated by Ruth's next words. "So, bubbele, how's my book coming along?"

"I'm sure your book is coming along fine. Mine's not doing so well. I keep running into roadblocks."

Her tinny, speakerphone voice made my eardrum cringe. "You must give me something. Three chapters, at least, by Friday."

Three chapters. My first draft covered about that much. "I'm struggling with it. Do they have to be good?"

"No, unless you want to keep your contract." She had a hint of amusement in her voice.

"I was afraid of that."

Ruth's fingers tapping on her desk spelled out my epitaph in Morse code. She took the phone off speaker. "What's this mishegas? Why can't you finish the book?"

"I've been a little distracted." I filled her in on the events of the past week, then held my breath, waiting for the ax to fall.

"I think the husband did it for the money."

I emptied my lungs and put my phone on speaker. Pouring coffee had always qualified as a two-handed job for me, unless I happened to wear brown that day. "You and everybody else, including the police. I think they suspect me too."

"Hah. Why?"

I slid the pot back onto the warming plate. "They found part of my pen at the crime scene, and I gave Aletha a copy of *Double Trouble* with a stupid inscription about why I'd kill someone. It was a joke, but they didn't think it was funny. And they claim someone told them I'm having an affair with her husband."

"Are you?"

"*What?* No, Aletha was my friend."

"What are you going to do?"

I dumped enough of my favorite powdered vanilla creamer into my coffee to turn it beige. "I'm not sure. I wish I could figure out who did it. The cops aren't getting anywhere."

"What's stopping you? You write the mysteries, don't you?"

Ruth never measured her words. One of the things I loved about her. I dipped a teaspoon into the sugar bag, twice, leaving little brown balls behind. "I plan my stories in my head. I know who did it before the body hits the ground. Beats me where to begin investigating a real murder. Besides, it might be dangerous."

"Where to begin? At the beginning, yah? Use your imagination."

I inhaled the bouquet as if the mug contained expensive red wine instead of store-brand java. "You make it sound so simple."

"Hmmm... maybe. You might be right, though. It's dangerous. Let the police do it."

"Are you kidding? They suggested the husband killed

her so he could run off with me. If they railroad him, the real murderer will get away, but I'd still be implicated. So, danger or not, I have to clear my name."

"You are young, Jennifer. You have much to learn, but much spirit, also. Ach, such spirit I had once, but that was long ago. What I missed in brains, I made up for in spirit. But what you miss in brains might get you in trouble if you're not careful."

I paused at the steam spiraling out of my cup, but ventured a careful sip. "I know. That's what I'm worried about."

"So, where's your creativity? Think about it for a minute. What started all this?"

Good question. What instigated the situation? Only one reason Aletha had a boat to stand on, outside her house on the lake, that Saturday afternoon. "The contest. Without the money she won, there's no house and no boat. But it makes no sense. What can an essay contest have to do with Aletha's death?"

"Probably nothing, but isn't that why they call it a mystery? So, solve the mystery. After you get me those three chapters."

"I will." And, with luck, my missing brains wouldn't get me into too much trouble.

My conversation with Ruth left me energized. My creative juices flowed for the first time since Aletha died. It took me two hours to do a rough edit of chapter one, leaving it better, if not quite there, yet. Four days to get it, and two more chapters, right. Four days to save my future. No pressure there.

Ruth's words echoed in my head as I paced around the apartment: *Where to begin? At the beginning, yah?*

Yah, at the beginning. The contest. I'd never figure

out what was going on without more information about the Your Life contest.

A quick internet search produced the expected promotional blurbs and winner announcements. I went forward a few pages and found an obituary for another contest winner from earlier this year. My heart jumped into a higher gear. Two contest recipients died in less than a year, which threw the coincidence possibility into question. Publisher's Clearing House where all the winners seemed to be senior citizens, maybe, but an essay contest for people wanting to start new businesses? That would be quite a coincidence indeed.

But why kill contest winners? And why Aletha?

Someone might have a problem with the winners. Or, somebody at the contest had a predicament solvable by eliminating them. *Who knows?* Either way, this could be the clue I'd been looking for.

I wiped my palms on my thighs. I had to find a way into the contest offices. But, how? They didn't host tour groups. I could apply for a job. No, not fast enough. Who could ask questions of the right people without raising any eyebrows? A cop? Private investigator? A journalist. Scott's old ID remained in my desk drawer. He'd told me nobody ever paid attention when he flashed it. If I held it right, people would see nothing but *Sutton Chronicle* across the top. What's the worst that could happen if someone noticed? They'd throw me out. It was worth a shot.

I picked up my phone, dialed the number on my laptop screen, made it through three different menu selections, and survived long enough to reach a human female in communications. I told her I wanted to get their reaction to the death of their latest contest winner.

She replied she couldn't give a phone interview, but offered me an appointment at two.

Pay dirt. I hung up and called Brittany, who didn't share my enthusiasm when I told her what I had in mind.

"Why do you want to do that?"

"Because I need to start somewhere. I've spoken with Marcus and Tim and haven't learned anything useful. I have to take a different approach."

No response. I shifted the phone to my other ear.

Finally, she said, "I understand, but you're a writer, not a detective. You don't know what you'll be walking into."

"You're right. However, I have to do this for Aletha. And me."

She sighed into my ear. "Fine, but I'm coming with you."

"What? Why?"

"To cover your back, of course. Every good reporter has a photographer, right?" Her childish giggle tickled me.

"True, except I've seen your pictures."

"Ha, ha! Nobody else is going to see them, though. It's all for show."

"Okay, although I only have one badge."

"No problem, I'll use my Town of Riddleton ID. At least the picture and name will match."

"All right. We have a plan."

With a few hours to kill, I opened chapter two for an edit, but the words on the screen bounced off my brain into the atmosphere. I closed the chapter. A blank page appeared in its place. I typed Interview Questions across the top. What did I want to learn, and how could

I obtain information without tipping the communications director off to my agenda? What agenda did I have? To learn something which might help me figure out who killed Aletha and why. Might the contest, or someone involved with it, have a connection with Aletha's death? Probably not, but somebody had to know something. One clue to point me in the right direction. Either way, it was worth the trip, even if nothing came of it.

I enjoyed the drive to Blackburn. Surprising for a Monday afternoon. Normally, traffic made for a miserable drive. Brittany and I each stayed engrossed—I in my questions, and she in refamiliarizing herself with the Canon SLR her father had given her for her sixteenth birthday in the vain hope she would pursue his dream. She hadn't used it since high school.

I fingered Scott's badge while we trekked from the parking lot to the tall, glass-sided building.

Deep breath in, slow breath out. Head up, shoulders down.

Your Life headquarters encompassed the top floor. An elevator opened onto a deep-pile, burgundy carpet, which retained our shoeprints. The plaques underneath declared the gold-brushed picture frames, on the cloth-covered walls, held original works by local artists.

I caught Brittany's eye. "You think they have anything left to pay the winners?"

"No, it all went to the interior decorator."

The platinum-blonde receptionist directed us to a pair of double doors. Shadowy bare walls on the other side contrasted with the sophisticated reception area. We hesitated long enough for our eyes to adjust to the dimmer light, and total silence caused the hair on my arms, and the nape of my neck, to stand at attention, as if hidden eyes watched every step. Tension made the trip down the short hall five miles long.

A brass plate attached to the third door on the left read "Communications." I opened it.

A woman in black pants and a blue polo shirt came around a desk. "Ms Dawson?"

"Yes." I gestured toward Brittany. "This is Ms Dunlop. She's going to take some pictures for me."

"Certainly. Come with me, please."

She led us back down the hall to a door on the right, at the end, marked "Managing Director." "Mr Sikazian wants to speak with you himself." She knocked and opened the door.

Nobody occupied the maple desk, which guarded the inner sanctum. A desktop nameplate declared it the property of Mrs Edna Babbitt, and a door behind belonged to Albert Sikazian.

"Someone will be with you in a moment." The woman returned to the hallway.

I turned to Brittany and mouthed, "What the heck?"

Brittany put her hands up and shrugged.

A middle-aged woman appeared from the inner office, engrossed in a file. The hem of her black skirt fell below the knee, and her jacket was buttoned over a frilly white blouse with a cameo brooch pinned to the collar. Somehow, she managed to navigate on stiletto heels, which sank an inch deep into the carpet with each step.

Impressive. I would've broken my ankle getting out of my chair in those shoes. I wiggled my toes in my roomy, sensible flats, which matched my navy-blue pantsuit and baby-blue blouse. Quite professional. Great imitation of a journalist.

The woman, Mrs Babbitt I assumed, had pulled her gray-black hair into a bun so tight she appeared to have had one facelift too many, yet not one hair had come loose.

I swallowed hard and approached. Maybe she only gave a bad first impression.

She peered at me over horn-rimmed half-glasses. "Can I help you?"

"Yes, ma'am. My name is Jennifer Dawson, from the *Sutton Chronicle*. I have an appointment with Mr Sikazian."

She sniffed. "You're late."

I'll bet she's fun at parties. "No, ma'am. We've been here waiting for you."

"Didn't you see the sign?" She gestured to a piece of cardboard taped to the corner of the desk. *For Service Ring Here.* There was an arrow pointing to a white button attached to a wire stapled down the height of the desk. "If you had pressed the button, I would've known you'd arrived, and you wouldn't be late."

And if the communications lady had told me about it, I'd have pressed the button. Somehow I'd died and been reincarnated as a Catholic school third-grader. "Yes, ma'am. I'll know better next time."

"Humph. You'll be lucky if there's a this time. Let me see if Mr Sikazian can still speak with you."

Mrs Babbitt left us in front of the maple barricade. Penitents awaiting papal dispensation.

The phone rang; someone answered it. Mrs Babbitt came out and announced Mr Sikazian would see us shortly, looking like she'd just sucked on a lemon.

137

Brittany and I sat in the two available chairs.

"What's going on here?" Brittany asked in a low voice.

"I don't know, but it's making me nervous."

Mrs Babbitt studied her file.

I leaned toward Brittany. "Take some pictures to make it seem like we know what we're doing."

Brittany raised her camera and snapped the shutter a few times, training the covered lens around the office.

I caught her arm.

Brittany jerked her head around. "What?"

"Take the lens cap off."

She slapped a hand over her mouth, while I removed the cover.

"Try it now, goofy."

While she took shots of the waiting room, I eyed the phone on Mrs Babbitt's desk. When Mr Sikazian picked up for another outgoing call, it became obvious we'd played this the wrong way. My mother always said the squeakiest wheel gets the grease. Dana Davenport wholeheartedly agreed. I'd never demanded much attention, but I'd developed a knack for small talk. Painful, mind-numbing small talk.

I nudged Brittany. "I'll get us in. Watch this."

She raised an eyebrow.

I ambled over to the desk and let Dana take the lead. "I see he's on the phone again."

No response.

"You know, I've always wondered where the world would be today if the telephone hadn't been invented. Haven't you?"

Mrs Babbitt lowered her folder long enough to reply, "No," and returned to her reading.

Time to turn on the charm. "Really? Huh. I mean,

138

think about it. Look at all the people who can't live without a telephone. I know some people who will, one day, need to have their phones surgically removed from their hands."

She glared at me over the tops of her half-glasses. I smiled my best. "Please have a seat Ms—"

I offered my hand. "Dawson. Jen Dawson. It's very nice to meet you."

"Ms Dawson, please have a seat."

"Don't mind if I do." I picked up her nameplate and propped myself in the empty space. The edge of the desk dug into my thigh, but the horrified look on her face made the discomfort worthwhile. "Babbitt. How interesting. What kind of name is that?"

"Get off my desk! Can't you see I'm busy?" She snatched the nameplate out of my hand and thumped it down.

"Oh, I'm so sorry. Have I been keeping you from your work? I won't make another sound. I'll be a little mouse. You won't hear another squeak out of me." I feigned a return to my seat, but picked up the picture frame from the corner of the desk, instead. I stepped out of range of her reaching fingers. Mrs Babbitt, all smiles in front of a white, two-story colonial with a fresh coat of paint. "Is this your house?"

She sat up in her chair. "Yes, it is. Now, give that back, please." She came close to a smile but painted over it with annoyance.

Hallelujah. I'd found Mrs Babbitt's soul. The picture was the sole memento in the room.

"It's beautiful. Is it here in town?"

"It's in Valley Hills. Now, if you don't mind, I have work to do." She stood and held out her hand.

"Is your husband a doctor or something?"

"No, the house is mine. I'm not married."

"Your nameplate says you are."

"Not that it's any of your business, but it eliminates unwanted attention. Now, please give me back my photograph and sit down."

The Mrs Babbitt we all knew, and nobody loved, had returned, so I handed it over.

Valley Hills. One of the most expensive subdivisions in the area. Executive assistants must earn a lot more than I thought. Maybe I should look into it as a fallback position.

The light on the console blinked off. "Well, look at that. Mr Sikazian's off the phone. Can you see if he's ready to see us, now?"

"Gladly."

A minute later, we followed her into the office.

That's what I call service.

CHAPTER TWELVE

The room resembled a lodge with dark paneled walls highlighted by English hunting scenes and a three-foot bass on a plaque dominating the area over a well-stocked bar. A buck's head, with antlers large enough to make him the coat-check deer at the football stadium, observed from the wall behind us. A sweet aroma of pipe tobacco conflicted with my apprehension. My father carried that smell when he held me while my mother bandaged my often skinned knees. Some of my earliest recollections.

The scent rose from the tall back of a leather chair behind an oversized mahogany desk, which was empty except for a blotter and tray with pens and paper clips, a telephone, and a computer. The desk gleamed with a mirrored finish. Beyond the chair, a glass outer wall overlooked the Blackburn skyline.

Without turning, Mr Sikazian said, "Thank you, Edna. That will be all." Still facing the window, he continued, "I am sorry to have kept you waiting. Time gets away from me sometimes."

Brittany and I exchanged glances. He'd delayed our appointment while he stared out the window? How did that kind of man become managing director of anything? And, why did he insist he meet us himself? The communications director had scheduled our interview. Once again, I had a lot more questions than answers.

I shifted my weight from one foot to the other and drummed my fingers on my thigh until his seat swiveled in our direction.

From the surroundings, I'd expected a tall, aristocratic type, complete with Errol Flynn mustache and cold pipe. What I got was, well, Santa Claus. An identical twin of Kris Kringle. Of course, Kris wouldn't have clutched a half-empty crystal highball glass at two in the afternoon.

"Please have a seat, Ms Dawson." Sikazian struggled to his feet.

"Thank you." I dropped into one of the armchairs, which complemented the massive desk.

Santa had dark-blue circles under his eyes, which contrasted with the alcohol-induced rosiness of his cheeks and nose, everything surrounded by stark white hair and a well-groomed beard, accented by full, rosy lips. He drained his glass and lumbered to the bar for a refill.

As the parody in pinstripes squeezed by, I shifted to the far side of my seat. Did Santa's drinking problem have something to do with Aletha's death? Or did too many elves call in sick today?

He slid back into his chair and peered over the rim of his tumbler. "All right, Ms Dawson, if that even is your name. Would you care to tell me who you are, and why you are here?"

Brittany froze with her camera in front of her face.

My jaw dropped.

Sikazian sipped his drink. "Ms Krieger, the communications director, looked into you right after she hung up. I assume you know what she found."

I plastered on a poker face. Brittany sat down beside me.

Sikazian settled his glass on the blotter. "So, what is it you want from us?"

Brittany whispered in my ear. "Just tell him the truth. All he can do is throw us out."

Right again. "Aletha Cunningham was a friend of mine."

He smoothed his beard with one hand, picked up his glass with the other. "Edna told me about the terrible accident. It was a tragedy."

"The police think it was a bomb, not an accident."

His fingers tightened around the tumbler, which transformed his manicured nails from pink to white. "That complicates things."

I scooted forward in my chair. "What do you mean?"

He waved his free hand. "We have never had one of our award recipients die before. It causes difficulties with…'

Never? What about the obituary I found? Perhaps, Santa had a secret that had nothing to do with my Christmas gift this year.

Sikazian set his drink on the blotter again, and folded his hands on the desk. "I am sorry for your loss, Ms Dawson, but I still do not understand why you are here."

"My friend is dead. I need to know what happened and why. This seemed a logical place to start."

"Perhaps you should allow the police to decide where

to start." He reached toward the phone. "I'm not going to call them, but Edna will escort you out."

I jumped up. "Wait, please."

He wavered. His index finger hovered over the intercom button.

"I haven't been honest with you."

Sikazian lowered his arm. "Go ahead."

Think fast, Jen. "Aletha was my friend, and I do care about what happened to her, but the truth is, I think this will be a great plot for a novel. My publisher is breathing down my neck, and I'm desperate. I didn't know what else to do."

Sikazian studied me. "You are a mystery writer. I am not sure how we can help, but I am willing to try. My wife enjoyed your book very much, and she would never forgive me if I refused to help you. She has been awaiting your next one with great anticipation." He rose from behind the desk. "Come, I will show you around a little."

The trip might not be such a bust after all. The tour will give me time to get more information out of Sikazian.

The office door swung open. Mrs Babbitt stormed in. "May I have a word, Mr Sikazian?"

"What is it, Edna?"

Her face tightened into the familiar scowl. "In private!" She spun on her heel.

The blood drained from his face.

The instant the door closed behind Sikazian, Brittany snapped pictures of the desk, and inside the drawers she could reach. I picked up a double-sided picture frame on the file cabinet, careful not to smudge the silver finish. On the left, a photo of a woman who resembled Suzy Homemaker more than Mrs Claus, with two identical little girls in matching pink, mid-eighties dresses. On the right, they transformed into radiant women of the new millennium. Sikazian's wife and children. Did they know of his troubles? They seemed too happy to be part of his troubles, but anything was possible. A picture might be worth a thousand words, but it never told the whole story.

We hustled back to our chairs, and the door clicked open behind us. Sikazian returned to his desk with surprising speed. My heart pounded. I fought to steady my respiration.

It didn't matter; he never looked in our direction. "Please excuse the interruption."

"No problem. Is everything all right?" With luck, he'd tell us something useful.

"Yes, of course. Edna had a question about the audit."

"Do you get audited often?"

He lifted his empty glass, frowned, and set it back down. "Not really. We have a general audit every year, with a detailed inspection of the books every five years. That was my predecessor's downfall."

Santa's too, if his alcohol consumption means anything.

"In what way?"

"I am sure you have noticed he had very expensive tastes." Sikazian gestured toward the furnishings. "Unfortunately, the decorating money had been earmarked for other things." His lips twisted into a poor imitation of a smile. The glass wobbled in his hand.

"Audits can be difficult to deal with sometimes."

His gaze eluded mine. "Yes, but I thought we would have more..." He turned halfway toward the window.

"More what, Mr Sikazian?"

He scowled. "People to help us prepare, but several have departed recently, and we were unable to replace them in time." Sikazian came around the desk and stumbled as if he'd stepped on one of his own shoelaces. "Shall we go?"

Mrs Babbitt's magnified eyes followed us as we passed her desk. I resisted an urge to turn and stick out my tongue. A tiny step toward maturity, which remained my long-term goal, although Peter Pan would always be one of my heroes.

We stepped into the eerie, shadowed hall across from a door marked Security. "This is a good place to start," Sikazian said. A wall of television screens assaulted us, each with a different scene. Yup, one of Sikazian's office, too. *Oops.*

A blank-faced man with piercing eyes, in a steel-gray uniform complete with sidearm, nightstick, and handcuffs stood in front of the display. A tag over his right breast pocket read, "Security Chief." "Good afternoon, Ms Dawson, Ms Dunlop, we've been expecting you."

I lifted my eyebrows and glanced at Sikazian.

"Nothing happens around here without clearance from security. I am still looking for a camera in the men's room."

I searched for bathroom cameras in the display. Couldn't find any. "You mean you can't even give an interview without clearance from security?"

"No. That is why we have had so much trouble replacing personnel."

"I'll bet." Each room had a camera, with two in the corridor. No wonder my skin tingled when we came down the hall. Big Brother watched everyone around here.

Why didn't Security-bot tell Santa about our foray through his office? Perhaps he already had. Either way, Sikazian led us back into the corridor without hesitation.

We passed through other offices, learning little of note, despite my many questions. Not that they weren't answered. No signs of deceit or attempts to hide anything. And, unlike most workplaces I'd encountered, many more smiles than frowns. I guess Santa Claus for a boss created an atmosphere of perpetual Christmas cheer. For everyone but Santa, and his chief elf, Mrs Babbitt.

Public Relations gave me a promotional packet about Your Life and the annual competition, complete with video. Thousands of contest entries each day, separated in the mail room, journeyed straight to judging, and in receiving and payments, we learned how they processed the entry fee checks of one hundred dollars each. The hundred-and-fifty-thousand-dollar awards were deposited into each recipient's bank account every year for five years.

It was a brilliant setup. A for-profit charity organization. People paid money for the opportunity to win enough to start the business of their dreams. But the project had to be something that helped others in some way. Everybody wins. Well, almost everybody. The two winners who died were losers in the end.

The instant we entered accounting, the air became heavier, sound muted. Staff members wore overcoats of tension, along with the red-rimmed eyes of sleepless nights. Even the space itself, devoid of frivolous decoration or personal mementos, differed from the rest of the offices. The only actual place of business, in this place of business called Your Life headquarters.

I dragged leaden air into my lungs while Sikazian eyeballed the room.

A man with rolled-up shirtsleeves and tie askew burst through the door behind us. "Does anyone have change for a five? I lost my last dollar in the damn…" When he turned in our direction, his face reddened. "I… I'm sorry, sir. I didn't know you were… I didn't mean…"

Sikazian let loose a chuckle, which sounded nothing like ho, ho, ho. "I understand, Craig. I have probably lost fifty dollars in those damn machines myself." He reached into his jacket and removed a hand-tooled leather billfold from his inside pocket. He extracted five crisp one-dollar bills, exchanged them for Craig's crumpled five, and made no show of smoothing it out before he slid it into his wallet. "Oh, by the way, Craig, this is Jennifer Dawson and Brittany Dunlop. They are working on a story about our organization. Ladies, Craig Marshall is the beleaguered head of our accounting department."

I held out my hand. "Call me Jen."

Craig shook it, his grasp strong, but not crushing. "Nice to meet you. I'll be right back. If I don't get something to drink, I'll die." He nodded to Sikazian before he returned to the canteen for another round of vending roulette.

As Sikazian returned his billfold to his pocket, a folded piece of paper fell and landed beside his polished brown wing tip. I mumbled something about a loose shoelace and knelt. While retying my navy-blue oxford, I retrieved the scrap and, against my mother's teaching,

148

slipped it into Brittany's camera bag. A clue? Or a receipt for his dry cleaning. I'd find out which the first chance I had.

Sikazian took my hand in both of his. A little creepy, in an antebellum sort of way. I resisted the urge to pull back. "It has been lovely to make your acquaintance, but I must get back to work."

Alcohol lingered between us. "Thank you for the tour of Your Life. It's been very interesting and informative." Not informative enough, though. At least, not yet.

Sikazian bent at the waist in a semi-bow, his reserved elegance a throwback to the nineteenth century. More suited to the gilded glory of the reception area than the drab confines of the accounting department. "I am glad you enjoyed it. I hope you find the answers you are looking for. Craig will escort you out, since Security requires everyone to be accompanied in this area."

He shuffled away, and I pulled Brittany close. "Take all the pictures you can. I have a feeling something's going on here."

When Craig returned, he signaled me to join him at his desk. At least, I assumed he had a desk under there somewhere. My kind of guy—average height, average build, and disorganized. Decent-looking, too. Still, I suspected underneath he had a mind sharp enough to slice overripe tomatoes without spilling one drop of juice.

"Sorry to keep you waiting," Craig said. "It's been a helluva day." He gestured toward the chair beside his desk. "So, what's your article about?"

"It's not an article, actually. I'm a novelist and I thought the contest might provide an interesting backdrop for a book. Do you have time for a couple of questions?"

149

Dishonesty had become quite natural to me. I'd have to watch that.

His smile revealed somewhat crooked teeth. "I can squeeze in a few minutes for you. We lost a recipient last weekend, and the paperwork is a nightmare. I'm getting started on it now, so I don't get bogged down the way I did last time."

Why had Sikazian said a winner had never died before? "You lost a prior recipient? Would you mind elaborating?"

"It was tragic. A woman from Georgia died in a car accident earlier this year. I worked late for two weeks getting everything straightened out, but I learned my lesson. I'm not going through that again. Especially on top of this godforsaken audit."

"What was the woman's name?"

Craig frowned for a moment. "I'm sorry, I don't remember."

My mind went blank. Come on, Daniel, don't fail me now. "You must be a pro at handling these audits by now."

"True, but I got this job because the last guy wasn't prepared. I'm not interested in giving it back the same way." He glanced at his watch. "Now, if there's nothing else, I have to get back to work."

"Just one more question, if you don't mind."

He nodded.

"Do you think there's any connection between the deaths of the two recipients?"

He raised his eyebrows. "The idea never occurred to me."

"And now that it has?"

His gaze held steady. "I don't see how they could be related, but stranger things have happened, I suppose."

"What happens to the prize money when a winner dies?"

"The money's attached to the project being financed by it. So, whoever gets control of the project gets the remainder of the payments. And an immediate payment to help with expenses. To keep the project afloat until the next scheduled payment comes in."

"Thank you for your time. You've been very helpful."

Craig escorted us to the elevator and watched until the doors closed for our trip down. We rode in silence. The memory of hidden cameras dictated our actions.

I relaxed a bit as my car key slid into the driver's side door lock. Brittany waited for me to let her in. I smiled and waved from inside.

She mouthed, "Open the door." When that didn't work, she held up her camera bag.

It was fun to mess with her occasionally. She often returned the favor. I unlocked the door.

"I thought that might do it." She settled into the passenger seat, pulling her ankle-length floral-print skirt out of the way of the door before it closed.

"Absolutely. I need those photos."

"I love you, too."

I filled Brittany in on the conversation I'd had with Craig while she photographed the office. "Now you know everything. What do you think is going on here?"

"All we have is bits and pieces. No way to see how they fit together, yet. Or if they have anything to do with Aletha's death."

I negotiated our entrance onto the highway. "Who do you think killed Aletha?"

"I don't know. Have you heard from Russell?"

"No." The empty place reappeared in my chest. "Why do you hate him so much?"

"I don't hate him." She hesitated. "Something about him bothers me."

"I think you're jealous." I shot her a sidelong glance and sealed my lips against a smile.

"That's crazy. Why should I be jealous?"

"He's smart, attractive, and he likes me."

"What's your point?"

"You're not used to having to share me with anyone."

"Jennifer Dawson, you are my best friend. I would love for you to settle down and be happy. Besides, I liked Scott, didn't I?"

Yeah, and look how that turned out. Not Brittany's fault, though.

"Anyway, enough of that. You know, I'm beginning to think it might be Tim after all."

"Why?"

"He had motive and opportunity, and he's lied about several things. It looks bad, you know what I mean?"

She shifted in her seat to look at me. "It's all circumstantial. It doesn't mean he killed her. Besides, if they had any real evidence, the police would've arrested him already, right?"

"Probably. Olinski seems out to get him. Me too. Speaking of Olinski, he's still pretty cute. I'll bet I know somebody who might be his type, now."

"I have no idea what you're talking about. And there's no way I'm interested in one of your rejects."

I risked a quick glance in her direction. "I didn't reject him. He dumped me, remember? Accused me of abandoning him when he needed me most."

"Even more reason for me to have nothing to do with him."

"Why not? He might be perfect for you. I can see it now, Brittiella and Prince-Not-So-Charming riding off into the sunset to live happily ever after."

She crossed her arms. "Forget it. You're not playing matchmaker for me. Besides, he's been a real jerk to you. And I'm not ready to start dating again."

"Aw, come on Brittle." I used the hated nickname to irritate her. "You'd look great in that pointy hat and only one shoe."

"Sure, okay. You've lost what's left of your mind. This conversation is officially over."

We chatted about her family until I dropped her off at the library. She got in her car and I drove home. I had a whole lot of bits and pieces to fit together.

CHAPTER THIRTEEN

Brittany and I drove separately to Aletha's memorial service Tuesday morning, since I had an appointment at the lawyer's office afterward, and she had to work. I arrived first. Cars on the street near the bookstore ranged in style from an old beat-up Nissan—mine—to a brand-new Lincoln Town Car, shiny and black. I'd parked behind a steel-gray Mustang convertible and my car resembled a poor stepchild in comparison. Still, so was Cinderella once, and look how she turned out.

Russell stood next to his Honda, dapper in his black suit, light-gray shirt and charcoal tie. All the blood in my body converged in my face. He had the bad-boy good looks of Leonardo DiCaprio, in the role of Frank, in *Catch Me If You Can*, and I feared the personality to match. Despite my best efforts, his charm would save him from my anger, as I suspected it had worked with others many times before, and he knew it.

Russell smiled, giving no indication he had any idea he'd upset me.

I rubbed the back of my neck. "Hi, stranger, how've you been?"

He took in my appearance and raised his eyebrows.

"Not as good as you, I see." He cradled my hands. "I sure have missed you the past few days."

My body responded to his touch, despite my desire to remain aloof. I turned away to hide the heat in my cheeks. Betrayed by my own flesh. At a funeral of all places. He tried to put his arm around me, but I pulled away from the intoxicating scent of his Axe body spray. "Oh, really? I've been around. What about you?"

"I went to see my mother and came straight here to surprise you. And pay my respects to Aletha's family, of course."

He's full of surprises all right. Or, perhaps, something else.

I wrapped my arms around my chest. The reason we stood here settled in my heart like a stone.

"I had to get away for a while. You know how that feels. Riddleton can suffocate you if you let it. Small town with small minds. You and me? We're different. We know there's a whole world out there waiting for us to join it. That's one of the things that drew me to you in the first place."

I cleared my throat and trickled my fingers across his arm. For the first time, someone understood me. Even Scott never appreciated me the way Russell seemed to. And Olinski didn't get me at all. Not really. Of course, back in high school, I didn't get me either.

"Look, I know you're upset about what happened the other day, but I can explain."

"Go ahead."

He brushed a rogue fly off his jacket sleeve.

I struggled to ignore his long, slender fingers and the image of them on my body.

As if able to read my mind, he put his hands on my

shoulders. "I was upset about what happened to Aletha and should have waited to see Tim. I lost my cool. Then you showed up. I didn't want you in the middle of it."

"Why didn't you explain that when we talked outside? Or take any of my calls?"

He peered at me from under dark eyebrows. "I didn't understand what I was feeling myself, and my mother has bat ears. She'd have us married before we even knew each other's last names."

"I know your last name. You mean you don't know mine?"

He hung his head. The way he peeked up at me sent blood rushing to all the wrong places. His dimples disappeared into a smile. He had skated out of trouble once more. The curse of his impish charm. *Curse for me, that is.*

Brittany arrived at just the right moment, nodded at Russell, and took my arm. We trudged into the bookstore together. Russell followed. An aromatic mixture of chrysanthemums, gladioli, and snapdragons struck me the instant the door closed behind us. Vased flowers adorned every flat surface and several standing sprays divided the room at the kids' section.

Olinski and Havermayer stood in the Art corner and observed every person who entered. My skin prickled and I refused to look in their direction. To acknowledge them meant to concede they considered me a suspect. Not today.

We signed the guest book on a stand by the door. Aletha's family had removed the tables and lined the chairs in rows on both sides of an aisle. At the front of the walkway, next to the coffee bar, stood a podium beside an ornate stand with a simple silver urn on top. Aletha's ashes. I gulped, and my shoulders bowed.

The first three rows of seats filled with family and friends. Eric, Angus, and Lacey whispered together in the fourth row. I nodded to them and slid into a chair about halfway toward the front on the opposite side of the aisle. Russell joined me.

Brittany motioned toward Tim, who stood in a small cluster of mourners near the podium. "I'm going to pay my respects."

I turned back to Russell. "What were you and Tim discussing the other day?"

He shifted in his seat. "He accused me of having an affair with Aletha, as if that would ever happen."

Russell, too? Another example of Tim's jealous streak. "Nothing's impossible."

"That was. I can't understand why, but she loved that man." He nodded at Tim. "She was my boss, nothing else." He shifted again and crossed his legs. The romance books on the wall to his right held his attention. Why did he seem so uncomfortable?

I turned away.

His gentle finger under my chin turned my head back toward him. "I'm serious. I had no kind of personal relationship with Aletha. Besides, I'm only interested in you. Weird, silly, unpredictable you."

Daniel would believe him. I wanted to, also.

"Why would Aletha have encouraged me to ask you out if I was having an affair with her?"

She did want us to get together. Her eyes sparkled whenever the subject came up. My heart rock shifted and impelled a lump into my throat. I cleared it with a fake cough. "Tim must have a reason for accusing you."

Russell kicked at the chair in front of him with his black wing tip but didn't make contact. "His overactive imagination. The most personal conversations Aletha and I shared were about how much she loved him, and how he drove her crazy with his jealousy. If she called a repair guy to fix the sink, he'd accuse her of flirting with him. Tim's nuts."

"Maybe, but is he crazy enough to accuse someone of killing his wife by accident, while trying to kill him?"

Russell's eyes opened wide. "He said that?"

"Yes. And, what's more, I think he really believes it."

"If he accused me of killing Aletha while trying to murder him, he's certifiable." He waved his hands as he spoke.

When I turned away, Brittany sat down beside me, and Tim had his gaze on Russell, pure rage in his eyes.

The pastor stepped to the podium. I sighed and scrutinized the veins in the backs of my hands. The one other funeral I'd ever attended had a quite different atmosphere. Brittany's grandmother had suffered for many years, so relief prevailed over grief. And no questions about how she died.

The mystery of Aletha's death had dominated my mind for much of the last ten days. Now, once well-controlled emotions came bubbling up like Mountain Dew in a can I'd dropped right before I opened it. Aletha had transformed everyone she met. I'd only known her for a few months, but I'd never forget her. Not because the police suspected me of involvement in her murder, but because she believed in me.

By the time we'd recited the Lord's Prayer, my composure had returned. Two of Aletha's brothers spoke, and Tim took a turn until he became too emotional to continue. Grief or guilt? When the service ended, people gathered in small groups to share memories of Aletha.

Her family had a faith I couldn't fathom. Their devastation had an underlying peace to it. They believed—no, knew, their sister had gone to a better place. The subject of religion never came up in my house as a child. Of course, nobody grew up in the South without some familiarity with it. Either way, I had no idea where Aletha had gone, only that she'd left me and I missed her.

I approached the Riddleton Runners. Eric sported a black suit and white shirt with a gap in the collar two fingers would've fit in without any interference from his neck. Lacey wore a black dress, elegant in its simplicity, while Angus buttoned and unbuttoned his navy-blue suit jacket. I squeezed his arm.

"How are you holding up?" Eric asked.

"Well as can be expected, I guess." I turned to Lacey, who'd had a closer relationship with Aletha than any of us. "How are *you* holding up?"

She intercepted a tear. "I'm sad. And I feel guilty. If I hadn't worked for her that day...'

Angus put his arm around her. "It's not your fault."

Eric nodded. "We're working hard to find the person responsible."

I put my hand on his shoulder. "Any news on that front?"

"We have a few leads. The State Law Enforcement Division has the bomb fragments."

"What have they found?"

"You know I can't tell you that." He tugged at the loose shirtsleeve cuff around his wrist.

"What if I share information with you? How about a trade?"

Eric scrunched his eyebrows together. "No trades. Spill it."

"Fine. Marcus Jones doesn't have an alibi for the day Aletha died."

Angus unbuttoned his jacket again. "Who's that?"

"Aletha's ex-boyfriend who spent time in prison for armed robbery. I had dinner with him and his family on Saturday."

Lacey's mouth fell open. "How did that happen?"

"His mother's a fan."

Eric broke in. "Fan or not, the detectives spoke with him Sunday, and he was at the movies with his kids that Saturday afternoon. His mother backs him up. Sounds like an alibi to me."

"Well, his four-year-old says it was Sunday, not Saturday."

"Even if it's true, who'll believe a four-year-old?"

"I do." I spotted the detectives in the back of the room.

Havermayer examined the crowd while Olinski studied Tim. The detective cared about getting his man. Dogged determination had always been one of his best qualities. Even in high school. He should've been a Mountie. At least Dudley Doright would've considered other possibilities. Tim Cunningham had become the catch-of-the-day special in Stan Olinski's restaurant. The worm that might get him to bite.

As Olinski continued to observe Tim, my anger edged close to the surface, but we needed to call a truce. He had to get over the past and I had to get over my resentment of how he'd treated me ever since. At least enough for us to communicate on a basic level. How else could I find out what the police had learned?

I sauntered over to interrupt his one-sided staring contest with Tim. "How goes the investigation, detective?"

He smoothed the wrinkled lapel of his brown jacket. The same suit he wore at my apartment? From the look of it, he'd slept in it every night since.

"The investigation is progressing quite nicely, Jen."

"Really, how so?"

"I feel comfortable saying we about have enough for an arrest."

I wiped my sweaty palms on my pants. "An arrest?"

"Correct. Within the next day or two."

It couldn't be me if he was telling me about it. "Who is it?"

Olinski's nostrils flared. "I can't discuss an ongoing investigation."

"Okay, what's the motive, then?"

"Maybe you should ask one of your friends. Or better yet, don't." He marched toward the door.

I tightened my hands into fists. The more I dealt with him, the angrier he made me. I missed the days when we could finish each other's sentences. Sometimes.

Brittany had donned her social butterfly suit, so when Olinski cleared the doorway, I followed him out. Beyond the crowd gathered on the sidewalk, Tim conversed with Marcus Jones. I tried to see Aletha's husband through Olinski's eyes, but the picture of a cold-blooded killer eluded me. I couldn't see Marcus that way, either, so which one did Olinski and Havermayer have their eyes on? Hard to tell, but Olinski was spellbound by their conversation.

The level of animation rose between the two men,

with lots of gesticulation and finger pointing. Tempers flared and voices rose. When Tim shouted, I hurried in his direction. Marcus shoved Tim away and strode toward the corner, where Russell caught up with him.

How had they met? I turned to ask Tim, but let the question drop at his puzzled expression. Instead I asked, "What was that all about?"

"He had the nerve to accuse me of killing my wife. Him, of all people. He should be the prime suspect, not me." Tim kept an eye on Marcus and Russell as they strolled toward the Mustang. "He claims he's had no contact with Aletha since he went to prison, but I don't believe him. I can't prove it, but I'm positive he's seen or at least talked to her since then. Since the contest, even."

"What makes you so sure?"

Tim stiffened as Russell approached us. Over Russell's shoulder, Marcus leaned against the hood of his car.

"How do you two know each other?" Tim asked Russell.

"Aletha introduced us when he was at the store one day. Why?"

Tim and I exchanged glances. I took off after Marcus, who had started the Mustang's engine. He waited for me to catch up. I leaned on the canvas roof, catching my breath. The eight-cylinder Ford rumbled through my arms and made my fingertips tingle.

"What's up?" he asked, but I put him off with my index finger. He snickered. "You need to get in shape, girl."

I collected enough air to activate my vocal cords. "Don't I know it."

"You'd probably drown in my daughters' kiddy pool."

"Believe it or not, I can hold my breath for an astonishing amount of time. The kiddy pool would be easy."

"Sure fooled me."

"I used to practice in the bathtub."

He twisted his lips and raised an eyebrow.

"I know. I was a weird kid. Still am. Besides, I was an only child. I had to entertain myself somehow."

He stared at me.

I patted the roof of the Mustang. "Nice car. Trade in the Grand Am?"

"Nah. Borrowed it from a friend."

"Wish I had a friend with a car like this I could borrow."

Marcus shifted in his seat. "So, is this why you came running over here? To ask me about the car?"

"No, I wanted to make sure you were okay."

"I'm fine. Why wouldn't I be?"

"I don't know, that shouting match with Tim maybe?"

His hands tightened on the steering wheel. "He accused me of killing his wife. Hell, everybody knows he did it."

"Do they? You tell me."

He narrowed his eyes. "What do you mean?"

Spitting a bluff into the wind, I said, "Think about it. You used to be involved with his wife, wanted to be involved with her again, but she turned you down. Now, she's dead. What would you think?"

"I didn't kill her, he did. So we couldn't be together. Aletha told me he thought she was gonna leave him."

Gotcha. "Was she?"

He hit his palms on the wheel. "No. I called her the night before she died. I told you, she loved him. Hell if I know why."

Yet, she'd seen a divorce attorney. And Marcus had been in contact with her. Another falsehood outed.

Could I trust anything he said? "Why did you lie to me? You told me you hadn't spoken with her."

"I was scared. If you told the cops I was talking to her, they'd arrest me for killing her. I'd never hurt Aletha. Never!"

"So, maybe Tim was right, and you were trying to kill him, but got Aletha instead."

"Huh?"

His confusion appeared genuine, but I couldn't know with any certainty. "Tim has a theory that whoever killed Aletha was after him, but Aletha was on the boat, instead."

"Man, what kinda bull is that?" He jabbed the air with his index finger. "I didn't kill Aletha, and I sure as hell didn't try to kill him."

"Did you tell Tim that?"

"I tried. He wouldn't let me get a word in. Besides, what's the point? The cops ain't gonna believe me."

"Did you tell Tim you thought he blew up the boat?"

He barked laughter. "Hell no! You think I want to be next?"

Why couldn't these guys get their stories straight? Olinski was about to arrest someone, but I couldn't believe either Marcus or Tim had anything to do with Aletha's death. I'd better find out what the detective had based his decision on, pronto.

CHAPTER FOURTEEN

Marcus pulled away in his Mustang as Russell joined me at my Nissan. He put his hand on my shoulder. "Nice car."

The Mustang was cool, but I patted my Sentra instead, just to mess with him. "I kinda like it."

"I can see how attached to it you've become. Have you ever considered getting a new one?"

"Are you kidding? This is the new one. The old one? Now, that was a beautiful car."

"Never mind. I give up. You're incorrigible." He mussed my hair, a gesture I despised but forgave with reluctance as I smoothed it back down again. I suspected that would turn into a new normal for me when it came to Russell.

I stifled an urge to stick my finger in one of his dimples. "Nope. I can't even spell that." I sat on the side of the driver's seat with my tiptoes on the ground.

"Why'd you go running off, Jen?"

The sun's rays framed his face. A devil in an angel suit. "I wanted to check on Marcus. Make sure he was okay."

Russell cleared his throat and swallowed. "What did he say?"

"Not much."

He inspected his unsullied manicure. Russell had about as much chance of dirt under his fingernails as I did of cleaning out my hall closet.

"So, what's your take on all this?" I asked.

"I don't know what to think."

"You must have a theory. Everybody else does."

He tapped his fingers on the car. "Did I tell you Aletha called me that Saturday morning to tell me she was going sailing with Tim? Talk about a big surprise. I didn't think she'd ever get on the boat."

Russell knew about the planned excursion. Who else did? "What time was that?"

"I don't know, eight or so." He squinted into the sun. "It was the last time I ever spoke to her." His voice came out soft and low.

"Did she always update you on her plans for the day?"

"She needed me to let Lacey in and leave her a key to lock up when she closed."

"I wish we could think of something to help us figure out who did this."

"I told the police everything I know. They were waiting for me when I got home Saturday night."

He took my hand. "I need a distraction. What are you doing for dinner tonight?"

"Eating. What'd you have in mind?"

He brushed a hair off my forehead. The spot his finger touched tingled. "How about something romantic? You know, a candlelit dinner for two at your favorite restaurant."

"They don't allow candles at McDonald's. Something about fire codes."

Russell pulled me up to him. His amused gaze brought fire to my face. His dark eyes sizzled. I held my breath. He leaned toward me until my lips trembled under his gentle kiss.

I stepped away. "Okay, how about my second favorite restaurant then?"

"That depends. What is it?"

"My place. I make a mean cheese omelet." The instant the words came out, doubts took their place.

He smiled. "Now we're talking."

Nausea twisted my stomach. I scrambled for a way to revoke the invitation without a messy scene. No luck, so I ran with it. "Cooked with my very own hands. I don't do that for just anyone, you know."

"I'll bet. You'd make too many enemies that way."

I moved as if to punch him and he covered up. "Smart aleck. Be at my apartment at seven sharp and bring wine."

"What kind goes with eggs?"

"Nobody cares anymore, remember?"

"You've never met my mother. I guess I'll stick with white. That egg would've been a chicken eventually."

Now that's a yummy thought.

Russell got in his car and drove away, and I strolled back inside to find Brittany deep in conversation with one of Aletha's brothers. She frowned.

When I approached, the tall, bald man introduced himself. "Ronald Simpson. Aletha's oldest brother."

"Jen Dawson. I'm sorry for your loss."

"How did you know my sister?"

"I used to spend a lot of time here. We became friends."

Ronald jammed his hands into his pockets. "This

167

place was her dream. That's why we decided to hold the memorial service here. To honor her." He looked around the store. "She did a wonderful job with it. I hope she was happy."

An odd thing for him to say. Had he never been here before?

I glanced at Brittany.

She pursed her lips. "Did you know Aletha was estranged from her family?"

"No, she never mentioned it." In fact, I didn't remember her ever talking about her family, other than a few anecdotes from when they were kids.

"We haven't seen or heard from her in years. Not even after she won the contest," Ronald said.

"No, she told me all kinds of old friends and family she hadn't seen since she was a kid contacted her after she won. They crawled out of the woodwork. Her words, not mine."

Brittany nodded. "They contacted her, but she never responded."

A vague idea grew in the back of my mind. I touched Ronald's sleeve. "Do you have any idea why?"

He swallowed hard. "I have no idea. There was tension in the beginning. Tim isn't the man I would've chosen for my little sister to marry, but she was headstrong. Once she made up her mind, nobody could talk her out of it. But none of that explains why she cut us off after the wedding."

My heart welled. Aletha could be stubborn at times. "I can see that. If you don't mind my asking, what did you have against Tim?"

"I heard he'd been in some trouble as a kid. Didn't know what for since he was underage, but he spent a good chunk of time on probation. I didn't want him dragging Aletha down like that other guy did."

Marcus. Ronald clearly didn't like him much either.

He continued, "But we went to the wedding and tried to stay in touch afterward. Making the best of it, but she wouldn't answer the phone or return our calls. I even went to the house once and Tim wouldn't let me in. Said she was sleeping. Finally, I just gave up."

Could this be what Vangie hinted at on the phone the other day?

Brittany pulled out her phone. "Gosh, it's late. I have to go to work." She turned to Aletha's brother. "Ronald, it was very nice to meet you. I only wish it could've been under better circumstances."

He nodded and turned away.

Brittany took my arm and guided me to the door.

The notion floating around the back of my head came into full bloom. "You think Tim might have been controlling Aletha's contact with her family?"

"I don't know."

"I'll find out, that's for certain."

We reached Brittany's car, and she fished around in her purse for keys. "Where did you disappear to?"

"I followed Olinski out and ran into the Three Stooges."

She raised her eyebrows.

"Tim. Marcus, and Russell." I filled her in on my conversations with each of the three and ended with Russell's invitation. The words came out in a rush. "He's coming over for dinner tonight."

Her mouth fell open. "Are you crazy?"

"Why do you say that?"

Brittany unlocked her car. "Did he mention why he

169

didn't call you like he said he would? Or explain why he treated you the way he did at the bookstore?"

"Yes and yes."

"What does that mean?"

I deposited my hands on my hips. "What's wrong with you?"

She tucked a stray hair behind her ear. "I don't trust the guy. I have a feeling you're falling for him without knowing him. It worries me."

"I am not falling for him."

"Oh, yeah?" She searched her purse again. "I think there's a mirror in here somewhere."

I flushed. "Okay, I'm a little interested. What's wrong with that?"

"I don't know. That's what bothers me." She gave up searching. "Where's he been?"

After my repeat of his story, she had nothing to say.

"I take it you don't believe him?"

"I don't know what to think." She stared over my head. Then, she blinked and focused on me. "Have you decided who killed Aletha yet?"

Nifty change of subject. She'd get back to it, though. "Miss Scarlet, with the knife, in the conservatory."

Brittany shook her head and climbed into her car. "I'll see you later."

I waved.

The Riddleton Runners came out of the store at the same time I opened my car door. I slammed it shut again. "Hey, guys, wait a minute."

They stopped while I caught up. "Eric, I've heard Tim Cunningham has a criminal record."

"Yeah, I think someone around the station mentioned something about it."

"I was wondering what he'd been arrested for. Anything violent, an assault, a domestic dispute?"

He frowned. "I don't know. It was something juvenile, and the records are sealed. What are you getting at?"

I turned to Lacey. "Did Aletha ever say anything to you about Tim being controlling?"

She stared into the distance. "Not directly, but I wondered about it sometimes."

Angus rocked back and forth on his heels. "What made you wonder that? It never occurred to me."

"I majored in psychology in college, and I noticed some of the signs." Lacey inspected her Louis Vuitton shoes. "I invited her to get together away from the store a couple of times, and she was kind of weird about it. Made up obvious lies. I gave up trying."

Eric touched my arm. "What are you thinking?"

"Aletha's brother told me she's been estranged from her family since she married Tim. Perhaps someone should speak with him about it."

He squeezed his lips into a line. "I'll look into it. Tell the detectives, at least, and see what they think."

"Thanks. Let me know what they say." I turned back to Lacey. "What did the attorney say when you called him?"

She crossed her arms. "As we expected, nothing. They wouldn't even confirm she was a client, although I got the distinct impression they knew exactly who she was."

"Why?"

"Well, what they said was they weren't allowed to divulge client information. If she wasn't a client, why would they say that?"

"Good question. It might be a standard response, though."

Nothing more I could think to ask, so I climbed into my car and left for my date with Fiero and Coleman, Attorneys at Law.

The office occupied the top floor of a two-story building, three blocks from the courthouse in downtown Blackburn. I climbed through the peculiar silence and well-trodden stairs creaked under my feet. My experience at Your Life headquarters made me examine the corners for cameras. Nothing but my imagination pushing invisible fingers up and down my spine.

I opened a wooden door with a frosted-glass window and stepped through the doorway into a satire straight out of the forties. Minus the coat rack waiting for a fedora. However, a red-headed receptionist chomped gum like a Guernsey chewing its cud, while she filed her nails behind a battered, oak desk. Only a desktop computer and multi-line phone represented the twenty-first century.

"Can I help you?" The redhead put the finishing touches on her left pinky.

Doubtful. "My name is Jennifer Dawson. I'm here for the reading of Aletha Cunningham's will."

She pressed a button on the phone and announced my presence. A moment later, a short, chunky man in an immaculate gray suit opened the other door. He'd plastered his cropped black hair with enough gel to immobilize an ant farm, and a bushy mustache hid his upper lip. A built-in soup strainer. *Yum.*

He extended his right hand. "Ms Dawson, I'm Jason Fiero. It's a pleasure to meet you, although I wish it could've been under better circumstances."

I pumped his squishy hand. "I agree."

Fiero led me to a conference room where Tim and Ronald sat at a large, round table. Their scowls made it clear they hadn't anticipated my presence. I took a seat next to Ronald.

Fiero pulled a sheaf of paper out of a manila folder. "Does anyone have any questions before I begin?"

We shook our heads.

"Very well, let's get started." He droned out a bunch of legalese about as stimulating as a recitation of who begat whom in the Bible. With luck, it wouldn't take as long to get through. I clasped and unclasped my hands under the table. The question of why I was there ran on a continuous loop in my mind. After an eternity, Fiero came to the reason.

To Tim, Aletha had left their house with all its furnishings. To Ronald and her other living siblings, she bequeathed various family heirlooms left to her by their parents. After a deep breath, Fiero continued, "And, to my good friend, Jennifer Dawson, I bequeath my bookstore, Ravenous Readers, with all inventories, because I know she loves it the way I do and will carry on the mission I set out to accomplish in Riddleton."

Under his breath, Tim mumbled, "I can't believe she actually went through with it!" He jumped to his feet and stomped out the door.

I sat there with my mouth open.

CHAPTER FIFTEEN

I spent the entire ride home from the lawyer's office in a battle with the late-afternoon sun in my eyes, and myself. Ravenous Readers now belonged to me. I wiped tears away. The whole concept was overwhelming, and Aletha's thought process escaped me. What did I know about the business end of a bookstore? She entrusted her baby to me with a likelihood I'd let her down. My knuckles blanched under the pressure of my grip on the steering wheel. I'd move forward with my favorite movie line in mind: "Failure is not an option." I refused to fail her, or myself.

Tim's reaction to the news suggested I might not have to worry about it any time soon. He would contest the will, although he didn't seem surprised at Aletha's decision. Why did he want the bookstore anyway? He'd showed no interest in it until a few minutes ago. He and Aletha had argued about it the night before she died. Perhaps they'd had other disagreements on the subject, one of them so big she didn't want him to have it. Maybe, he only cared about the remaining prize payments or wanted to sell it or both. Perhaps that's why Aletha made the choice she did.

Since I had little control over how the bookstore saga would play out, I pulled into the Piggly Wiggly and focused on what to fix for dinner, instead. The omelet idea was fun, but I settled on grilled steak, some shrimp, baked potatoes, salad, and apple pie. A menu impossible even for me to screw up. Well, maybe not impossible.

A quick look around my apartment showed me I had five hours' worth of cleaning to do in the four hours until Russell's arrival. I pulled on my miracle sweats, retrieved dirty clothes from the floor, and gathered the myriad of old receipts and scraps of scribbled book notes, which decorated the coffee table.

The inspiration to locate the other Your Life recipient who had died came while I scrubbed the bathroom sink. Guess this cleaning thing had an upside after all. Lots of time to ruminate.

I stopped cleaning, picked up my laptop, and typed "Your Life contest" into the search bar. A reference to the audit seized my attention in the list of results. I opened the story.

Audit Manager Retires
Thomas Pendergrass, Senior Audit Manager for Pendergrass & Associates, a Blackburn accounting firm, announced his retirement today, after 37 years with the company. His departure will not be official until the end of December, and he intends to use the time to train his replacement, Anthony Moriarty, formerly of Anderson, Blackstock, and Gould.

Pendergrass & Associates has served local businesses, such as Tomorrow's Tavern, Midland's

Antiques, and the Your Life contest, since 1927.
Peter Morrow, Managing Partner, believes the
necessary alterations to the audit schedule will
improve the company's ability to serve their long-
standing clients and new businesses.

A change in the audit schedule could've caused the
Sikazian and company freak out. The audit could now
be earlier than expected.

I backed up to the results page again. More skim-
ming, more results, still no answers. Finally, on the third
page, I found a story entitled: *Savannah Woman Latest
Contest Champ.* Craig had said the person lived in
Georgia. The Associated Press blurb declared Ida Clare
Green of Savannah, Georgia, "thrilled and excited."
Only a newbie reporter could come up with something
that lame. Still, everyone had to start somewhere.

The minutes I had left to clean ticked away while I
searched for Ida Clare Green's obituary, again. Too bad
I didn't pay more attention the first time I read it. Didn't
know I needed to until Sikazian denied it ever happened,
though. I still had to do the living room, at the moment
cloaked in papers, books, and empty candy wrappers,
as if a high-school chemistry lab had exploded. I guess,
if I had to, I could shove everything into a closet until
Russell went home. Of course, I'd have to make room
in the closet first. It would take less time to clean the
living room.

The obituary appeared on page six of the results. Ida
Clare Green had died on March twelfth of this year.
No reference to how she died, but the Independent
Presbyterian Church held the service on March nine-
teenth at two in the afternoon.

No way Sikazian didn't know about this. Why did he lie? She died before she'd collected her second payment, but he claimed to know nothing about it. As Ruth would say, something here wasn't kosher.

I googled the church for the phone number.

"Good afternoon, Independent Presbyterian Church. This is Velma, can I help you?"

Can I have some pancakes with all that syrup?

I asked about Ida Green.

"I've only recently moved here from Macon, and I don't believe I ever met Ms Green. Let me ask Pastor Beauregard."

The second hand swept more minutes of the clock. Russell would arrive soon. At this rate, I might not have time for the closet or the living room. I could stuff everything under the couch.

"This is Reverend Bubba. Can I help you?"

A preacher named Bubba? Only in the South. "I wanted to ask you about the funeral service you held for Ida Clare Green, in March."

"I remember."

I released a breath. "You knew her?"

"Not at all. She wasn't a member of the church. Her neighbor asked me to perform the service."

Strange he'd remember her then.

"Do you know how I can reach the neighbor?"

"I'm afraid Mabel died three weeks ago, after an extended illness. She'll be missed, but there's not much we can do when the Lord calls one of us home."

So much for that. "Can you tell me how Ida died?"

He paused. "She lost control of her car during a thunderstorm. Ran into a power pole and died instantly."

I tried to walk off my frustration, pacing around the

room. "Is there anything else you can think of, Reverend? Did she have any other friends or family?"

"May I ask why you're interested in Ms Green?"

Think, Jen. "I'm writing an article on the Your Life contest and Ms Green is one of two contestants who have died without warning."

"I see. Well, the only person to attend the service, other than church members, was a man with a beard who came in late and sat by himself in the last pew. Later, I heard he claimed to be Ms Green's father. He even had a recent picture of the two of them together."

"What's unusual about that?"

"Mabel told me she didn't have any living relatives. That's why she was handling all the arrangements. And he didn't accompany us to the cemetery. It seemed strange."

Indeed. "Did anyone happen to get his name?"

"I don't know, but he might've signed the guestbook. Nobody wanted it, so we kept it in case someone asked for it later. Hold on."

The clock ticked away more precious minutes. I didn't have many left, so I put the potatoes in the oven.

"His name is Kingsley Franklin. Mean anything to you?"

"No. Do you have an address?"

The pastor deciphered the Savannah address scrawled next to the name. I thanked him for his help.

My hand shook as I set the phone down. Was Ida's death definitely an accident? No way to know at this point. What if Ida and Aletha's deaths were related somehow? That would eliminate the coincidence factor. And what about Craig Marshall? Where did he fit in? I had no idea, but, for the first time, it seemed I'd made some progress in the investigation.

Next stop: Savannah. Something there wasn't kosher, either.

I went back to work on the living room until the phone rang. Brittany's picture filled the screen. I swiped.

"Hey, watcha doin'?"

"Getting ready for my date. What are you doing?"

"Not much. I wanted to talk to you about this morning."

I carried the phone into the bedroom. "I need to get dressed while we talk, so don't worry about the heavy breathing, okay?"

She huffed into the phone. "Gee, and I thought you liked me."

"Get real." I reached for a pair of jeans. "Oh, I found the obituary for the other person who died, again. Got some details this time."

"Really? That's great. What did you find out?"

As I dressed, I described my conversation with Reverend Bubba and concluded with my intention to do some on-site investigating. Victorious in the struggle with my shoes, I reached for a red silk blouse to finish off the ensemble.

"Did you ask Reverend Bubba if Ida's father resembled Santa Claus?"

Sikazian? "It never occurred to me. Besides, he couldn't kill a roach with a steamroller. Maybe it was Edna Babbitt in disguise."

Brittany's guffaw made me yank my phone away from my ear. "I can see that."

"I know, right? Either way, I'll find out when I get there tomorrow."

"What if there's something sinister going on?"

"I imagine it's a coincidence, but I have to know straight up." I carried the conversation into the bathroom.

"I think you should stay out of it. There could be trouble."

"I can't imagine how. The best I can tell, all Ida and Aletha have in common is the contest. If someone at the contest has something to gain by killing off the winners, going there is the best way to get more information. And since I'm not a contest winner, I should be okay." Unless the murderer wanted the projects too. In which case, the bookstore could be my downfall.

"I guess, but I'm not fond of the idea of you going alone."

"Come with me, then, if you're so worried about it." She didn't respond, so I continued, reaching for my toothbrush. "Come on, it'll be fun."

"I can't. I have nobody to cover the library," she said with a hint of regret.

"What about Lacey? Can she help you out?" I squirted toothpaste onto the brush and stuck it in my mouth.

"She has a doctor's appointment. Besides, we have a school group coming tomorrow; I can't take off." Irritation replaced regret in her tone.

"Party pooper." I spat toothpaste into the sink, and on the mirror, the counter, and my sleeve. "So, what did you want to talk to me about?"

Brittany took a deep breath. "I'm worried about you. Now more than ever. I have this spooky feeling something bad's about to happen. Why don't you let the police check out the Savannah thing?"

I scrubbed at the spot on my sleeve. I didn't have time to change my clothes, or any clothes to change into. "Because I can't trust Olinski to take me seriously. He's always accused me of having an overactive imagination, and I haven't seen anything to convince me his feelings have changed. Everything will be fine. I promise."

"You don't know that."

Good grief. "When did you become psychic?"

"I don't have to be. It's clear you're in over your head. Promise you'll be careful."

I ran my fingers through my hair out of habit, then had to smooth the tufts. "I'll be as careful as possible. Good enough?"

"I mean tonight, too. With Russell."

What in the world? "I will. Don't worry; I won't let him take advantage of me. Much. Besides, I didn't have time for a shower, so he'd be a fool to try."

"I'm serious."

"I promise I'll be careful. Okay?"

"It'll have to do."

I had no chance to think about what she'd said. The doorbell rang. Russell, ten minutes early.

Deep breath in, slow breath out.

CHAPTER SIXTEEN

I checked my hair in the mirror again, then ran to peek through the peephole. Russell stood in the center of the reverse telescope in a burgundy oversized sweater and cream-colored pleated slacks, showing off his profile. He could make a potato sack sexy. My pulse pounded in my ears. I hauled in a lungful of air and opened the door.

He smiled. I opened my mouth, but nothing came out.

He offered me a single red rose. In his other hand, he held two bottles of wine—one white, one red. "May I come in?"

Blood rushed into my head. "Of course, I'm sorry." Like a schoolgirl with her first crush, my face caught fire, and I had to clasp my hands together so he wouldn't notice how violently they shook. *What's going on?* "Thank you for the rose. It's beautiful." I gestured toward the balcony. "Would you start the grill while I put this in some water?" I ran into the kitchen and leaned on the counter.

By the time I put the flower into a tall glass, I'd collected myself enough to face him. Russell had a fire blazing in the balcony grill, and the bottle of red breathed on the table. He moved with a cat's grace, quick and sure-footed, and even brought his own corkscrew. Scott had all the polish of a hippo in comparison. And I wouldn't even get started on Olinski.

Russell caught me in mid-ogle and grinned.

I avoided his gaze. "I bought a couple of steaks and some shrimp, although I've never tried to grill them before."

The sun framed him like a stained-glass version of the Madonna and child. "No problem, I have. I'll put them on right before the steaks are done."

When the coals glowed under an even coat of ash, he laid the meat on the grate. I sliced cucumbers and tomatoes for the salad. The evening air drifting in through the open balcony door had cooled somewhat with the slow decline of the sun. We said little.

While the steaks cooked, Russell opened the bottle of white wine and we sat on the couch.

"Did you have a nice visit with your mother?"

He handed me my glass. "Nice as possible, I guess. Mother can be difficult at times."

"Can't they all? I think mine wrote the book on the subject." The white Moscato flowed down my esophagus. Warmth wafted back up, bit by bit.

"They coauthored it, then."

At eye level, the sun sparkled through the pale yellow liquid in my glass. "What about your father? Did you see him too?"

He pressed his lips together. "I'd rather not talk about him, if you don't mind."

I drained my glass and held it out for a refill. "My mother remarried after my father died. I wished she hadn't."

Russell straightened the creases in his pants. "Why?"

"My stepfather and I don't get along very well. I was eight when they got married, and he never treated me like his own child, although he tried to put on a show when my mother was around. I wrote to escape. Turned out I was pretty good at it, so I stuck with it."

"Pretty good?" He chuckled. "Not what I've heard."

"Don't believe everything you hear."

"I'll try not to, but people are pretty insistent. What else do you like to do?"

"I spend most of my time writing, actually. Although, I do love old movies."

"Have you ever been sailing?"

"Never even thought about it." His words wandered around in my head. I didn't drink often. I'd better slow down or risk another foolish episode.

"You'll have to come out with me sometime. I have a friend who lets me borrow his boat once in a while. Do you swim?"

"A little. I haven't had much opportunity to practice."

"We'll have to work on that." He stood up. "I need to check the steaks and put on the shrimp. I don't want dinner to burn because I'm running my big mouth."

I brought him a plate for the meat and set the table.

Russell deposited the mouth-watering, browned-to-perfection steaks next to the salad I used for a center-piece, and disappeared into the bathroom.

I pulled the potatoes out of the oven.

He returned to the table with his wristwatch in his hand, his fingers elegant and graceful. Not words often associated with a man's hands.

"Something wrong?"

"No, not really. I got some water on it, and I don't want it to get under the crystal. I hate when it gets foggy."

"It's a beautiful watch."

He twisted the gold flex band to wipe out another drop and held it out for me to see. "Thank you. It was a graduation present from my mother."

The intricate scrollwork on the face caught my attention. Handcrafted, I'd wager. I flipped the watch over and found initials engraved on the back. "Who's RCB?"

Russell shook his head. "It's supposed to be RCJ, but when I took it back to the shop, it turned out the guy who did the work had been mooning over his new girlfriend, Brianna. You see what came out. The manager offered to replace it, but it was the third time the guy'd made that kind of mistake. I didn't want him to lose his job, so I told him not worry about it."

I brushed his cheek with a kiss and handed back the watch. "That was nice of you."

He snapped the watchband over his left wrist. "This steak looks delicious. Let me get the shrimp and we can dig in."

We ate in silence, for the most part, and Russell helped me clean up. When the dishes retired to the cabinet and the kitchen sparkled again—twice in one day set another record—I brewed fresh coffee to accompany the apple pie I'd bought for dessert.

"I've been doing all the talking so far. Let's talk about you for a change." He parked himself on the couch beside me and stretched his long legs out in front of him. He could even make casual sexy.

I cuddled next to him. "Again? What do you want to know this time?"

"Whatever you want to tell me, I guess. What do you do when you're not writing?"

"Mostly think about what I'm going to write. I've recently taken up running, though. Sort of."

He propped his arm on the back of the couch. "Sort of?"

I told him about my adventures with the Riddleton Runners, and when I described my introduction to Angus, Russell snorted coffee up his nose.

When he'd recovered, he asked, "Are you going to run in the 10K?"

"I'm thinking about it. Right now, I'm more worried about what I'm going to do with the bookstore."

"What do you mean?" He sat up straight.

"Aletha left me Ravenous Readers in her will."

Russell turned to face me, eyebrows together. "Aletha left you the bookstore?"

"You seem upset." I poked him in the arm. "Don't worry, I'm not gonna fire you."

He smiled, but the skin around his eyes remained smooth. "I'm not upset at all. She said something about changing her will, but I didn't think she'd actually do it. She was angry." He refilled his glass. "I'd much rather the store go to you than Tim. He'd sell it the first chance he got, to buy another expensive toy."

"I'm glad. I was looking forward to working with you." I pulled on my earlobe. "How about we discuss this over dessert?"

He followed me into the kitchen. "What are we having?"

"Apple pie. Like Mom never used to make."

"Mmmm. My favorite."

We munched pie and sipped coffee, and sat too close together on the couch. The room spun lazily, and I should've shifted away but didn't. Instead, I rested my head on the top of the couch and folded my hands over my belly, relaxing into the moment. My mind buzzed with all I'd learned today. "I found out last year's contest winner died in a car accident earlier this year. I'm going to Savannah tomorrow to check into it."

Russell shifted away. "You think that person was murdered too?"

"No, I'm not saying that. That would be way too weird. Only, Sikazian, the contest director, told me a recipient had never died before. I thought it was a strange thing to lie about."

"Maybe he forgot."

"Possibly, but an old man tried to pass himself off as the woman's father at her funeral. He even had a picture of the two of them together. None of her friends had ever heard her speak of any relatives, and he didn't accompany the procession to the cemetery."

"Could be they'd had a falling-out and she didn't talk about him. Who knows?" He held my hand in his slender fingers. "I wish you wouldn't go."

I intertwined my fingers with his, our palms met, and mine tingled. "Why?"

He kissed my knuckles one at a time, and the ensuing shock wave made my toes curl. "I don't think it's safe."

"If I didn't know better, I'd think you really cared." I poked him in the side with my free hand.

He put his arm around my shoulders and lowered his face to mine. "I do really care."

Electricity sizzled between us as he covered my mouth with his and brushed my lips, scattering promises of more to come. A fireball grew in the region south of my navel. He gazed into my eyes and nothing existed but him.

Until the phone rang and the moment evaporated.

"Let it ring," he said.

"Let me see who it is. It might be important."

He released me with reluctance. I hurried to pick up the phone. Tim's name filled the screen, and the passion drained into the air. *Do I want to talk to him?* No, but he might have information about Aletha. I swiped the screen.

"Hi, Jen. I wanted to apologize for my behavior this afternoon."

Really? I broke off a kiss for this? "It's okay. I understand you were in shock."

"Still, it's no excuse. I'm sorry."

I turned to Russell, mouthed "Tim," and shrugged.

He pressed his lips together and waved bye-bye.

"Apology accepted. Look, I have to go—"

"Olinski didn't even speak to me at the memorial. I think it's a good sign, don't you?"

I took a deep breath and let it out slowly. "Maybe. Speaking of Olinski, do you still have that necklace I gave you?"

"Yes, why?"

"You need to give it to him. It might be evidence."

"I doubt it, but okay. I'll turn it over to him tomorrow. Why don't you come with me, in case he wants to speak with you about it?"

"I would, but I'm going to Savannah tomorrow to look into a few things. I'll call you when I get back, okay?" I disconnected the call.

I slid back into position beside Russell, but anger had replaced the passion in his eyes. "What's wrong?"

"I wish you hadn't told him about the trip."

"Why?"

"I don't trust him."

"That's okay, he doesn't trust you either." I smiled and squeezed his arm. "I'll be fine. I don't think he killed his wife."

"But you don't know for sure. Plenty of evidence points his way, and the police think he did it."

"Come with me. You can be my bodyguard."

He pursed his lips and considered me through narrowed eyelids. "You know, I might do that."

Sweat appeared on my palms. "Really? That's great. I didn't want to make that long drive alone."

"Now you don't have to." He stood and glanced toward the door.

No, sit back down. "Where are you going?"

"I have some things to do at home. I'm going out of town tomorrow, you know." He winked at me.

"Yeah, so I've heard." A granite slab replaced the fizzling fireball. "What time do you want to leave in the morning?"

"I'll pick you up at eight. Is that too early?"

"No, I'll be ready."

"Great. I'll see you then." He kissed me on the forehead and ducked out the door.

I splashed the last of the white wine into my glass, turned on the TV, and dozed on the couch. Plans for the bookstore coasted through my head.

I awoke to the blaring news and fumbled for the remote to turn it off, my head pounding, mouth dry. I found the right button, but a newscaster filled the screen.

"The man found dead at the Moonlight Motel last night has been identified as thirty-three-year-old Craig Marshall, head of the accounting department of the Your Life contest. The cause of death is still unknown. Anyone with information about this incident should call..."

CHAPTER SEVENTEEN

The alarm clock produced no music on Wednesday morning, only shock jock chatter, which I hastened to silence. Annoying but effective. No way to fall back to sleep after that racket.

I put the finishing touches on my coffee routine and entertained second thoughts about the trip, but Savannah might hold the secret to the connection between the contest and Aletha's death. The newscast from last night cemented the idea.

Craig is dead. The guy I'd spoken to on Monday had died in a seedy motel frequented by drug dealers and prostitutes. What business could he have in place like that? He seemed too much of a straight arrow to me.

And was it a coincidence he died so soon after Aletha? Two people, both affiliated with the Your Life contest. What could an accounting manager have in common with a contest winner? If Craig's audit preparations produced something incriminating, the perpetrator could also work for the contest. Someone who had something to lose if the information came out. Sikazian had the most to lose, but Santa seemed too pathetic for a killer. Mrs Babbitt maybe, not him.

And what did Aletha have to do with any of it? Perhaps the connection lived only in my imagination.

Back to the coincidence theory. Not my favorite, but I had no way to prove otherwise.

Although the concept made my jaw clench, I had to call Olinski. I turned his business card over and over in my hand while I waited for the detective to come to the phone.

"What can I do for you, Jen?"

He listened to my theory about the possible connection between the deaths of Aletha and Ida, and his silence bounced off my eardrums. I needed to believe he took me seriously but couldn't convince myself of it.

"Sounds like your imagination's running wild again. This isn't one of your novels. Stop looking for things that aren't there. However, since I've got you on the phone, I need to ask you some questions about your windfall."

So much for taking me seriously. "Windfall?"

"Aletha Cunningham left Ravenous Readers to you in her will. Why would she do that?"

Here we go again. I dropped the card onto the coffee table. "She said it was because I felt the same way she did about books. I guess she knew I'd follow through on her plans to get more kids into reading. Also, I think she might've been planning to divorce Tim."

Olinski cleared his throat. "Yeah, we heard about that. Did you know she was going to leave the store to you beforehand?"

"No. It was a complete surprise."

"She never mentioned it? Hinted at it?"

I paced my apartment track. "No, never, and I'm

192

pretty sure her brother had no idea either. Her husband might've suspected, though."

"What makes you think so?"

"Something he said about her having gone through with it."

"You know, if you knew about the will, it gives you a pretty good motive to kill her."

And there it is. "Not really, since I know nothing about running a bookstore. I have no idea what's involved, or if I even have the time to take it on. I have my own obligations to worry about. Deadlines to meet."

"Hmmph. I'm sure you'll figure it out."

My voice went up a decibel. "How about you figure out why people affiliated with the Your Life contest keep dying in suspicious ways?"

"Jen, you need to stay out of this. Let us do our jobs."

One more decibel. "*Stay out of it?* You keep making me a suspect, remember? I'm in it whether you or I like it or not."

"We haven't accused you of anything. We haven't even brought you in for questioning. Leave it alone before you force me to do something I don't want to do, like arrest you for interfering in a police investigation," he said, sounding like my fourth-grade math teacher when I got the same problem wrong for the third time.

My pitch returned to normal. "I'm trying to help. If the deaths are connected, this could be a lot more complicated than me killing Aletha for the bookstore. Are you interested in justice or closing the case? I'm trying to do the right thing, but you're not listening."

"Enough." Controlled anger accentuated his voice. "I want to close the case by solving it. But think about it for a minute. What if you're right? What if there is a connection? It's dangerous for you to be involved. I don't want to see you get hurt. So, for the last time, forget about it. Please!"

Two beeps confirmed the end of our conversation. Just as well. I had to get ready.

The shower's drops pelted my neck and shoulders, driving some of my tension into the Riddleton sewer system. Soapy clouds appeared on the pale-blue tiles, as if drifting across the sky, and I let my mind drift with them. I almost believed Olinski when he claimed to care about my well-being. Almost. The possibility he only worried about me messing up his investigation lurked in the back of my mind, though. Since I never could tell what he really thought, trying to figure him out was exhausting.

By seven fifty, I'd dried and dressed. At eight fifteen, I patrolled my apartment. A caged lion stalking the clock. *Where's Russell?* My ego still stung from his abrupt departure last night, and I fought to maintain enthusiasm for the day's adventure.

At eight thirty, my impatience won out. I called and roused him from a sound sleep.

"I'm sorry. I've had a rough night."

I tried to convince him to stay home and sleep it off, but he insisted on coming with me. So I spent another forty-five minutes pacing my apartment. I had to burn off some of the frustration, or the long ride to Georgia would make me crazy. Well, crazier, anyway.

When Russell knocked on the door, shock replaced anger as I found him propped against the wall with his eyes closed, complexion pasty-white, his by and large perfect hair limp over his forehead. When I touched his arm, he opened his eyes, smiled, and offered a half-hearted wave.

"You look terrible."

"Thanks. That's what I was going for."

I chuckled in spite of myself. "Are you sure you're up for this?"

"Absolutely. Just a little indigestion, and I didn't sleep much last night, but I'll be fine. Promise."

"Come on." I took him by the elbow. "We'll take my car so you can nap on the way. Maybe you'll feel better by the time we get there."

"We'll be more comfortable in mine."

He had a point. It made more sense to take the roomier Honda, and the county garbage truck had less trash inside it than my Nissan. "All right, but I'm driving."

Russell settled into the passenger seat. "Believe it or not, I think the worst has passed. A little rest, and I'll be fine."

Fine. Right. His face resembled curdled skim milk. "Have you taken anything?"

"Yeah, I took some pink stuff. I'll be feeling great soon."

I had my doubts, but what could I say? "Okay, but if it gets worse, let me know. Keep in mind, if you throw up in the car, I'll beat you senseless. After you're better, of course."

A lone clump of mud on the driver's side floorboard stood out against the black carpet of the otherwise immaculate Honda. If nothing else, I should keep him around for his housework skills. My car had seemed dirtier than this when I drove it off the lot. I turned to tease Russell about it, but he'd begun to snore.

I stopped for an egg McMuffin and coffee, and his

eyelids fluttered, but he never opened them. I stole glances at him the whole way down the highway. Yup, still breathing. My maternal side awoke from its life-long hibernation and wanted to crawl into his seat to hold him while he slept, but my realistic side won out. We'd never get to Savannah that way. So, I settled for stroking his hair back off his forehead.

Brittany spoke the truth. My feelings for him ran deeper than I wanted to admit. Why did that worry her so? What did she see that I didn't? I had no idea. In fact, I still didn't know why she beat up Timmy Hardwick when he stole my finger paints the first day of kindergarten. Or, why she'd appointed herself my protector ever since.

We reached I-95, and Russell stirred but relaxed again when I completed the interchange. I fiddled with the radio, but found nothing but pitchmen, preachers, and top forty playlists. Having my fingernails pulled out with pliers would offer more entertainment value.

I pulled in for gas in Savannah, and Russell woke up. I consulted my GPS while he disappeared into the men's room. It had taken two and a half hours to drive the hundred and fifty miles. Not bad.

When Russell came back to the car, his eyes appeared bright and focused, and his pallor had succumbed to a little color. We searched for Kingsley Franklin's Gwinnett Street address. According to the app, I could take Bay Street to Martin Luther King Jr. Boulevard. Seemed simple enough. Of course, it would take a level of finesse I didn't have to get him to tell me why he'd impersonated Ida Green's father at her funeral. Still worth a try.

We arrived at our destination with only one hitch

when the GPS tried to send us through a dead-end street.

Kingsley Franklin's home doubled as a convenience store.

"What do you think?" Russell surveyed the parking lot.

Two guys in their twenties leaned against the wall on either side of the door in a redneck imitation of the lions in front of the New York Public Library. I couldn't read the insignia on their greasy baseball caps, and their jeans exhibited more black than blue. "Not much."

"Maybe there used to be a house here and they tore it down."

The cracks in the building's foundation and black-streaked roof shingles indicated otherwise. "It wasn't within the last year."

"What do you want to do?"

"I think I'll go inside and talk to them. Perhaps they've heard of him."

Russell leaned against the car, arms folded across his chest, as I approached the entrance with false bravado and braced for a reaction from the guys holding up the wall. Nothing happened. Russell must've appeared more of a threat than possible in his current condition.

When I opened the door, a blast of cold air stung my eyes, and they had to adjust to the gloom. The world once more came into focus, and I stared at auto sundries on hooks. A true convenience store, it had a little bit of everything: pine-scented air fresheners, circuit testers, battery terminals. On the shelf below: quarts of motor oil, antifreeze, and dollar-ninety-nine bottles of windshield washer fluid for only two dollars more.

At the front of the store, a cashier with orange,

leathery skin leaned on the counter, and the roots of her tinted blonde hair matched the scarred Formica beneath her forearms.

I ventured in her direction, and shallow breaths allowed me to avoid inhaling any more of the mildew-laden air than necessary. Beneath my feet, the floorboards creaked ominously, mushy in places under the yellowed linoleum.

As I reached the counter, the clerk turned to address a plump, middle-aged man seated at a desk in the corner. He had the color and vigor of the sheaf of papers he held in his hand, and his Hitleresque mustache twitched in time with the woman's whiskey-coarsened voice. A rabbit sniffing for carrots. A large, dumpy rabbit with matted fur. I drummed my fingertips on the cracked countertop and checked out the mummified chicken on the hot bar.

At last, the dumpy rabbit-man gestured for the woman to turn around. She did and knocked a Slim Jim display to the floor. Sparks from her eyes flew at me. *What did I do?*

"Can I help you?" Her tone made it clear she didn't mean it. In fact, it didn't even crack the top ten on her priority list.

I poured on the charm. "I'm looking for a guy named Kingsley Franklin. He gave me this address, but I must've written it down wrong. Do you know where I might find him?"

"Never heard of him."

She could've at least pretended to think about it. "What about a woman named Ida Clare Green?"

She glared at me. "Nope."

I pointed to the rabbit-man. "What about him?"

She scowled and turned around. "Hey, you ever heard of Kevin Thompson or…" She stopped and looked at me. "Who was the other one?"

I bit the top layer of skin off my tongue. "Ida Clare Green and Kingsley Franklin."

Dumpy stared at me, translating my words into his native language, though he had no trouble with anything the clerk said. In the end, he shook his head and returned his attention to the papers before him. I wasn't sure if he'd never heard of them or didn't understand the question. Either way, I wouldn't find any help here.

As I turned to leave, the cashier stopped me. "Hey, aren't you the lady that wrote that book? You know, the one with the twins?"

"Yes, that's me."

She flashed nicotine-stained teeth at me. "I loved that book. So, when's the next one coming out?"

So, she was capable of carrying on a conversation when she wanted to. I inhaled and clenched my jaw. "Soon, I promise."

When I climbed back in the car, Russell wrinkled his nose. "You smell like chicken."

I lowered my window. "Today's special."

"What did they say?"

"Never heard of him."

He opened his window, too, which allowed a slight breeze to wash away some of the stench. "I vote we get some lunch and decide what to do from there."

"You're hungry?"

He patted his flat abdomen, which I suspected would look even better without the shirt over it. I looked away. "Starving. I feel like I haven't eaten in a week."

"What did you have in mind?"

He peered out the passenger-side window. "Anything. How about the Burger King across the street?"

"Sounds good."

Russell ordered a Double Whopper Combo. We slid into one of the blue plastic booths and I nibbled at my Whopper Jr. and fries while he bolted down his food in silence. An invisible wizard had brought him back to life with a magic wand. Or a magic French fry. Only when the last bite had disappeared did Russell acknowledge my existence. "What do you want to do now?"

"I'm not sure. I had a feeling the guy was a fake when I decided to come here. I expected some sort of inspiration, but I'm still waiting." I struggled to focus.

He drummed his fingers on the table. "I'm more of a perspiration kind of guy. We ought to try a different method."

"Like what?"

"That depends. What do we know so far?"

My sticky hair fell into my eyes, and I smoothed it back into place. "We know Ida was killed in a car crash, and Kingsley pretended to be her father at the funeral."

"Okay. Why would he do that?" Russell stopped tapping and sat back.

I avoided his gaze to keep my hormones at bay. "The main reason I can think of is to get her inheritance."

"Exactly."

I massaged the back of my neck. "But how could he have known she didn't have any other living relatives?"

"I don't know, but he must have." Russell rubbed his smooth chin the way some men stroked their beards. "And he used the picture to prove they had a relationship."

"Where did the picture come from? They had to know each other."

"Unless he Photoshopped it."

I squirmed in my seat. "Okay, so where do we go from here?"

He flashed his dimples. "I've got some ideas."

I narrowed my eyes at the innuendo, although tempted. "There has to be a way we can find him. The fact he gave a fake address is more suspicious to me than his impersonation at the funeral. He has to be hiding something."

"Well, he needs a way to get the money, if that's what he's after."

I snapped my fingers. "The contest pays off by direct deposit. He would have to have a bank account."

"Then, all we have to do is find the account."

"And I know the person to help us."

Russell cocked an eyebrow.

"My neighbor Charlie. He's a huge computer geek. It'll cost me the longest dinner of my life, but I'm sure he'll help." If nothing else, his attire du jour would take my mind off his lack of conversation skills. "I'll give him a call and get him started on it."

My attempt went straight to voicemail, and Charlie's mailbox had reached capacity. I'd have to discuss it with him when I arrived home this evening.

"Maybe we could try to get more information about Ida Clare Green, which might lead us to Kingsley. Since we're here anyway, might as well do everything we can."

"It's worth a try. What do we know about her?"

"Not much. What I do know, I got from the church where her funeral was held."

I pulled out my phone and called the Independent

Presbyterian Church. No answer and no way to leave a message.

"Well, in that case, milady." Russell stood and held out his hand. "Methinks we'd best get home ASAP."

I took his hand and slid out of the booth. "Methinks you're right. But first I need to use the little princesses' room."

"I'll wait for you outside."

When I ambled out into the sunshine, Russell, who'd waited by the door, said, "I can't believe how hot it is today. I wish I'd brought some shorts."

I wiped humidity off my forehead. "Yeah, me too. Actually, I wish we had some time to enjoy it. I'll bet there's a lot more interesting things we could do in this city."

He dropped his arm around my shoulder, which tingled in response. "Duty calls. Let's go home and put Charlie to work." As we reached the car, he pointed to the windshield. "Hey, what's that?"

Someone had tucked a folded sheet of paper under the driver's side windshield wiper. I pulled it out and unfolded it while Russell peered over my shoulder. Printed in large block letters were the words:

KINGSLEY FRANKLIN WILL BE AT THE RIVERBOAT DOCK TONIGHT AT 10:00. COME ALONE AND NO COPS UNLESS YOU WANT TO WRITE YOUR OWN OBITUARY AND YOUR FRIEND'S TOO.

CHAPTER EIGHTEEN

Russell snatched the note. "That's it." He reached for the Honda's door handle. "We're going straight to the police. This is too much."

"Forget it. I'm going to the meeting. Alone!" No way I'd relinquish control of this expedition.

"The only place you're going is home, after we talk to the cops. You got it?"

My blood pressure threatened to blow out the top of my head, turning me into a human volcano. "Excuse me? If you want to go, here are the keys."

"That's dumb. How will you get back? It's a long walk."

"Not your problem."

He reached for my arm.

I pulled away.

"Don't do this, Jen." His solemn brown eyes softened, voice pleading.

I wavered, then strengthened my resolve. "I'm going to the meeting. Aletha is dead. Somebody has to stand up for her, and I seem to be the only one interested in doing that."

He pointed his index finger at my nose. "That's what

the police are for. You're nuts if you think I'm gonna let you do something so stupid. I care about you. You asked me to come with you to keep you safe. Remember?"

Tempted to bite the challenging finger, I took a step forward instead. He stepped back. *Score one for me.* "You're nuts if you think I'm gonna leave when I have a chance to find out what's going on here."

His fire-engine-red face stiffened. He took several deep breaths, then said, "Think about it rationally. Why leave a note? Why not talk to you here and now? And why ask to meet you at night, in a deserted place? This guy could be a psycho for all you know."

"So could you, for all I know."

Russell smiled. "True, but we'll leave the fun stuff for later." He took both my hands in his. "I don't want anything to happen to you. I've been looking for you all my life. Let the police handle this."

Looking for me? A guy like him?

Withdrawing, I sat on the hood of the car with my arms folded to put some distance between us. No way he would charm me out of my decision. "The police won't be the least bit interested in this."

Russell gripped my shoulders, his face relaxing. "How do you know? We can explain the situation. Tell them how important this is. At least give them a chance to look into it."

I peeled his hands away and held them. Soft, smooth, uncalloused palms, which had never seen a minute's manual labor. "I know. My roommate in college received threatening notes and she took them to the police. They ignored it, and three weeks later she was attacked in the parking area. They caught the guy and, even then, insisted the notes had nothing to do with it. The guy's handwriting didn't match or something stupid like that. Like you can't change your handwriting by holding the pen a little different. The note said 'no cops.' How do we know he's not watching us right now? If I want to learn anything, I have to go by myself."

Russell disentangled his fingers and brushed the hair off my forehead. He looked into my eyes. "The information won't do you any good if you're dead."

His gaze hypnotized me, but I wouldn't fall for it. "I'll be fine."

"I know you believe that. Didn't we have this conversation last night?"

"Now that you mention it. Too bad we can't use the same solution."

He squinted into the afternoon sun. "Maybe we can."

"How?"

"I'll go with you."

"You can't. The note said come alone, and I'm not in the mood to write my own obituary. Yours either. I have a headache."

"You *are* a headache." Russell poked me in the shoulder. "What if he doesn't know I'm there?"

I looked at the sky, and blinked against the glare. "You mean you'd hide somewhere?"

"Sure, why not?"

That might be a workable solution. "What if he follows us?"

"I'll hunker in the back."

"It's too risky, Russell." I rested my hands on my hips.

"I'll be careful. You're not going alone. One way or the other, I'm going to be there." His jaw bulged, but his eyes remained soft.

Perhaps a witness wouldn't hurt anything. "Okay."

He grinned. "Good."

My shoulder muscles stiffened, and my head had a vise locked around it. We'd have to make it work.

"Now that's settled, what do you want to do?" I slid off the Honda, leaving a wide, clean swath on the hood. It hadn't seemed that dirty. I brushed off the back of my pants.

"First of all," he checked his watch, "ten's pretty late for us to be driving back home. I think we should get a room for the night."

Warmth rose up my neck, and my mind raced. Not ready for that, yet.

As if he could read my thoughts, he put up his hands. "We can get two rooms, or separate beds, whatever. We're already tired and the meeting is late. It won't be safe to drive home after."

"Fine. Where do you want to stay?"

"I saw some motels on Bay Street right before we made the turn. Why don't we try one of those?"

Deep breath in, slow breath out.

We ended up in one room, with two beds, and split the bill. Housekeeping wouldn't get to our room for another couple of hours, so we had some free time.

"Why don't we go to the meeting place and scope it out?" I asked.

"You're sure you don't want to go to the police?"

"Positive. I think we've covered that pretty well already, don't you?"

I found the shortest route to our destination on my phone. It took about fifteen minutes to get there. The boardwalk had a full complement of tourists and locals enjoying the late summer sun. We took pictures for three different couples—one each from Germany and Australia, and one from Idaho—in the shadow of the large, white riverboat replica with *Savannah River Queen* painted on its hull.

Russell bought a couple of Creamsicles from a sidewalk vendor. We hung over the rail that separated us from the river, dripped ice cream, and basked in the slight breeze. The sun glistened on the water.

"So, what do you think?" He followed a boat in the distance.

I turned to face the crowd. "I think it's not going to be anything like this tonight. This place will be deserted."

"I know, but I don't see anywhere someone could hide."

"Which means there's no place for you to hide, either. You'll have to stay in the car."

"At least, whatever he does, it'll have to be out in the open."

"Yup, but hopefully, he'll only want to talk."

"Here's to talk." Russell pulled the last of his ice cream off the stick with his lips.

The room had the typical, modern motel motif, with nondescript wallpaper and carpet to match. Restful autumn colors: orange and harvest gold. A prairie landscape stretched the width of both beds, bolted to the wall. Even the air lacked substance.

I flipped through the regulation Bible and guidebook in the nightstand, while Russell flipped through all two-thousand channels on the television. Five minutes alone together and we already ignored each other. Not a good sign.

Neither of us wanted to go out, so we settled on pizza delivery for dinner. Pepperoni and mushroom on my half, sausage and black olive on his. We ate in silence. I fought fatigue while Russell continued to channel-surf. I once asked Gary why men did that, but his response—what do you care, bring me another beer—didn't help much.

I swallowed three slices of the medium and dozed off. When I woke up, the empty pizza box lay beside Russell, spread across the other bed, asleep. A scene more for a couple with fifty years of marriage behind them. Good or bad? *Beats me.*

Wide awake, the planned meeting front and center in my mind, I took a walk so as not to disturb Russell with my inability to sit still. I passed the long row of identical orange doors on my way to the lobby. Each room had its own story. Maybe a couple engaged in an extramarital affair behind one door, a bank robber who ducked the police behind the next, and a woman with her two kids hiding from an abusive husband behind the one after that. The Davenport twins could spend months solving all the potential crimes in this place. Lots of fodder for a novel. If I ever finished the one on my desk at home.

The motel lobby provided little variance to the monotony, so I used the opportunity to call Brittany at work on her one late night of the week. The muzak version of "Hello Dolly" entertained me until she came to the phone. *I can name that tune in three notes.*

"Don't fuss. I'm still in Savannah. We're spending the night and coming back tomorrow."

"We?"

The picture of Russell the way I'd last seen him,

stretched out on the bed, made me smile. "Russell came along to protect me from the bad guys."

"I'll bet. Rushing things a bit, aren't you?" Her sarcasm flowed over the airwaves.

The phone weighed down my hand. "It's not what you think, Brittany."

"Oh? What else could it be?"

I couldn't understand the shrill pitch her voice had taken on, but I also didn't want to fight. I had to tell her about the note on the windshield.

"Are you crazy?"

I must be, since everyone kept asking me that. "I'm trying to find something to convince Olinski Tim didn't kill Aletha and neither did I. Someone else connected to the contest died, and a strange man showed up at her funeral. Also, Craig died under suspicious circumstances. I—"

"Wait! Craig died? When did that happen?"

"The other night, at some motel in Blackburn. It was on the news. I don't know how or why, though."

She sighed. "That's a shame. He was a nice guy."

"He was, which is why I need to find the link, if there is one. Is that so hard to understand?"

"No, but what good will it do if you get killed in the process?" Angry Brittany had returned. Someone I'd had to contend with more often these days than ever before.

I leaned against the wall while we talked. My customer satisfaction survey response would include a request for chairs in the lobby. "Why would anyone feel threatened by me? I'm nobody, and I don't know anything. Besides, I'll be surprised if he even shows up."

"Everyone thinks they're invincible until they're a statistic."

"You read too much."

"And you write mystery novels. You should know better," she said. "Call the police. They can protect you."

"If I show up with the police, you think the guy's gonna come out waving his hands in the air?" I stood up straight and shifted my weight from one foot to the other.

She changed tactics. "What does Russell think of all this?"

"He doesn't like it any more than you do. He's insisted on going with me so I'll be safe. Happy?"

"It's a start, but I still think you should let the police handle it." Her voice relaxed. "Besides, who's going to protect you from him?"

"What makes you think I want protection?" I said with a giggle.

"That's what I'm worried about."

"No cause for alarm. We have separate beds."

She fell right into our old routine. "As did Ricky and Lucy Ricardo. So, where did Little Ricky come from?"

I shifted my weight again, legs twitchy in anticipation of the night's adventure. "They shoved the beds together. The ones in our room are anchored to the floor."

Brittany chuckled. "I feel much better now. You're grown, do what you want. I just don't want to see you get hurt."

Only the meeting with Kingsley Franklin occupied my mind right now. "I don't want to see me get hurt, either, but I don't think it'll come to that."

"I'll take your word for it. But, do me a favor, call me when you get back to your room tonight so I'll know you're all right."

"I can do that. If I'm not lost in the throes of passion, that is. Otherwise, it might have to wait 'til morning."

"I'm serious. If I don't hear from you by eleven, I'm calling the police, okay?"

The phone slid in my sweaty fingers. "I promise, I'll call you by then, no matter what."

It felt like an army of ants crawled down the back of my neck, as if someone watched me put the phone back in my pocket. *Big Brother down here, too?* The desk clerk concentrated on the lobby television, and nothing outside the window seemed amiss. I must have absorbed Brittany's paranoia and added it to my own.

My phone rang. It was an unknown number. I swiped on the second ring.

"Jen."

The familiar voice raised the hackles on my neck.

"What can I do for you, Olinski?"

"I've got a better question. Where's Tim Cunningham?"

I swallowed part of my anger. "How would I know?"

"He's not with you?"

Russell's sleeping face popped into my mind. "He's certainly not with me. I have no idea where he is."

"The evidence points to you and Tim working together to get rid of his wife. Did you help him?"

An icicle dripped down my backbone. "You should know better than to even ask me that. I have no idea if he killed his wife, but I'm certain I didn't help whoever did, and I'm not having an affair with Tim Cunningham."

"Well, I've got three witnesses who say you are."

"That's ridiculous. When did you start listening to gossipmongers?"

Olinski breathed into the phone. "I didn't want to

have to do this, Jen, but you need to come in for questioning tomorrow morning."

"What are you talking about? You know me. I'd never hurt anyone."

"It doesn't matter what I know. I have to do my job. I want to see you at the station at nine o'clock."

Is he for real? "I'm not in town right now, so it'll have to wait."

"It's not a request. I'll come and get you if I have to."

"Good luck with that."

Silence. Finally, he asked, "Where did you say you were?"

"I didn't." I hung up.

CHAPTER NINETEEN

Russell was snoring softly on the bed when I returned to the room, but the conversation with Olinski had boosted my stress level to twelve on a scale of one to ten. His existence put me on high alert. The one person, besides my mother, who could infuriate me to that degree.

I sat at the table by the window, the curtains open enough to watch the traffic go by. The half-moon hung low in the sky, and despite the glare from the city lights, a few stars twinkled. I lost myself in the peaceful view, making out the Big Dipper, the Little Dipper, and Orion, the hunter. If I could sit here gazing at the stars forever, I'd have the perfect life.

Another day bites the dust. The words to the Queen song with a similar line ran through my head, and I had to force myself to focus on something else. Unfortunately, the replacement involved Tim Cunningham. Why had he disappeared? Not the action of an innocent man, no doubt. Could I have been that wrong about him? And Olinski still insinuated we'd killed Aletha together. I'd be amused if he didn't have the power to arrest me for it. The meeting tonight might provide my chance to prove to Olinski I wasn't a flaky writer with no sense, who had no clue how the real world worked.

What connection could there be between the mysterious Kingsley Franklin and Ida Clare Green here in Savannah, and Aletha Cunningham and Craig Marshall in South Carolina? They didn't seem to have any relationship, yet my gut screeched otherwise. What did Ida Clare Green and Aletha Cunningham have in common? They'd both won the Your Life contest and they'd both died. There was something missing in between. Perhaps, Craig Marshall had discovered something someone had killed him over. Something that knitted the threads together.

A red strobe light flashed across the sky. An airplane star. *Where's my ticket?* I needed a change. My old routines didn't work anymore. I'd spent too much time treading water, so maybe I needed to learn how to swim. *But where to start?*

Russell groaned and I turned toward him. His hands and eyes twitched. Was it a nightmare about me? Paranoia. My favorite neurosis. Dr Margolis hadn't helped with that one.

He turned over and settled again. I hated to disturb his much-needed rest, but we'd have to leave soon. If I went without him, he would worry, but, more importantly, my safety hinged on his presence. I needed to find out who'd killed Aletha, but was I willing to die in the process?

I touched Russell's shoulder. He dreamed on. I gave him a harder tap and called his name. He opened his eyes, but they remained unfocused.

"Hey, sleepyhead. Time to get up."

He stretched his arms above his head and smacked his hand on the headboard. "What time is it?"

I chuckled and checked the nightstand clock. "Not quite nine thirty. We have to leave in a few minutes."

He shook out his hand. "I can't believe I slept so long. What've you been doing all this time?"

His hair stuck out and little lines from the bedspread crisscrossed his face. My heart tap-danced. I inhaled to slow my breathing. No time for that now.

"Contemplating the meaning of life. Watching my nails grow."

"Sounds wonderful."

"It's tedious actually, all the brainwork and everything. Gives me a headache." The banter slowed the tension that rippled through my muscles a tiny bit. I tapped my fingers against my leg, made myself stop, and tapped my foot instead. Pathetic.

"I'll bet. Let me throw some water on my face and I'll be ready to go."

He tossed the towel he'd used to dry his hands on the bed, then we stepped out into the balmy September night, the air heavy with moisture, but not chilly. In another month, I'd need a jacket, but I'd enjoy that. I liked to pretend autumn in fact existed here, even though it didn't.

When we got to the car, I opened the back door for Russell to get in.

He stopped. "What are you doing?"

"I'm letting you hide in the back, the way you said you would."

"Here? Why can't I wait until we get there?"

Adrenaline-produced sweat soaked my T-shirt under my arms, and I spoke with manufactured composure through gritted teeth. "Because we might be followed.

I'm supposed to go alone. You hide in the back. That was the deal."

"But how do you know he isn't watching us right now?"

"I don't, but what do you want me to do about it? Pull the car into the room? You get in the back or you don't come. What's it gonna be?"

He released a drawn-out breath.

My chest tightened. He only wanted to help. "I'm sorry, but I want a chance to talk to this guy. I don't want to blow it."

"I know. I'll behave." He relocated a canvas bag from the floor onto the seat.

"What's that?"

"My workout clothes." He shifted the satchel farther back.

"I never work out. Other than my Saturday morning run. And that's a stretch since I've only been once. Unless, you count my failed attempt the other day."

Russell squeezed into the space behind the driver's seat. "I believe you, but aren't you glad you're not the one trying to fit back here now?"

I mussed his hair and pushed him. "Nobody ever said playing knight in shining armor was easy."

"Ha, ha."

"I'm sorry you're so uncomfortable. Let's get going."

I retraced the journey from this afternoon, parking on the street by the waterfront, where Russell would have a clear view of the meeting place, and my car wouldn't stand out as the only one in the parking lot. The silent, still air settled on me like a cloud. A chill ran down my spine.

My phone read 9:57. I got out of the car and crossed the street to the cement area, which served as a boardwalk, and the *Savannah River Queen* loomed over me, adorned by the fog that drifted across the water. No sign of Kingsley Franklin. I sauntered down the length of the boat and trailed my hand along the rail. Nothing to do but wait. The moon flitted between the clouds, and the misty reflection gave the river a marshy look. Minus cattails and rotten logs, plus the sheen of motor oil and floating trash. The haze could never hide that, although it did hide Russell's car from view. If I couldn't see him, could he see me? I hoped so.

By ten fifteen, I'd given up my patrol and stood with my foot propped on the lower rail, staring out over the water. The guy probably wouldn't show up, but it was worth a few more minutes to know for sure. The waves lapped against the boat, and it swayed an inch or so out on its tether. I pulled on the rope, and the boat came back to the dock. A power rush from having moved so large an object with my bare hands thrummed through my body. A macho moment.

I tipped my head back to see more of the vessel, and my imagination provided the music and bunting which would've accompanied the gentlemen in spats and the ladies with their parasols. The lower deck would house the gamblers with their cigars and marked cards, and the huge wheels paddled them all down the Mississippi. Only Mark Twain was absent.

Footfalls behind me made my body tense. I caught a glint of metal out of the corner of my eye, and something hit my jaw. My head snapped around. Strong arms pinned mine. I kicked wildly, connecting with bone and creating enough of a distraction to break my arm free. An odorous rag covered my nose and mouth. I held my breath.

I pulled at the arm that held me. My heel crashed into a shin, but it elicited only grunts. My heart raced, and sweat stung my eyes. I twisted away, but the hand across my mouth jerked my head back. My neck cracked. Pain shot through my skull. My nose burned from the rag's acrid fumes. Tears leaked from my eyes. My lungs ached for air. Frantic, I inhaled, searing my throat. Everything went black.

When I came to, icy water filled my mouth and nose. My sinuses burned and I flailed my arms, fighting to remain on the surface. A tremendous unseen force pulled me under. Water closed over me. I sank toward the bottom of the river.

My heart pounded, and I concentrated on equanimity. Why hadn't I learned how to swim better? *God, please give me the chance and I promise I'll practice.* I'd grown up without religion, but no atheists existed in a foxhole, or at the bottom of a river.

I stopped sinking. The moonlit surface shimmered far above me. I pulled my arms through the water to head for it. But I didn't move. Something held me by the ankles. I reached down to my feet. It felt like thick rope, which supported some sort of weight on the bottom. I floated, tethered above it like one of those fish-tank divers. Tiny bubbles swirled around me, clinging to my skin. If I could get the rope off, I might have a chance. Could I hold my breath long enough?

I needed Tim Cunningham, the rope king. *And where was Russell when I needed him?*

My frozen fingers stiffened, unable to pull the rope from my ankles. The murky water blinded me. Something bumped against my legs. Fish. An effort to jerk away burned the rope into my flesh. The bones in my ankles crunched together. Pain shot up my legs. I bit my lip and drew blood.

I swayed with the current, the rope pulling my feet away from my ankles. The many years of practice in the bathtub would come in handy at last. How long could I hold my breath? Two minutes, maybe three. How much time had already elapsed? Twenty seconds. Possibly, a little more. My lungs thought it was twenty years as the pressure built. I had to monitor the time as it passed.

One Mississippi, two Mississippi, three Mississippi.

The thick rope bound my ankles. I pulled at the cord, but my hand slipped right off. Lights danced in my eyes, and my lungs balked against the force from within.

Eleven Mississippi, twelve Mississippi.

With numb fingers, I examined the rope. No frayed spots, the thing appeared brand new. Why did that seem important? *Oh God. Help me.*

Rough fibers cut into my skin.

Twenty Mississippi, twenty-one Mississippi, twenty-two Mississippi.

I had to concentrate.

My fingers worked at the cord while the words *new rope* played through my mind. What had Tim said about new rope?

Thirty-five Mississippi, thirty-six Mississippi.

It stretches. New rope stretches when it gets wet, but only if it's not synthetic. *God, please don't let it be synthetic.* I had to make the rope stretch enough to get away.

I yanked my feet in opposite directions, but my thighs cramped, and I had to stop. I inserted as many of my fingers as would fit between the rope and my ankle and pulled hard. When I removed my hand, more room existed between my feet. The rope was made of natural fibers. *Thank you, God.* I had close to enough space to get one foot through.

Forty Mississippi, forty-one Mississippi.

A minute left, at most. My lungs screamed for air. I fought the impulse to breathe.

Forty-five Mississippi, forty-six Mississippi.

I pulled my left foot up to the rope, but it stuck. I kicked my feet and tried the finger trick again. Still nothing. Running out of time.

Sixty-five Mississippi, sixty-six Mississippi.

My lungs ached. My heart's staccato beat vibrated in my belly. I would have to breathe soon, one way or the other. I released a few bubbles and tried to jerk my foot out again. No good.

I pulled on the rope and struggled to kick off my shoes. My feet had swelled, but in the end, the Nikes dropped to the bottom.

Seventy-eight Mississippi, seventy-nine Mississippi.

One chance left. My lungs would hold out no longer. When I yanked on the rope, my left foot squeezed through the space. I would make it. Then, the noose tightened around my right ankle.

Ninety Mississippi, ninety-one Mississippi.

Time had run out.

Air seeped out of my lungs and I jerked on the rope one final time. My endurance gave way in one large bubble at the same time as my foot came out of the loop.

The water turned faded gray, dotted with sparkling lights. I kicked toward the surface.

CHAPTER TWENTY

I broke through the surface and vomited water hinting of motor oil, fish, and rotten vegetation. I gulped for air and coughed, each breath a fiery agony, each heartbeat a knife in my chest. Water lapped against my chin, and I lowered my head into a makeshift back float.

I had to get out of the river. I turned in a slow circle to get my bearings. My sodden jeans sucked me down. The moon hid behind a cloud. Eerie darkness blanketed me. Waves lapped against the receding riverboat, which gave me a sense of direction while the current carried me farther downstream.

A call for help resulted in a pitiful croak even I couldn't hear. No cavalry would save the day this time. I was on my own. No, I had the twins to help me. What would Dana do? She'd fight.

My eyes adjusted, and a large dark object materialized near the riverbank. I couldn't tell if it progressed with the current. I kicked my sluggish legs and propelled myself toward the target. My breath came in short, rough, gasps.

The cloud slid across the sky, and the moon peeked

out far enough to illuminate a small dock, which listed to one side. My next destination.

I drifted and dogpaddled for what seemed hours, but the moon hadn't moved from its position, the city lights in the distance had come no closer. My arms carried lead weights, and the muscles in my back cramped.

The dock loomed ahead at last, and I kicked toward the nearest pylon, then wrapped my arms around the creosote-covered wooden post. My neck muscles relaxed, which sent fire up the back of my scalp. I closed my eyes.

Spasms rippled through my shoulders. Would I have enough strength to climb out of the water?

I gripped the edge of the platform with my right hand and summoned the energy to do the same with my left. I hung on by my arms, my shoulders rebelled. A ragged groan escaped.

When the spasms faded, I had to move or fall back into the water. I forced my stubborn arms into action and pulled my upper body onto the weatherworn boards, resting my weight on my forearms. Barnacles dug into my flesh.

I heaved myself farther onto the dock. Bent over the boards, I lay quivering.

I rested until I regained enough strength to swing my left leg onto the dock. A surge of pain in my hip joints almost catapulted me back into the river. I cried out and bit my bottom lip. Blood dripped down my chin.

It took three more tries until I could lift my leg high enough to get my knee on the edge. Uncontrollable trembles forced a bucket of river water and pizza out of me onto the pier. I ran a rough tongue over my lips. The cool breeze lowered my body temperature, but unable to make my muscles work, I curled up and dropped into peaceful oblivion.

When I came to and tried to sit up, I disgorged what little remained in my stomach. Pain lit up every nerve ending in my body, and my mind reeled. Where was Russell? Had my attacker killed him first? No, I would've seen or heard something. Unless it happened while I was unconscious. I had to find him, but before I could do that, someone had to find me. No way I could spend the rest of the night wandering the empty streets looking for help. Sitting up was enough of a challenge already.

My rubber-band legs balked under the weight of my saturated clothing. I forced myself onto my elbows. A huge wolf came toward me.

I shook my head, and water crackled in my ears. Not a wolf. A German shepherd. "Here, boy!"

The wolf dog's ears perked up and he stepped toward me.

Please be friendly.

The little adrenaline I had left fluttered in my belly, without enough power for real fear, though. No fight or flight, this time.

When he drew closer, I could see milk-laden teats hanging from his stomach. He was a she, and she had puppies.

She stopped six feet away. I lay still. She watched me with eyes that reflected green in the moonlight. A magnificent animal—black and tan, with a touch of silver on her muzzle. Well cared for. She took another step toward me. I lifted my hand and she stopped.

"Go get help, girl. Jenny's fallen in the well."

The dog sat and cocked her head. She hadn't seen *Lassie.*

I shivered in the muscle-tightening, bone-chilling cold. With her muzzle between her front paws, the shepherd studied me while I coughed. Then her ears twitched, she jumped up and turned back in the direction from which she'd come.

"Wait, don't go."

She glanced at me over her shoulder.

"Princess!" A woman's voice. "Princess, where are you?"

The dog took several steps.

The last of my energy went into the struggle to sit up. My abdominal muscles screeched in protest. "Help!" Loud enough for canine, but not human ears. I coughed again.

"Who's there?" the woman asked from the darkness. "Princess?"

The dog issued a deep rumble of a bark. A terrifying sound.

The woman whistled and Princess trotted away. Her milk-burdened belly swayed beneath her. I was on my own again. Good thing I didn't have enough energy to freak out.

I eased back down and closed my eyes. My head throbbed with each heartbeat, which lulled me to sleep. A car door slammed, then voices, then nothing.

I opened my eyes at the sound and propelled myself onto sore, splinter-filled elbows. A flashlight beam bobbed toward me. The cavalry at last?

My head slid back onto the boards and a freckled face, topped with bright red hair, shimmered over me. Eric? Nah, couldn't be.

"Jen, are you okay?"

I responded with another cough. My lungs burned.

"Lacey, call 911." Eric squeezed my hand. "Hang on, Jen, help is on the way."

It was him, and Lacey too. How did they find me? Not that it mattered right now. I squeezed back. A verbal response would require more strength than I had.

Red lights reflecting off the clouds signaled the arrival of the ambulance, and a paramedic brought me a blanket, which did little to quell the irrepressible quivers.

At the hospital, the smiling blonde nurse gave me a blanket from a warmer. As I thawed, pain hummed through my muscles. She helped me undress. I'd torn three fingernails down to the quick in the skirmish with the dock. I'd never worried about protecting my nails, but that was a bit much, even for me.

My clothing oozed the delectable aroma of fishy motor oil. When the nurse handed me the plastic bag, I searched for a trash can. No use for those clothes again. Strangely, I didn't care. Not even about my favorite Nikes sitting at the bottom of the river. Eric would be thrilled, though. He'd have the chance to pick me out some new ones.

None of those things seemed to matter anymore. I'd almost died, and the warm blanket and the gown, which flapped open in the back, had become my new best friends. *Sorry, Brittany.*

The doctor examined my swollen, bruised hands along with the rope burns on my ankles. My core temperature registered a tropical ninety-four degrees, which sealed the decision to admit me for observation. Fine with me, as long as it included a warm bed and sleep.

A cop, R. Murphy as described by the silver nameplate on the flap of his breast pocket, came in to question me while the nurse finished my admission paperwork. I could barely lift my head off the pillow, but cooperation might help me find out what they'd learned about Russell. He took out his notebook. "Ms Dawson, can you tell me what happened to you tonight?"

I gave him the condensed version of the day's events, along with a description of Russell and his car.

"You should've contacted us when you got the note. You're lucky to be alive."

"I know." I licked my lips and tried to swallow. Did they have anything to drink in this desert?

"Can you describe your attacker for me, please?"

I turned my head, which sent the world around me into a spin. I closed my eyes to quell the nausea. "I didn't see him. He grabbed me from behind. I have a vague memory of something shiny and a sharp pain in my jaw before he put the rag over my mouth, but nothing else."

He looked up. "Shiny? Like what?"

I started to shrug my shoulders, but a bolt of pain changed my mind. "A watch, maybe? I don't know."

The nurse came back. "We're ready for you, Ms Dawson. Officer, I'm afraid you're going to have to leave. You can talk to her after she gets upstairs."

"I'm finished." He flipped his notebook closed. "Ms Dawson, if you think of anything else, call me at the station. A detective will be by in the morning, after we finish processing the scene, to get your statement. If we find out anything, he'll let you know."

He handed me a business card and turned to leave. I stopped him. "Officer?"

"Yes, ma'am?"

I lifted my arm to push my greasy hair off my

forehead, but a painful tug stopped me short of success. "What about Russell, the guy who was with me? I'm worried about him."

Officer Murphy looked at his shoes, then back at me. "We'll be on the lookout for him."

"You have to find him. He was watching me from the car. The attacker must've gotten him first or he would've helped me. Please, he might be lying somewhere bleeding." Or taking my place at the bottom of the river.

He exchanged a glance with the nurse. "We'll let you know when we find out anything, ma'am. Have a good night."

"Are you ready to go?" Blondie gestured to the wheelchair.

No way I would even consider riding in that thing. "I can walk."

She patted the back of the seat. "Hospital policy. Nobody with a plastic bracelet moves without wheels. Besides, do you want to walk around with your bottom out in front of your friends?"

"I guess not." I tried to sit up, but my muscles had stiffened. I could only turn my head to the left, and my right shoulder wouldn't support any of my weight. With Lacey and Eric on either side, I edged off the exam table and sank into the chair.

I focused on my hamstrings to take my mind off my ankles and shoulders. Each bump of the chair sent a lightning bolt through my entire nervous system. A steamroller had run over me.

Blondie settled me into a private room, and by the time the floor nurse had finished with my vital signs and completed the paperwork, it neared two in the morning. No part of my body moved comfortably. Some parts didn't move at all. I gave up.

Lacey sat in the chair by the window and Eric sat on the edge of the bed. "You feel like talking?" he asked.

"For a little bit, maybe. I'm tired."

"I'll bet," Lacey said.

I scooted up in the bed a fraction of an inch, then quit. "How did you guys find me?"

Eric rubbed his hands down the front of his jeans. "Brittany called me when she got off the phone with you."

I turned to Lacey. "And, you?"

She smiled. "He called me for company. We saw a woman with a dog and she told us she'd heard something by the river, so we checked it out, and there you were."

"And you guys drove down here to do what exactly?"

"To have your back, of course. That's what friends are for," Eric said. "Why did you come here?"

The story came out as rehearsed, and I didn't expect much of a response. No matter, as long as they agreed to help with the search for Russell. Not much I could do from a hospital bed.

Lacey replied first. "So, you think Russell's still out there somewhere, a victim of whoever attacked you?"

"I do."

Eric and Lacey exchanged glances.

"All right," Eric said. "We'll see what we can find out and check in with you in the morning. I'm pretty sure you're going to be discharged first thing. We'll take you home."

"Thank you."

They turned out the light when they left, and the pain medicine kicked in. My mind reeled. What had happened to Russell? Someone had to find him. Find his car. And, when they found his car, they might find my assailant.

I had to call Brittany. The phone sat on the nightstand. I rolled over to my right to get to it. Pain stampeded through my shoulder and I turned onto my back. Guess I hit the water hard. Hit something, anyway.

Still, she would worry, so I tried once more. Not the toughest task I'd ever had to accomplish, but pretty close.

I dialed her number slowly. The only phone number, besides my own, I knew. Her sleepy voice answered on the sixth ring.

"Hey, I wanted to let you know I'm okay." The pain meds had made me woozy. Great stuff.

Brittany's voice took on a tender note. "I was so worried. How are you?"

I dropped my head onto the pillow, eyes crossing. The phone lay beside my ear. "Great… now. Eric and Lacey are here. They're going to bring me home in the morning."

"Naked? Eric told me you threw away your clothes. I'll bring you some of mine."

"Thanks." I pulled the phone closer to my ear, and a hand meandered in front of my eyes. Mine? Yup, it coasted at the end of my arm. I giggled. "I need shoes, too. Mine are at the bottom of the river. Your doll feet are too small."

"Don't worry, I'll take care of it. Get some rest and I'll see you in the morning."

I wiggled my fingers. Squishy, white worms. Or sea

anemones atop the water. "Britt, something's happened to Russell."

"Something better have because, if he's okay, I'm going to kill him myself."

I giggled again. "Funny, I had the same thought. Are you on pain meds, too?" Before she could respond, I continued, "You were right. I should've listened to you. I'm sorry."

"I never thought I'd hear that from you! Forget about it. Hindsight's twenty-twenty, right? I'm glad you're okay. I don't know what I would've done if I'd lost you, too."

I didn't deserve her kindness. She rated a much better friend than me. I tried to scratch my nose, missed, and poked myself in the eye. I didn't even feel it, though. What did they give me? "I don't know what I'd do without you."

"That's the drugs talking. Besides, if you keep pulling these kinds of dumb stunts, you might have to find out."

"You're right. I'm sorry I've been so selfish."

I fell asleep with the phone on the pillow beside my head.

CHAPTER TWENTY-ONE

The nurse's aide returned to my room to take my vital signs at six the next morning. I told her since I could talk I must have some, but she insisted on the actual readings. If my injuries didn't kill me, this schedule would. My last experience in the hospital had been my birth. They must not have let me sleep then, either.

I dozed back off at six fifteen and, at seven thirty, they woke me for breakfast. The greasy bacon smell made my stomach flip, so I rejected the glutinous mishmash in favor of my next pain shot. No luck. The nurse brought me a pill instead, and the tray remained untouched. I used the bed controls to sit up but couldn't turn my head in any direction, nor raise either arm above the level of my shoulder. I saved a test of my legs for dessert.

I drank a little orange juice, which my arid mouth appreciated but my stomach tried to send back to the kitchen. As I couldn't eat, I turned over, and the movement plucked every muscle string I had. The cacophony of pain that ensued made AC/DC sound like the Philadelphia Philharmonic. The medication had better kick in soon.

Eric and Lacey arrived around eight, drained and disheveled, as if they'd kept the same sleep schedule I had.

"How are you feeling?" Eric asked.

"About as good as I look, I'm afraid. What have you learned about Russell?"

"Not a whole lot, but Lacey did find a small piece of rope in the parking lot. It could match the one that held you down, but we won't know until the divers bring it up from the bottom of the river. Maybe your assailant used the same rope to tie Russell up, too."

"I guess we'll see."

Lacey smoothed the blanket over my legs. "When is the doctor supposed to release you?"

"I'm not sure, but Brittany's going to drive me home. I don't have any clothes to wear, and this gown doesn't cover even the bare essentials."

Eric chewed on his lip. "Okay, then we'll see if we can learn anything else here, and meet you back in Riddleton."

"Sounds good. And thank you."

Lacey squeezed my shoulder. "Let us know if you need anything."

"I will."

At nine, the doctor came in, examined me and decided, while battered and bruised, none of the damage was permanent. I begged him to send me home, where I could at least get a little rest, and he agreed to discharge me. Although I did have second thoughts the instant I tried to move, but the hospital stood between me and what had become my number-one priority: finding Russell. Something had to have happened to him. Why else wouldn't he be here?

When Brittany arrived, she helped me sit up and dressed me like a toddler, although I couldn't kick my legs and scream. They had yet to invent pain medicine that worked that well.

She finished with my shoelaces, and a thin, gray-haired man in a black suit with a badge around his neck came in. His pinched, sallow face told the story of too many investigations conducted in the local cop bar.

"My name is Detective Edwards. I need to ask you a few questions." He spoke as though he had a mouth full of marbles.

"I told the officer everything I know last night."

He nodded and pulled the obligatory cop notebook—in much better condition than Olinski's—out of his pocket. "It's for your statement."

With luck, I wouldn't have to repeat the tale two or three more times. I recited it from the start and finished with, "Have you found Russell Jeffcoat?"

He focused his dishwater-blue eyes on me. "We located his car, abandoned on a side street not far from where we found you. Do you know anything about it?"

Why would I? What did he think, I drove to the spot, tied myself up, and jumped in the river? Maybe I became wet and sore drowning Russell. "Uh-uh. Any sign of him?"

"No, but there were some bloodstains in the trunk. Forensics sent samples off for testing, but we won't know anything until tomorrow. Any idea whose blood that might be?"

Blood in the trunk? Was Russell injured? "All I know is what I've already told you. Do you think he's been murdered? Have you checked the river for his body?"

"Not yet."

"He has to be somewhere." I clenched my fists, and agony radiated from my swollen fingers. Somebody had to care besides me. I'd ended up in the river, why not Russell, too? And whose blood covered the trunk of his Honda, if not his?

"I have a 911 call from last night I want to play for you. Tell me if you recognize the voice."

"Okay, go ahead."

The detective tapped a few buttons on his phone and a woman's voice said, "911, what's your emergency?"

"You have to help me, please. My friend is being attacked."

My heart pounded. "That's Russell."

The call continued. "Sir, what's your location?"

"I'm at the dock."

Rustling sounds and a car door opening.

"Hey! What are you doing? Stop!"

"Sir? Sir, are you all right?"

"Let me go."

A man shouting. Call disconnected.

Orange juice surged into my throat. I slapped a hand over my mouth. Brittany snagged the basin on my tray table and held it for me while I retched. The nausea passed, and I took a sip of water to settle my stomach.

Edwards dropped the phone into his jacket pocket. "Are you all right, Ms Dawson? You recognize that voice as Russell Jeffcoat?"

I nodded. "You have to keep looking. He's in trouble." If it's not too late.

The nurse came in with my discharge papers, uninsured stamped on the top of each page. When I finished mortgaging my soul, she handed over my copies and left. Someone would return in a few minutes to wheel me out.

I turned to Detective Edwards. "Are we finished, detective? I want to go home."

"I have all the information I need, but you can't leave, yet."

"Why not?"

"Detective Olinski is on his way."

"What for?" I struggled to sit up.

"I'm sorry, Ms Dawson. I have to keep you here."

Brittany helped me stand. "You're kidding, right?"

I bit my already sore lip. My breath came in shallow gasps. A cough surged up, and I held my breath.

Edwards hooked his thumbs in his belt loops, which exposed his service automatic. "And you are?"

She ensured my stability on the edge of the bed, then turned to the detective. "Brittany Dunlop."

"Ms Dunlop, I have my instructions."

The door to my room swung open, and Olinski came in. Today, he wore a wrinkled blue suit and mirrored sunglasses shielded his brown eyes. He showed his badge and ID to Edwards. "Stan Olinski, Riddleton PD."

Detective Edwards shook his hand. "Frank Edwards."

I made an aborted attempt to stand. "What's this all about?"

Olinski lowered his sunglasses. "I warned you how this would play out. You're wanted for questioning in the murder of Aletha Cunningham. Are you ready to go? Don't make me arrest you."

Arrest me? Was I really a suspect? I picked at my sole unbandaged fingernail and searched my brain for a way out of this mess.

Brittany stepped up. "Look, Olinski, Jen's been through a lot. Why don't I drive her back and you can follow us to make sure she doesn't escape?"

"I'm sorry, I can't allow that." He removed his sunglasses. "Besides, I don't think either one of us is up for a car chase today. Do you?"

"There wouldn't be a car chase. You have my word. And you know I never break my word. At least, you should."

"You might be overcome by temptation." His grin melted his eyes until he put his glasses back on.

"I doubt it." When he didn't budge, Brittany said, "All right. Where are you taking her?"

"Back to Riddleton. You can follow if you want."

"Count on it."

They eyed each other, and Olinski turned away first. *Score one for Brittany.*

He took me by the elbow. "Come on, we need to get going."

"I'm not going anywhere with you." I jerked away, my shoulder squealed, but I had to find out what had happened to Russell. The Savannah police department didn't care about his disappearance.

"You're going. *How* is up to you." He stood with his hands on his hips. His jacket pulled away from his side and his gun peeked out. That maneuver must have led off chapter one in the detective's intimidation handbook.

I ignored the sting in my legs, stood, and steadied myself against the bed. "Leave me alone."

He tried the soft approach. "Look, Jen, I know you've had a rough night, and I'm really glad you're okay. Come back with me. We'll talk for a little while, and you'll be free to go. If you keep this up, I'll have to arrest you. You don't want to stay in jail, do you?"

I abandoned the bed, stood up straight, and swayed like a skyscraper on a windy day. "I have to find out who did this to me."

"Leave it to Detective Edwards and the Savannah police." The detectives exchanged glances and Edwards nodded.

The cops hadn't accomplished much so far. No way I could trust Russell's, and my, fate to them. "Right. And what about Russell?"

"Everybody wants to find Russell Jeffcoat, right now."

I had to stall for time to figure a way out of this. "Where's your sidekick?"

"Who?"

"You know, Detective Starchy."

Olinski chuckled. "Detective Havermayer is continuing the investigation in Riddleton. It won't take two of us to escort you back, will it?"

My mind searched for possibilities and couldn't find any. Even Dana couldn't help this time.

"Will it?"

"All right," I said. "Let's go."

Olinski's face relaxed. "That's better. Believe me, this is for the best."

Detective Edwards put his hand on Olinski's shoulder. "Detective, can I speak with you outside for a minute?"

The detectives stepped into the hall.

Brittany took my hand. "It's going to be okay."

"If you say so. Britt, nobody cares about Russell's disappearance."

"Sure they do. They consider his disappearance as serious as your attack."

"Well, it sure doesn't seem that way to me."

She tucked a hair behind her ear. "Believe it or not, I understand. I'm going to see what's going on. I'll be right back."

"All right. Can you help me to the bathroom first?"

She took my arm, and we shuffled to the bathroom next to the hallway door. She released me. "Are you okay?"

"Yup, I'm good." I backed through the doorway; Brittany went to find the detectives.

I turned toward the sink, and the room spun like a tornado had sucked up the hospital. The edge of the hand basin balanced me as I slid down the wall to the cool, tiled floor, and closed my eyes. Eventually, the whirlwind spat me back out.

When I opened my eyes, Brittany squatted in front of me. "Are you okay?"

I made a feeble attempt at a grin. "How can I tell?"

She patted my shoulder. "Do you want me to get the nurse?"

"No, I'm fine." I used the wall, and Brittany, for support and drove myself upright.

Brittany held me until I found my feet and took a step toward the door.

"Where do you think you're going?" Brittany asked.

"I'm going to find out who's behind all this."

"You're not going anywhere but back to Riddleton." *Not her too.* "Why?"

Brittany brushed the intractable hair off my forehead. "Olinski says the safest place for you is with him, and this time I have to agree."

"What about finding Russell?"

"You're in no condition to do anything."

"I'm fine." And I was, for a ninety-year-old.

"How do you do, Fine. I'm Queen Elizabeth."

I tried to curtsy with the same result as last time. I toppled over, but Brittany caught me.

"Nice to meet you, Your Majesty. Are you gonna help me, or what?"

Olinski and Edwards came back into my room. Olinski held his glasses in one hand and rubbed his eyes with the other. I couldn't decipher the tight expression on Edwards's face as I hobbled toward the bed.

"What happened?" Olinski asked.

Brittany looked at me, then back at him. "Just a little dizzy spell."

"I'm okay."

Olinski put his glasses back on. "Are you sure you don't want me to call a nurse or something?"

"Yes."

"All right then, let's go."

My mouth fell open. "You mean you were serious?"

CHAPTER TWENTY-TWO

I fidgeted in the back seat of the unmarked car, and the midday sun targeted my left cheek like an ant under a magnifying glass. Olinski refused to remove the handcuffs. My shoulders shrieked. Why had he insisted on them in first place? Revenge for my refusal to stay home like a good little girl and for going off to college without him. I owed Olinski some gratitude, but after the events of the past twenty-four hours, I didn't have much left besides anger. Perhaps, a little humiliation.

I'd done it this time. Olinski could hit me with interfering in a police investigation, even obstruction of justice. Unless, he was serious about me being a suspect in Aletha's murder. Pretty sure the first two were both misdemeanors, but I still might end up in jail, which had no place on my to-do list for this lifetime. The third could put me away for life or stick a needle in my arm.

The sunlight pierced my eyes, so I closed them and rested my head against the glass. I basked in the warmth like a cat on a windowsill. At least, there were no bars on it, yet.

Olinski jerked open the driver's side door. "Ready?"

"When you take these stupid cuffs off."

"Keep dreaming."

I tried to explode his head with my mind. No luck. "They're hurting my wrists."

"You should've thought of that before."

Before what? I kicked the back of his seat. "I won't try anything. I'm not a hardened criminal, you know."

"Everybody's gotta start somewhere." He smiled into the rearview mirror and enjoyed the illusion of some control over me. Well, maybe more than an illusion. For now.

Fine. I pulled my legs onto the seat and leaned back to take a nap.

When I awoke, a gas pump filled my window, and Olinski had disappeared. Tired, sweaty travelers crisscrossed in front of the car. Although, they couldn't see my handcuffs, mortification, tempered only by anger, made me squirm.

I had to get out of here. I could crawl over the seat to get to the door that actually opened from the inside, but my arms tingled and burned, while my head pounded out a beat for them. I willed myself to try it anyway, until Olinski approached the car with two plastic bags.

He opened the door and smiled. "Look who's awake. Did you sleep well?"

"What do you think?"

"If you promise to behave, I'll take those handcuffs off."

I glowered, but had no choice. "Okay."

"Repeat after me. I, Jennifer Dawson—"

"This is stupid."

"You want your hands back?"

Yes, to strangle him. "Fine. I, Jennifer Dawson..."

His grin expanded. "Excellent. I, Jennifer Dawson, do solemnly swear…"

"Do solemnly swear…"

"To behave myself completely…"

I had to force my fingers to relax. "To behave myself completely…"

"And give Detective Stan Olinski no trouble of any kind."

"And give Detective Stan Olinski no trouble of any kind. Are you happy? Take the damn things off."

"Temper, temper. Say please."

I mumbled the word under my breath, lips still.

He turned sideways and cocked his head in my direction. "I'm sorry, I couldn't hear you. Did you say something?"

Behind my back, I made fists so tight the knuckles had to be white. "Please. I said please, okay? Did you hear me that time?"

Olinski released my seat belt. "Loud and clear. Turn around."

Easy for him to say. I maneuvered onto my knees, chin on the back of the seat. He pulled on my wrists, and the handcuffs fell away.

I kneaded the red, chafed skin. "Thank you. That was very human of you."

"You're welcome. I try to be human whenever possible." He reached into one of the bags. "Hungry? I brought you a sandwich. Ham and cheese. That used to be your favorite." He held the wax-papered lump over the back of the front seat.

He remembered. Which would have been sweet, if he didn't have an ulterior motive. Either way, last night's pizza had disappeared a lifetime ago. I could've played

243

my empty belly like a bongo drum, if I knew how to play a bongo drum.

We reached the end of the highway entrance ramp. I'd finished my sandwich and half the drink he'd given me. I coughed Pepsi onto the back of the driver's seat. I dabbed at it with my napkin, but the fabric had absorbed the sticky liquid, which delighted my mean, spiteful side.

Unlike my car, the floorboard had nothing on it, so I reached over the back of the seat to drop the empty wrapper into the bag.

Olinski smirked. "I had a feeling you might be hungry. There's another one in there for you."

I tore the wrapper off and devoured the sandwich like a lactating wolf. "Thank you." Probably should've swallowed first.

"You're welcome."

Momentarily energized, it was time to push the elephant out of the car. "So, does this sudden display of humanity mean you've forgiven me for having the audacity to do what I thought was best for me?"

"There was a lot more to it, and you know it. I thought we were going to get married. Settle down and have a family."

I met his pained gaze in the rearview mirror. "We dated for close to four years. Did you never pay attention to anything I said?"

"Of course, I did."

"All I ever talked about was going away to college and becoming a writer. You know that never could've happened if I'd stayed in Riddleton."

He completed the interchange onto I-20, then said, "I thought you loved me. God knows I loved you."

I did love him, and he knew it. My jaw clenched. "Not enough to support me and try to make it work."

"I didn't want to hold you back. There was no place for me in your world."

"You never gave me a chance." Even as I said the words, deep inside I had to admit he had a point. Sure, I would've finished school, but *Double Trouble* and all the rest of it might never have happened. Too many complications and commitments. "Okay, I get it. Sort of. But, if that's the way you felt, why are you so angry with me? It was your decision to break it off."

His shoulders rose and fell as he expelled a breath. "I guess, I wanted you to love me enough to stay and you didn't. Besides, you weren't supposed to be so successful. You were supposed to fall on your butt and come running back to me. I would've magnanimously taken you back. And then, we'd get married and start our family."

I had no idea he felt that way. What could I say? Daniel had nothing to offer, either.

"If it makes any difference, I'm happy your dreams are coming true. And, I'm proud of you." His voice was soft and low. A sound I hadn't heard in a very long time.

I brushed a stray tear off my cheek. "Thank you. It makes a big difference to me. I thought you hated me."

"I did, for a while."

"Why?"

"It was easier than loving you."

My turn to take a deep breath. "So, does this mean we can be friends? You're not so bad when you want to be."

"I'm not so bad period, if you give me a chance.

Besides, by now even you have to acknowledge you look guilty. I'm not saying you are, but there's enough evidence that Chief Vick insisted I bring you in."

I sealed my lips against the nasty reply barreling toward them. No point in messing things up. "So why am I here? Why couldn't you just wait until I got home? It's not like I'm a flight risk."

He scrutinized me in the mirror. "It was the only way to keep you safe. Whoever tried to kill you wasn't playing around. Do you have any idea why somebody wants you dead?"

Keep me safe? I wanted to believe him, but his abrupt change in attitude seemed implausible. "Besides you? No. If anyone I knew wanted me dead, it would've happened years ago. And isn't the attempt on my life proof I didn't have anything to do with Aletha's death?"

"Yes and no. Cunningham is still missing. If you two were in on it together, he could be tying up loose ends."

"You know better. I'd never be involved in something like this."

"It doesn't matter what I know or think I know. I'm not in charge, the Chief of Police is. I have to do what I'm told."

I stared out the window in search of answers in the scenery, but it passed too fast and revealed too little.

"What were you doing in Savannah?"

I crossed my arms and relaxed into my seat. My muscles had loosened, with only a little resistance from my shoulders. "One of the previous contest recipients died in a car accident. Two dead winners in one year are hard to ignore. And someone pretended to be the woman's father at her funeral. Nobody knew anything about him, and the address he gave was fake."

"And you think this is related to Aletha Cunningham's death?"

"I haven't found the connection yet, but it just about has to be. Otherwise, it's too much of a coincidence."

"Interesting."

Olinski seemed to be taking me seriously for once. He reached over and felt around the passenger seat, careful to keep his eyes on the road. "I forgot. Detective Edwards gave me this for you. Check it out and let me know if there's anything missing."

He handed my purse over the seat. I searched through it. Everything seemed there, but not the way I'd left it. "Somebody's been in it." I shifted a few more items around. "My keys are missing."

"Anything else?"

I searched again. "I don't think so. Everything's been taken out of my wallet, but thrown back in the bag."

"What do you think they were looking for?"

"I have no idea."

We parked in front of the Riddleton PD. Bile rose into my throat.

Welcome home.

Olinski had to help my uncooperative body out of the car, and I eyed the drugstore across the street. My pain med prescription was there waiting for me to pick it up. As I hauled my wooden legs up the stairs, I glanced at the abandoned bookstore next door and swallowed the slab that formed in my throat.

This is all for you, my friend.

Brittany waited in the lobby. She must've passed us when we stopped for gas. An officer spotted Olinski and beckoned him to follow.

Olinski turned to me. "Behave. I'll be right back."

Brittany came over and hugged me.

I rubbed my arms against the artificial chill. "What's going on?"

"I don't know, but something big."

"Why do you say that?"

She scanned the room. "The phone rang a little while ago, and all of a sudden, people were scurrying around like rats in a cheese factory."

"I wonder what the deal is."

"Me too, but it might not have anything to do with us." She put her arm around my shoulders. "How are you?"

"Beat up, but fine. Made some progress with Olinski, too."

Olinski trudged toward us. "This way, Jen. Brittany, this could take a while."

Brittany lifted her chin. "I'll wait. In fact, I'll run over and get your prescription for you."

"Thanks, Britt. You're a good friend."

"I know."

Olinski led me to a small room with a table surrounded by three chairs and the infamous one-way glass window. I waved at whoever stood on the other side.

He smirked. "There's nobody watching."

"And you're allowed to lie to me."

"True, but I hope you know me better than that."

"I thought I did, but now I'm not so sure. Let's just get this over with, so I can go home. I've had a tough day."

He read me my rights and made a point of glancing at the ceiling camera in the corner. "I'm required to inform you this interview is being recorded."

Message received. It didn't matter if someone watched the interview through the window, the whole thing would be recorded for posterity. Or to be used as evidence against me at trial. Neither option did much for my current mood.

"Do you understand these rights as I've read them to you?"

My eyes fired daggers at him. "Yes." So much for making peace. Back to the status quo.

"Do you waive the right to have an attorney present during questioning?"

Hmmm. Should I do that? Did I trust him enough? Maybe. "I'll waive a lawyer for now. Can I change my mind if I don't like the way you're handling things?"

He sat back in his chair. "Of course, but I have to tell you it'll make it look like you have something to hide. We're just having a conversation. Trying to clear up a few things."

Sure we are. "I'll take my chances."

He slid a waiver form across the table and I signed it.

Olinski folded his arms across his chest. "All right, let's get started. Tell me everything you did from two o'clock the Friday afternoon before the explosion until three o'clock on Saturday."

I went over it several times while Olinski listened for discrepancies in my story. All my time was accounted for, except when I was writing and napping between the bookstore and dinner with Russell, overnight when I passed out until I met the runners at the park, and the few hours between the run and lunch at the lake. Of course, if I'd known I needed an alibi for those periods, I'd have made sure I had one.

He finally switched the conversation to the pen found at the crime scene and Tim's disappearance. I had no new light to shed on those subjects, either. When he started again at the beginning, I'd had enough. Adrenaline-laced exhaustion weighed me down and I hurt all over.

"I'm done, Olinski. I've said all I'm going to say without a lawyer."

"If you call in a lawyer, this conversation has to get official. Right now, we're just talking. Giving you a chance to tell your side of the story." He peeked at the camera, again.

What was he trying to tell me? Was he only saying these things to placate the chief? Regardless, I wasn't taking any chances. "I've told my side of the story three or four times already. Am I under arrest?"

Olinski watched the door for several seconds. Nobody came in. "No."

I stood up. "Then I'm free to go."

"For now. Come by in the morning to sign your written statement."

He escorted me back to the lobby, where Brittany fidgeted in a plastic chair.

"Wait here for a minute."

Brittany looked at me and I shrugged. "No idea where he's going, unless he's asking for permission to arrest me."

"Would he really do that?"

"I wish I knew."

Olinski reappeared, head down and shoulders slumped.

Guess the answer was "No." His obvious disappointment irked me, however. Did he hate me that much? I thought we'd worked things out.

"Ladies, would you come with me, please?"

We followed him into his office. Two chairs sat in front of the desk, which had a chair of its own, but nobody sat. Olinski stared at the wall above my head.

"What's wrong?" I asked.

"Cunningham's dead. They pulled his body out of the Congaree River a few hours ago. He's been in there at least a day, maybe longer."

"Suicide?" Brittany asked.

Olinski rubbed his neck. "The medical examiner will tell us for sure, but it looks like he took a solid blow to the back of the head before he went into the water. His clothes were covered in blood."

My throat dried instantly, heart hammering. Vindication. Tim hadn't murdered his wife, but like the accused at a witch trial, he had to die to prove it. My hands shook, and my lungs trapped the air in them. Both Aletha and Tim had died. My life had changed forever. The only way to make sense of it all would be to figure out who'd killed them, and why. I resolved to do that, no matter what it took.

Olinski smoothed the creased lapel of his blue suit jacket. "Where were you the night before last?"

You gotta be kidding me. "You think I killed Tim? A few hours ago, you thought he tried to kill me."

"Every coin has two sides. Where were you?"

"Home. Asleep."

"Can anyone corroborate that?"

I narrowed my eyes. "I was alone."

His lips twitched. "Not much of an alibi."

Was he just going through the motions or did he really believe I'd killed Tim? "I didn't know I needed one."

He looked away.

I cleared my throat. "What happens now?"

He focused his gaze on mine. "We start over and try to find what we missed, and you go home and stay out of trouble. If you don't, the chief will make me arrest you. I'm trying to help you, here. Please cooperate."

I returned his stare without comment.

"I mean it. Go home and forget investigating this thing before you get yourself killed. And you'd better have your locks changed, too."

I ignored Brittany's glance. "Britt can take me home."

"Not home. I think you should stay with me tonight," she said.

"Maybe. We'll see." I turned back to Olinski. "So, I can leave?"

"Yes, but only under those conditions."

I grasped Brittany's arm. "Great. Let's go."

CHAPTER TWENTY-THREE

Brittany eased away from the curb in front of the police department.

"Make a left at the end of the street."

She stopped at the corner and stared at me. "That's the wrong way."

I rubbed my temples. "Just turn left, please."

"Where are we going?"

I squinted through the windshield, and the sun aggravated my headache. "The Cunningham house."

She pulled over and crossed her arms. "I'm taking you home. You heard what Olinski said. There were conditions to your release."

"You will take me home. Eventually."

She scowled at me as if I'd whistled "Dixie" in the Library of Congress.

"Come on, Brittany. Someone just tried to kill me. You expect me to turn tail and run? You know me better than that."

"I expect you to do what you agreed to do."

"When did I agree to anything? He assumed I did. He should've been more specific. Maybe, gotten it in writing."

"You let him believe it, but you're right, he should've known better than to think you'd be straight up with him. You haven't been so far. It's not like you."

I expelled a long sigh. "I want to look around to see if I can find a connection to Aletha's death or Russell's disappearance. If there's anyone else there, I won't even get out of the car."

Brittany studied me over the top of her glasses. "Scout's honor?"

I held up the appropriate three fingers. "Scout's honor."

She poked me in the shoulder. "You were never a Scout, idiot."

"Neither were you."

The car accelerated to the left.

Police swarmed the Cunningham house. We slowed for the blockade at the entrance to the yard.

Eric stopped us. "This area is off limits."

"Why?" I could play dumb when I wanted to. Sometimes, even when I didn't.

"It's a crime scene. You have to turn around."

"We just left Detective Olinski. He knows we're here."

He peered at me through narrowed eyelids. "Which is why he called and made it a point to tell me not to let you in."

I gnashed my teeth and looked to Brittany for help. She studied her hands, which rested in her lap, the corners of her mouth twitching.

We proceeded back down the driveway toward the main road. Olinski had won again. What should I do now? And where was Russell? The part of my brain I kept locked up tight hinted he might have died in

Savannah last night. I couldn't accept that. Thoughts tumbled around in my head, but none of them made much sense. Even a call on the Davenports produced nothing. A blanket of fatigue covered me, and I huddled under it.

As we waited at the end of the driveway for the rush-hour traffic to clear, my eyes settled on the Cunninghams' brick mailbox. Something seemed off. I opened the window to get a better look and spotted the problem as the car rolled forward.

"Hey, stop."

"What's wrong?" Brittany jammed on the brakes and pitched me into my locked seat belt.

Pain shot up my neck. "I have to look at something."

I eased out of the car and hobbled to the mailbox. Halfway down, on the edge, something had gouged out a large chunk of brick and mortar and left traces of blue paint in its place.

A deep voice startled me. "Yeah, some guy came flying out of that driveway a couple weeks ago, whacked it and kept right on going."

The farmer's face displayed the deep crevices and liver spots well earned in a near century of arduous work under a subtropical sun. He had a peach-sized plug of chewing tobacco in his left cheek, and brown drool trickled from the groove at the corner of his mouth down to his bib overalls.

"Did you see what he looked like?"

"I did." He gestured toward the side of the road. "He had to stop over yonder to pull the fender off'n the tire so's he could drive." The farmer switched his plug to the other side and spat, missing the toe of his battered work boot by a whisker. He rubbed his mouth with the back of his hand and wiped his hand on the leg of his overalls.

Nauseated, I expected him to continue, but he needed a jump-start. "So, what did he look like?"

The old man stared at a dilapidated shack across the road I assumed belonged to him. "He was one a' them black fellas."

That narrowed it down to a quarter of the state's population. No help at all. I balled my fists at my side. "Can you remember anything else? How tall was he?"

"Oh, pretty tall, I reckon."

Thanks, pal. Big help. "Did you tell all this to the police?"

He spat again. "They never asked me."

They never asked him. Clearly, to volunteer was out of the question. Against the ancient farmer's code or something. At this rate, it'd take years for the man to provide any useful information, but I suspected it didn't matter. I happened to know a man with a damaged blue car. I thanked him for his help.

"Ready to go home?" Brittany asked.

I settled into my seat. "Not yet."

"We had a deal. Where do you want to go now?"

"Marcus Jones's house."

"Why?"

"Because he lied to me. Again."

As we approached Marcus's house, despair sucked the oxygen out of the air. I'd so wanted to believe Marcus had nothing to do with Aletha's death. That he'd turned his life around, putting his family first. But too much evidence pointed in his direction.

I climbed the steps to the porch. Vangie's eyes lit up

when she saw us. I asked to have a look at Marcus's car and she agreed readily. Leaving Brittany in her charge, I proceeded to the backyard. The blue Grand Am remained where it was before, still undrivable. I knelt to examine the right front fender and didn't care if mud smeared on my clothing. I'd never worry about mundane things like that again.

I stuck my finger into the space behind the bumper and pulled out some of the red substance I'd assumed was rust or mud. I held up the largest piece I could find, which had the telltale mottled appearance of brick. I stuck my finger back into the space and fished out mortar. Marcus had told me he'd hit a deer, but no animal left behind these traces. Maybe, a brick mailbox deer.

My mind spiraled as I dragged myself back to the house. I couldn't process too much more today. Tim had died, Marcus had lied, Russell had disappeared, the police now considered me the prime suspect in Aletha's murder, and someone had tried to kill me. Enough for one day.

Vangie and Brittany had gone inside, so I tapped on the peeling, painted door and entered.

Vangie called, "We're in here, honey."

I peeked around the doorjamb and found them in the darkened living room. Brittany had stuffed herself into the pillows on the faded floral couch, which consumed one wall. Vangie perched in a straight-backed chair in the middle of the room. In one corner, a beat-up brown leather La-Z-Boy faced a floor model TV, which had a nineteen-inch flat-screen on top.

"Come on in and rest yourself. Your friend's been telling me about your adventures the past couple days."

I searched for a place to sit.

Vangie motioned toward an overstuffed armchair, which had once matched the couch. "That used to be my husband's favorite chair. Now, nobody sits in it except Marcus. You can if you want."

"Thank you."

Vangie's grin warmed the room.

I settled in and bit my upper lip, searching for a way to broach the subject. I didn't have the energy for a Daniel-style tap dance, so I opted for Dana's full-steam-ahead method. "Vangie, where's Marcus? I need to talk to him."

Her face sagged, which added ten years. "Honey, I wish I knew. I last saw him yesterday, about six in the evening."

That behavior resembled the old Marcus more than the post-prison version. A bad sign. "Where did he go?"

"Why?"

"Because he might be in trouble." He might be involved in a murder. Perhaps, two.

Her eyes widened. "Please don't call the police. I don't know what we'd do if he went back to prison. Can you help him?"

"I can try, but you have to be straight with me. Where is he?"

"Don't know. He got a call, then he rushed on outta here, and I ain't seen him since."

"He didn't say anything?"

She shook her head. "I talked to his boss this morning, and he ain't even been to work since Monday. He took off Tuesday for the funeral, and he ain't been back since."

"Where are the girls?"

"A friend of his picked them up yesterday afternoon, but I ain't worried 'cause he's had them a bunch a times before. He's the best friend Marcus has, except for Billy. Now, all three of them hang out together."

The hair on the back of my neck bristled. "Billy?"

"He's a fella Marcus met while he was in jail waiting for his trial. They been best friends ever since."

Billy the Bomber. *Sorry, Tim.* "Vangie, who is Marcus's friend?"

"I can't remember his name. I been trying. I reckon I be getting too old. Marcus met him a couple months ago. That's all I can remember." She stared at the wall.

"I have one more question for you, and then we'll go."

She continued to stare.

"Vangie?"

No response.

I tried again, louder. "Vangie!"

She blinked her eyes. "What, honey?"

I blew out a hard breath. "I wanted to ask you one more question. Where was Marcus on the Saturday afternoon Aletha was killed?"

She turned away, a shredded tissue in her hands.

"He wasn't at the movies with you and the girls, was he?"

Tears welled in her eyes.

I reached over and patted her hand, then Brittany and I returned to the car.

Fatigue saturated me like too much syrup on a stack of pancakes. I'd dealt with so much in the past two days, but accomplished nothing. Battered, bruised, interrogated, and almost drowned, and the only result to come out of it was proof Tim didn't kill his wife.

Unless, he killed Aletha and someone else killed him, which didn't make much sense. Why would the person who blew up the boat kill Tim when the police intended to charge him with the murder? Perhaps, Tim had been meant to disappear, as if on the run, but his body had floated up. Another screwup?

When I left for Savannah yesterday morning, Tim Cunningham had killed his wife. Now, Tim had died and it seemed his accusations against Marcus might not have been so out of line after all. Could Marcus Jones, with the help of his friend Billy the Bomber, have killed Aletha? Maybe, if I'd listened to Tim in the first place, he'd still be alive. Maybe, I had as much responsibility for his death as the person who'd dumped him in the river. Maybe, it was just the exhaustion talking. Over the past two days, my waterlogged brain had received little sleep and even less nourishment. The answers danced out of reach. I couldn't grab them.

In the car, I stared out the window as the scenery flew by. The low sun cast an orange glow over the tops of the buildings as they passed.

"What are you thinking so hard about?" Brittany asked, finally.

I turned to face her. "I'm trying to figure all this out."

"How can I help?"

"I don't know. It seems I've got a whole bunch of stuff here, and none of it fits together, you know?"

"It's a jigsaw puzzle. All you have is a thousand pieces on the table."

"Exactly, except with a puzzle, you have the picture on the box to get you started. I have nothing."

"Run it by me. Sometimes it helps to talk it out."

What did I have to lose? "Let's start with Ida Clare Green. How does she fit into all this?"

"She's the one who had some guy pretending to be her father at her funeral, right?"

"Right."

Brittany merged onto the interstate, then asked, "Why would he do that?"

"My guess is to get the remainder of her prize money."

She glanced at me, quickly. "How does that work?"

"Remember the contest rules? If a contest recipient dies, whoever inherits the project associated with the money gets the remainder of the payments to keep it going. They also get an immediate payment to help with expenses so the project doesn't go under before the next scheduled payment."

"So, this guy would've already received one payment?"

"Right, but I can't get a look at Kingsley Franklin's bank account. I'm hoping Charlie might be able to help me."

Brittany frowned and tapped the steering wheel. "Do you want to deal with him?"

"I don't know any other computer geeks."

"Unfortunately, neither do I. Good luck."

We cruised into Riddleton and Brittany insisted we stop at the supermarket. No point in arguing. I climbed in the back seat for a nap, but really wanted to collapse into my own bed. Although, I should take a hot bath first.

Home at last, my Sentra sat in its assigned place, but the person who'd stolen my keys had ransacked it. I found napkins, pens, and other assorted junk located in the glove compartment on a normal day piled on the dashboard. Trash from the floorboard adorned the parking lot, and a closer inspection revealed slashes in the upholstery. The stuffing hung out, the carpet cut to ribbons, plus the inside door panels lay on the back seat.

Why would someone destroy my car? Tears scalded my eyes. I tried to blink them back, but they melted hot streaks down my face. I'd cried more in the last few weeks than I had since high school. Would this nightmare never end?

Deep breath in, slow breath out.

A quick search found nothing missing. The CDs remained in their cases, the stereo intact. Even the loose change I kept in the console glittered at me in the sun. Whoever did this wasn't a coin collector. Or a gumball aficionado. Theft wasn't the motive, and vandals wouldn't have bothered with the keys. Someone had searched for something. The demolished upholstery made it clear this particular person had a mean side. They'd taken my sense of security, but nothing else of value.

I turned around to find Brittany at the top of the stairs, an unfathomable expression on her face. I called her, but she signaled for me to come up. Something told me I didn't want to, but I hauled myself up the stairs, anyway.

My apartment door stood open. I stepped into the living room and froze, my heart tapped out a loud tattoo. They'd trashed my home, just like my car. A search for absent valuables would waste my time because I didn't have any and because nothing would be missing. At least, nothing I ever knew I had in the first place. Brittany dialed 911. My eyes burned, and my mind raced a version of the Indy 500 with no finish line.

My mother used to tell me that a day could only last twenty-four hours, and I could do anything for twenty-four hours. As a bulletproof teenager, I'd always agreed. Today, the floor rushed up to greet me, and I knew she'd had it wrong.

CHAPTER TWENTY-FOUR

Olinski arrived, while Eric and his new partner, Leonard, finished their report. Brittany let him in as I sat on the floor, arms wrapped around my knees. The closest I could get to the fetal position without somebody calling an ambulance. No way I would beat my mother to the crazy house.

He clapped his hand on Eric's shoulder. "Watcha got?"

"Hey, Blink. What are you doing here? No dead bodies around. At least, none we've found, yet."

Brittany and I exchanged glances. I suppressed a giggle, inappropriate given the circumstances. *Blink?*

My reaction earned us an evil look ejected from the corner of Olinski's eye. "Did you look under the bed, yet?"

"Yeah. I can't believe someone in a hurry would take time to stuff all that junk under there."

Olinski grinned and pulled on the lapels of his rumpled jacket. "They didn't. It always looks like that."

Eric punched him in the shoulder. "Oh, yeah? How would you know?"

That earned him a faux-glare from Olinski. "Did you go through it?"

"Are you kidding?"

"No. What if the Lost Colony of Roanoke is under there?"

Leonard chimed in. "Hey, maybe we should take another look. I hear there's a reward."

The men laughed. I stuck my tongue out at Olinski's back. Immature but satisfying.

"Forget it, Leonard. Get it in gear and let's go." Eric glanced at Olinski. "Rookies."

"How's he doing, anyway?"

Eric shrugged. "Okay, I guess. He complains a lot, but other than that, he's getting it."

Olinski made a slow tour around the room. He touched nothing but observed everything, the same way Havermayer had done. He winked at me, then turned back to Eric. "What have you found?"

Eric ran his fingers through his red hair. "Not much. Nothing missing as far as we can tell. We dusted for prints, but the guy must've been wearing gloves." He snapped his notebook shut and buttoned it into his breast pocket.

Olinski turned to me. "Any idea what they were looking for?"

"No, but it has to be pretty small given some of the places they've searched. I'm surprised they didn't check inside the toothpaste tube." I cleared mucus out of my throat.

Brittany handed me a water bottle.

Olinski returned his attention to Eric. "Canvass the neighbors. If you find out anything, let me know, will you?"

"Yeah, sure, Blink."

Leonard knelt and retrieved something from the

clutter surrounding the coffee table. He held up a small, square piece of plastic, rounded on the bottom with a rectangular hole cut near the top. "What's this?"

I'd never seen it before. "I have no idea."

Eric reached out his hand. "Let me see it."

Leonard handed it to him.

Eric frowned and turned it over in his gloved hand. "It's a plastic sail slug."

"A what?" Olinski asked.

"A sail slug. It's used to hold the sails in the track on a sailboat."

All three police officers stared at me.

My heart bounced against my sternum. "I don't know what that is or where it came from. It wasn't there when I left yesterday."

Olinski turned to Eric. "Bag it." To me, he said in a more serious tone, "You'd better hope we don't find your fingerprints on it."

"Don't worry, you won't."

Eric and Olinski stepped toward the door, out of earshot. I glanced at Brittany, then back toward the two men. Eric nodded agreement to something Olinski said, waved at me, and escaped out the door. Leonard followed.

Olinski returned to us.

"What was that all about?" I asked.

He raised his eyebrows. "What do you mean?"

"What were you and Eric whispering about?"

"Nothing. I asked him to take a couple of extra turns around here tonight to keep an eye on you. You had your locks changed, yet?"

"When did I have time? Besides, what's the point now? I'll get a locksmith out first thing in the morning."

He reached into the side pocket of his jacket and pulled out a gold-colored chain and a screwdriver. "I brought you this, just in case. I figured you might need it."

A chain lock. The kind movie thugs always break when they kick the door in. "It doesn't look very sturdy."

Olinski screwed the chain into the doorjamb. "It won't keep 'em out, but it'll slow 'em down a little. Put a chair under the doorknob or something. It's only for one night, right?"

Yup. I feel better now. "Right. No problem, Blink."

He screwed the slide plate into the door. "Very funny."

"Where'd you get that nickname, anyway?"

"It's a long story."

"We've got time."

He stepped back and scrutinized his handiwork. "All right. When I was a rookie, there was a sergeant who kept calling me Olinki instead of Olinski. Anyway, his wife was one of those born-again Christians and she wouldn't let him swear. So, every time he was looking for me, he'd say, 'Where's that blinkin' Olinki?' The guys thought it was funny, so they started calling me Blink, and it stuck."

"Clearly." I held my arms out to the side. "How do you like my apartment? I've been redecorating."

"It's an improvement."

My look plastered him to the wall. "Ha, ha. Want to help us clean up?"

His brown eyes twinkled in the overhead light. "Fat chance. I mean, I'm awfully sorry, but I have a prior engagement this evening."

Sure you do. "Well, before you run to your engagement, what about Russell? Have you heard anything about him?"

He knit his eyebrows together. "Well, as far as where he is right now, nothing, but there is something that might interest you."

My heart fluttered. I tried to swallow, but my mouth had no moisture in it. "What?"

Olinski studied the tops of his scuffed cop shoes. "We haven't been able to find anything to support his story about who he is and where he came from. It's like he didn't exist before six months ago. I'm sorry."

"He told me he was trying to get away from his father. Maybe, he changed his name so he couldn't be found."

"Could be. I don't know what to tell you."

That had to be it. My mind wouldn't accept anything else. Otherwise, he'd told me a story full of lies, and I'd have picked up on it. After all, it was my job to read people, right? Of course, it seemed I'd misread everyone else involved, so why not Russell, too? "Okay, so what have you learned about who killed Aletha? And Tim?"

He lowered his eyebrows again. "Will you please leave it alone? When are you gonna figure out these people aren't playing around? If you keep it up, you're gonna wake up dead."

I didn't bother to comment on the physiological impossibility of that prediction.

Olinski turned to Brittany. "Keep an eye on her. Don't let her get into any more trouble." To me, he said, "I'm sorry about all this, Jen."

"Thanks." At least he didn't say, "I told you so."

He stopped in the doorway. "And one more thing. Don't plan anymore trips for the foreseeable future. We need to talk about that—what did Eric call it? Oh yeah, sail slug."

Brittany closed the door behind him. "Jen, I—"

My emotional circuit breaker tripped. "I don't want to talk about it."

I focused my energy on the cleanup. I didn't want to talk, or think, about Russell Jeffcoat or sail slugs. Maybe, Scarlett O'Hara had the right idea.

My brain didn't have much break time, though. Someone knocked on the door.

Brittany opened it, and disco-king Charlie danced into the room, uninvited. Brittany disappeared into the kitchen.

Thanks for the help, Britt.

I interrupted, mid-step. "I'm not feeling well tonight, Charlie."

He clutched my arm. "What happened to your face?"

"I had a little accident last night. No big deal. I'm fine."

His face darkened. "What kind of accident?"

In his own way, he cared about me. Too bad I couldn't stand him. "Nothing to worry about. Everything's fine."

He looked me up and down and undressed me with his eyes. My skin crawled as if he'd touched me.

"You do look fine to me." He waggled his eyebrows.

I shuddered and covered my mouth. "I'm not in the mood."

"I can see why. I thought you might want to know who did this." He spread his arms wide, pirouetting.

"What are you talking about?"

He stuffed his hands into the pockets of his jeans. A low-key wardrobe day. "I saw the guy who tore up your car. I didn't know he got your apartment, too."

"Why didn't you call the police?"

"He was gone before I realized what was going on.

269

Besides, I figured you'd want to go after him yourself." He glanced sideways at me. "And maybe you'd need some help from me?"

The concept of the two of us playing detective together overloaded my neurons. "Who was it? What did he look like?"

"It's gonna cost you."

My jaws tightened. "I don't have any money."

He did a little soft-shoe. "Not money. Dinner."

Even worse. "I don't have time for this. Tell me who it was, or I'll reach down your throat and pull your intestines out. How's that for an offer?"

"I-I don't know his name."

"You said you knew who it was."

"I've seen him before. He was here the other night."

Russell? No way. "Come on, Charlie. What are you talking about? He was here when?"

"Tuesday night. Late."

I pulled out my phone and scrolled to a picture of Russell. "Is this him?"

Charlie frowned and squinted at the photograph. "I can't tell. It could be."

Nice try. "Forget it. You're full of it, as usual. I don't have time for this."

He put his hand on the door. "I'm serious. He was here Tuesday night. I swear it."

His gaze held steady on mine. He told the truth as he remembered it. Another unreliable witness. "What did he look like?"

"He was tall, with dark hair. Medium build. Wearing light pants and a dark sweater."

Charlie's description fit Russell. It also fit about seventy percent of the southern white male population

270

under forty. Russell remained somewhere in Savannah, in who knows what condition, with no transportation. He couldn't have trashed my car. Forget it. I had enough wild geese to chase already.

I shoved Charlie out the door and slammed it behind him. Except, I needed him to find Kingsley Franklin's bank account. I opened the door again. "Hey, hold up."

He smiled.

Brittany and I spent about an hour on the apartment, then I had to quit for the night. Too worn out and too sore. Everything else could wait. Besides, the bedroom didn't look much different than normal. I had to give Olinski credit for that observation. Of course, he got his information second-hand from Havermayer.

However, before we could settle in for the night, I had to make a phone call. My mother needed to know what had happened to me. I didn't want her to find out from someone else, although who would tell her, I couldn't fathom. Still, the possibility existed.

I steeled myself and pressed the button. "Hi, Mom."

"Well, this is a surprise."

She sounded happy to hear from me. I'd have to tread carefully. She'd set those kinds of traps for me in the past.

We exchanged pleasantries, which actually seemed pleasant for a change, until I could delay no longer. "There's something I have to tell you."

"Okay, go ahead."

Her voice seemed cautious, restrained. Not at all the hysteria I'd expected. If she could make that effort, I should too. I'd have to contain my ingrained knee-jerk responses. I gave her the CliffsNotes version of my experiences the last couple of days, and held my breath until she responded.

Finally, she did. "I want you to come stay with me until it's safe."

I lowered myself onto the couch. My eyes brimmed with tears. The hot, angry kind, which scalded my face on the way to my neck. The kind I couldn't stop until exhaustion set in. I struggled to regain my composure. "Thank you, but I couldn't do that. I can't risk putting you in danger. Besides, Gary would never go for it."

"I'll handle him. Don't you worry about it."

First time for everything, but I doubted she could. "I appreciate the thought, but I have to find Russell. He's still missing and nobody seems to care."

"I'm positive that's not true. Surely, the police are looking for him."

"You would think, but I'm not convinced. They haven't even found Aletha's killer, yet."

"Maybe, when they find one, they'll find the other."

Not you too. "Perhaps, but I don't think so."

"Jennifer, you have to stop this. Investigations are for the police. Leave it alone before something serious happens to you."

I promised to stay with Brittany until the danger passed. In return, she dropped the idea that I should come home to stay for the duration. Besides, I'd allowed Olinski to believe I'd let Brittany watch over me, so I might as well make an honest woman of myself. They had a point, although I'd never say it out loud. But that didn't mean I would give up on the hunt for Aletha's killer. If anything, the destruction of my home had solidified my resolve. The Davenport twins never quit, and I wouldn't either.

Brittany puttered in the bathroom, running water. I cleared a place to sleep on the bed. Rather than stay with her, I should ask her to spend the night here, with me. Whoever did this either found what they were looking for, or knew it wasn't here. That made this place safer than her apartment.

She appeared in the doorway as I finished with the blankets. "I've run you a hot bath. Go soak while I fix dinner. You'll feel better."

"You're the best friend anyone could ever have."

She blushed. "Nice thought, but the best friend you could ever have would be somebody just like me... who's filthy rich."

"Good point. But, somehow, I doubt someone who's filthy rich could turn out to be like you."

"True. Poverty does have its advantages." She pointed toward the bathroom. "Hit the showers."

"Right, coach."

I peeled off my clothes and eased into the water an inch at a time. One by one, my muscles loosened while the bubbles tickled my skin. Steam opened my clogged sinuses, and the moisture soothed my hoarse, dry throat. I could swallow and fill my lungs without coughing.

However, my apartment bathtub wouldn't allow for a good soak. Even though my last growth spurt had leveled me off at five foot six, I could either have my upper body under the water, or my legs, but not both. If I ever bought a house of my own, I'd make sure the bathtub fit my whole body. Had to keep my priorities straight.

I'd begun to doze when Brittany tapped on the door to call me for dinner. I had to vacate the sauna, against my will, to placate my stomach. I toweled off and threw on my sleep sweats.

Brittany had fixed an enormous pot of chicken noodle soup, and hot ham and cheese sandwiches. The melted Swiss dripped out the sides onto the plate. We ate in silence.

The edge off our hunger at last, Brittany asked, "What happens now?"

"I wish I knew."

"You must be close to finding out something someone doesn't want you to know." She swallowed the last bite of her sandwich, and dabbed her mouth with a napkin. Her perfect table manners would've infuriated Gary. Which thrilled me. Gary was a stickler for things he thought were important, but table manners didn't make the list.

I waved my spoon, a stray noodle stuck to the end. "I know, but what?"

"If we knew the answer to that, we'd know who the killer is."

I downed my last mouthful of soup and thrust the bowl away. "I don't even have a clue who the killer is."

Brittany picked up the empty dishes and carried them to the sink. "Apparently, the killer doesn't know that. Someone thinks you know too much. That's why you were attacked. They're not very bright, whoever they are. They should know by now, I'm the brains in this outfit. If anyone's going to figure out what's going on here, it's me."

"True, but then you'd be the target. That wouldn't work."

Her eyes twinkled. "Why not? I think I'd look good with a bull's-eye on my chest."

The laughter made my side hurt, but my stress level dropped to a lower plane than since yesterday morning. That's why we had friends. That, and the deliberate avoidance of subjects that made me fidgety and sick to my stomach, like Russell Jeffcoat. And sail slugs. Whatever the hell they were.

Perhaps, tomorrow, after some uninterrupted sleep, my mind would be clear enough to tackle the stickier issues I faced. Or I could just sleep through the day. That might work, too.

CHAPTER TWENTY-FIVE

I cleared off the table and enjoyed the kitchen cleanup, for once. The events of the past few days had given me a greater appreciation for the simpler aspects of life. I might make some guy a good little housewife, yet. Except I'd rather jump back into the Savannah River, oil, trash, and all.

Brittany put the last dish in the cabinet. "What should we do now?"

A good stretch took stock of my muscles, which seemed looser but still sore. "Nothing that requires movement. It's close to nine, so let's veg out. Watch a movie or something."

"Now we're talking. What do you want to see?"

I flopped onto the couch while she checked out the DVDs. My meager movie collection resided in the cabinet beside the television. We'd seen them a hundred times each, but a well-worn classic would work well tonight. "I don't care."

She pointed toward the DVD player. "What's in here, now?"

"I have no idea. Turn it on."

When she hit play, the first scenes of the Your Life

promotional video filled the screen. Brittany reached down to turn it off.

I stopped her. "I fell asleep on this the other night and forgot about it. Let's watch for a minute. There might be something useful on it."

Brittany shrugged and joined me on the couch. The narrator's voice mimicked Ted Baxter from the old *Mary Tyler Moore Show*. No wonder I fell asleep so quickly.

The fifteen-minute intro led into a video montage of the recipients' presentation ceremonies, first aired on television. Then, a guided tour of the headquarters, similar to the one we'd taken in person. When the narrator introduced the employees, I'd had enough. "Go ahead and turn it off."

While Brittany reached for the remote, the screen flashed to an employee family picnic. In one corner of the picture, Albert Sikazian and Edna Babbitt in part obscured a young, dark-haired guy with a bushy, full beard I could swear I'd seen before.

I grabbed her arm. "Hold on." I backed up to the picnic.

Brittany leaned back. "What's wrong?"

I leaned closer to the screen. "I know that guy, just can't place him."

"Could he be somebody you saw on the tour?"

Possible, but the man seemed more familiar to me than some random person I'd passed in the hallway three days ago. "It'll come to me, sooner or later. I'm going to turn it off."

I opened the movie cabinet and pulled out the first DVD my hand touched. *Hidden Figures*. A good one. I limped back to the couch, laying my head on my arm. When I closed my eyes, my body relaxed. The last couple of days had taken a toll. What was the next level past exhausted? Fried? Burned out? Whatever it was, I'd reached it.

Brittany woke me around ten. Coming out of the bathroom, I found her putting sheets on the couch.

"What are you doing?"

"You don't think I'm going to leave you here alone tonight, do you?"

My ego accepted the challenge, despite my promise to my mother. "I'll be fine. Somebody thought I had something they wanted. Now, they either have it back or know it's not here."

"I'm not leaving. What if it was something you knew, not something you had? Did you ever think of that?"

"I don't know anything. And why would they search my apartment looking for something I knew? That doesn't make sense. There's no reason for you to stay here and be uncomfortable all night. The police are making extra patrols, and I have a gun."

She arched her left eyebrow in that expression she used to annoy me. "What gun?"

"The one my father left me."

"Ha! You mean that old thing your great-grandfather brought back from France in 1918? That's no gun. That's an antique."

"I'll bet it still works." Maybe.

She held out her hand. "Let me see it."

I waded through the mess in the bedroom closet and pulled out the box with the Luger my great-grandfather had taken from a dead German officer at the end of World War I. At least, nobody found it during all the searches I'd been through lately. I handed it to Brittany, and the oily smell brought back memories of the stories my great-grandfather had passed down. Also in the box were two magazines, plus a pack of nine-millimeter ammunition. Did bullets have an expiration date? I had no idea. Olinski would know. I'd never ask him, though.

The insertion of rounds into one of the magazines turned out more of a challenge than I'd expected. The projectiles slid over the top to land on the floor. My thumb ached, and every time I had to bend over to pick one up, my head thumped. Easier to let Brittany stay, but I couldn't back down now. Eight painful rounds later, I handed the gun over.

Brittany turned the weapon over in her hand. "You sure you know how to work this thing?"

"I can figure it out. I wrote a story about gun control in high school, remember?"

She raised her eyebrows.

I clenched my teeth.

Deep breath in, slow breath out.

"How does it work?" she asked.

I picked up the loaded magazine. "You put this thing into the hole in the handle, pull the slide back to load a bullet into the chamber, and pull the trigger."

"Let me see you put it together."

Harder to do than I'd made it sound, but within a minute, I had a functional weapon, loaded and ready to use. I flipped on the thumb safety and put the Luger back into the box. "Are you satisfied, now?"

"I guess that's all right."

"Gee, thanks." I pointed toward the door.

Brittany stood firm. "You promised Olinski, and your mother by the way, you'd stay with me tonight. I don't care which apartment we stay in, but we're going to be together. I'm not leaving you alone."

I'd lost the battle, but still had the war to think about. "Fine. You win. How much do you charge for babysitting?"

"This one's on the house. I'm going to get some things. I'll be right back."

She returned while I rinsed off my toothbrush. I turned to her and smiled. "Thanks for everything, today."

She hugged me. "That's my job. You would've done the same for me. In fact, you did when I needed you the most. You uprooted your life for me when Frankie disappeared. Moved back to this place you despised, just to support me."

"I know, but still, I don't tell you how much I appreciate the things you do for me."

She ruffled my still-damp hair. She could get away with it, although I still loathed it. "Don't worry, I know. Now, cut out all this mushy stuff. It doesn't suit you."

Right again. I'd never been this maudlin before. Emotional overload. "Yes, ma'am."

"Say goodnight, John-Boy."

Another of our old routines. "Goodnight, John-Boy."

I inserted a chair under the front doorknob, stumbled to bed, and fell asleep before I could even consider not being able to.

CHAPTER TWENTY-SIX

I next opened my eyes at almost noon. I'd made it through the night without any attempts to kill or kidnap me. Except for a wicked headache, my body had recovered well—until I moved. A stay in bed for the day sounded quite appealing, but I had an appointment with my novel. Ruth expected the first three chapters today. Unfortunately, I had nothing ready to send. Maybe, Aletha's bequeath of the bookstore would end up being a good thing. It would give me a way to support myself when my writing career crashed and burned.

I limped to the bathroom, with the walls for support, desperate to walk without using my feet. No luck there.

The shower massaged my neck and shoulders. Honestly, another bath would've helped more, but it would take too long and I'd run the risk of an unscheduled tub nap.

I loosened up enough that I could turn my head and lift my arms. Progress.

In the mirror, dark-blue half-moons under my eyes announced I'd lost a prize fight, but at least they didn't hurt. Plus, combing my hair seemed only a little like medieval torture. Better than I'd expected.

On my way to prod the coffee maker into action, a brand-new lock on the front door caught my eye. Brittany must've let the locksmith in while I slept. I found a note from her on the kitchen counter.

Push the button and read this while you wait.

"This" described an envelope with the paper that had fallen out of Sikazian's wallet the day of our so-called interview with him. I'd left it in Brittany's camera bag and forgotten about it. While the coffee brewed, I tore open the envelope, which contained a ledger sheet, with payments to a company called RCB Enterprises SC interspersed throughout. RCB. Where had I seen that before?

I typed RCB Enterprises SC into the search bar of my browser. No relevant results. Only a bunch of stuff with one part or the other of the search parameter, but nothing with all of it together. RCB Enterprises SC as a business entity didn't exist. I called Brittany and set her to work on it.

I loaded the Your Life video again, and when the bearded man I didn't quite recognize filled the screen, I hit pause. He grinned, full-faced into the camera, while on his right, Edna Babbitt gazed up at him. His left hand rested on the shoulder of Albert Sikazian, but Santa seemed anxious to get away. And around the man's neck hung a tennis racket on a thin, gold chain. The same necklace I'd found at the crime scene.

Was Tim was murdered because he had the necklace that could identify Aletha's killer? A necklace I gave him. It was my fault he died. Except, how did the killer find out he had it? Also, that didn't explain why someone tried to kill me. Maybe the ledger sheet was more relevant than I understood.

Olinski had to know about this. I collected the DVD and ledger sheet and headed for the police station. We had a picture of Aletha's killer. We only had to identify him.

At the top of the police station steps, I turned toward the bookstore.

I think we've got him, Aletha.

The desk sergeant told me Olinski and Havermayer had gone out to the river to search for missed evidence in Tim's death, so I asked for Eric.

He examined the ledger sheet. " If this company really is a fake, this should be enough to get us a warrant for the contest's books. Great job, Jen."

"Thanks, but I got lucky. The contest director dropped it, and I picked it up."

"Sometimes it's better to be lucky than good, as they say."

"Is there a way we can take a look at this DVD I got from the contest? There's someone on it I can't identify who might be important to the investigation."

Eric led me into a room with a TV and DVD player. I popped the DVD in, fast-forwarded to the family picnic, and paused on the picture in question. "Does that guy look familiar to you?"

He leaned closer to the screen. "Maybe. Who is he?"

"I don't know. That's the problem. I think he might be Aletha's killer."

He stood up and locked his gaze on mine. "What makes you think so?"

"You see the necklace? I found it at the crime scene."

"What? Why are we just now hearing about this?" His scowl turned him into Opie Taylor's evil twin.

"Tim Cunningham said it might belong to a friend of Aletha's, and I believed him. I told him later to show it to Olinski. I guess he didn't."

Eric studied me with cold eyes, nostrils flaring. "I'll give all this to the detectives, and they can follow up. I suggest you lay low for a while. You could end up behind bars over this."

I'd stepped in it this time, without a doubt.

On the way home, I stopped in the Dandy Diner for a cheeseburger and a milkshake, as a panacea for my gross stupidity. Angus wiped the counter as I slid onto a stool and placed my order to go.

He passed it on to the cook and came around to sit beside me. "It's going to be a few minutes. We just finished cleaning up after a big order. We'll be caught up shortly."

"No problem. I'm in no hurry. Who's having a party?"

"I don't know. I've never seen the lady before. She came in by herself, but there was another guy in the car and two little girls in the back seat. Only four of them, but she ordered enough food for a dozen, at least."

I sat straight up on my stool. "What did the guy look like?"

"I couldn't see him. He was behind the wheel and had the visor pulled down."

When I arrived home, Charlie had planted himself in the parking lot. I turned in, and he skittered back into his freshly washed Ford Focus.

Please go away. I took my time in the hope he'd get tired and go back to his apartment. No such luck. He waited on the curb and rocked back and forth on his cowboy boot heels.

"Hi, Charlie." I didn't stop.

He followed. "Hey, gorgeous. What's the hurry?"

I pulled myself up the stairs.

He attacked. A wolf on a crippled elk. "Let me help you with that."

"It's only my lunch. I can handle it."

At the top of the stairs, I fumbled with my keys while I scrambled for ways to get rid of him. I could push him down the stairs, but I was already on Olinski's watch list, and a trip to jail would interfere with my plans. I didn't condone rudeness, but some people left me no choice. I shoved the door open.

"Thanks. See you later."

He stuck his foot between the door and the jamb. "Where are you going?"

I walked toward the kitchen. "I've got a lot to do."

The scowl on his face when he seized my arm, made my muscles tighten. "I'm getting tired of you leading me on."

Seriously? I jerked my arm away and rubbed my sore biceps. "I've never led you on. I've always been honest with you. You just don't listen."

"You're playing games with me, and I want you to stop it."

Pipsqueak. "Goodbye, Charlie." I shoved him out the door, closed it, and groaned. He had information for me. I jerked the door back open, again, to find Charlie in front of it, with a grin on his face.

"Forget something?"

"You know I did."

"It's going to cost you."

"Dinner. Yes, I know. What did you find out about Kingsley Franklin?"

He squeezed past me, proceeded straight to the couch, and propped his boots on the coffee table. "I found his account, and there was one deposit and one automatic transfer, like you thought. The deposit was from the Your Life contest for a hundred and fifty-thousand dollars."

"And the transfer?"

"The entire amount, to a company listed as RCB Enterprises SC. I did some research and it turns out RCB Enterprises SC is a shell company. I haven't been able to get any info on them, yet, but I'll keep digging."

I pumped my fist. Success. For once. "Thanks. I appreciate your help."

Charlie left, after a promise I'd have dinner with him Sunday night, and I called Brittany. She'd had no luck with information on RCB Enterprises SC, either. No surprise. All her avenues of exploration had legitimate origins.

"What are you going to do, now?" she asked.

I paced my apartment track. "I guess I need to call Olinski and lay it all out for him."

"Good idea. Maybe, he'll let you come along for the arrest when they put it all together."

"Doubtful. I'll call you tomorrow, before I head to Mom's party. You sure you don't want to come?"

Brittany laughed. "Positive. I'd rather have root canal without anesthesia. But I will if you want me to."

"No, it's okay. I'm tough, I can take it."

I ate my cold cheeseburger, washed it down with the melted chocolate milkshake, and picked up the phone.

Olinski answered on the third ring. "What do you want, Jen?"

"I guess you've spoken to Eric."

"I have, and I'm not happy right now."

"Well, hear me out, and you might change your mind."

It took close to ten minutes for me to finish the outline of my case. I laid it all out for him: the significance of the ledger, the necklace, the alteration of the Your Life audit timeline, Kingsley Franklin's bank account, and the death of Ida Clare Green. "All that's missing are the details. And, putting a name to the killer, of course. The necklace should be somewhere in the Cunningham house. DNA on it might solve the problem."

He breathed through a long silence, then said, "Unfortunately, it's all circumstantial, but you've given me a lot to think about."

I'll think about it—the ultimate blowoff. "I suggest you think fast. Russell could be in real trouble."

Duty done, I did the only thing I could now: write the three chapters for Ruth. While my recent experiences had helped me understand career success wouldn't fill all the holes in my life as I'd once believed, it remained an important part of what I wanted for my future.

I sat at my desk and read over chapter one. Pretty standard last-draft stuff. Insert comma here, delete comma there. Did I want to use that word? Maybe, I should use this one, instead. No, the first one worked better. Change it back again. And again. And again.

Dana fingered her mother's lovely roses, careful to avoid the thorns. Mom had planted the bush on the twins' first birthday.

No. Show, don't tell, stupid. Replace lovely with brilliant crimson. Better? Nope, vivid crimson, instead. Yes. Much better. On second thought, maybe just crimson.

A couple of hours later, I had three passable chapters to send. Monday morning, I'd find them back in my inbox, slashed to ribbons by Ruth's dedicated hand. A skilled surgeon with the sensitivity of Ted Bundy. However, I'd bought myself some time.

I settled on the couch to unwind in front of the TV for a few minutes, and promptly fell asleep. The phone rang in my dream for several seconds until I woke to the real thing. I reached for it, and glanced at the screen. Two in the morning.

Someone breathed into the phone. "Jen, this is Marcus."

I sat up, wide awake. "Where are you? Where are the girls? Are they okay? Your mother told me they were with a friend."

"They're here, and they're fine."

"Where's here?"

"I'm at the Cunningham house. Can you meet me? I need to talk to you. To explain."

"Why can't you talk to me, now?"

"Please! I messed up and I need your help. I can't go back to prison. And I can tell you how to find Russell, if you bring the paper."

"What paper?"

"You know."

"No, I don't. How can I be sure to bring the right one, if you won't tell me what it is?"

"The one you stole from Sikazian."

The ledger sheet. Which the police had. How did Marcus know Santa? A question for our meeting. "Is Russell all right?"

"Yes. Please come."

"Okay, I'll be there as soon as I can."

He wanted me to deliver the ledger sheet, in exchange for information about Russell, but something seemed off to me. What if it was a trap set to get rid of me because I knew too much? I was hands-quaking, mouth-too-dry-to-swallow, armpits-sweating scared.

Deep breath in, slow breath out.

CHAPTER TWENTY-SEVEN

I had to pull myself together. What would Dana Davenport do? She stayed cool no matter the situation. My perfect foil. She would call Olinski. So, I woke him in the middle of the night and took perverse pleasure in it.

"What's going on?" he asked, his voice barely audible.

"Marcus Jones called me. He wants me to meet him at the Cunningham house. He claims he has information about Russell Jeffcoat's whereabouts. He wants me to bring him the ledger sheet I found."

That woke him up. "I'll be there in half an hour. Make some damn coffee, and it better be strong."

Coffee sounded good to me, too.

While the coffee maker bubbled in the background, I flipped through my wardrobe. What did one wear to a middle-of-the-night meeting with a guy who might've helped kill my friend? Best to look tough. If I dressed to match my current emotional state, the whole thing would end in less than a minute, with me as victim number three.

I pulled out jeans, a T-shirt, boots, and a leather jacket with numerous zippered pockets, everything black. The boots and jacket, leftovers from my brief foray into the biker look during my junior year of high school, had resided, alone and lonely, in the back of my closet for years, but I could never bring myself to throw them away. Good thing.

The Luger I retrieved from the nightstand and tucked into an inside jacket pocket. Because of the eight-inch barrel, I couldn't zip it up. With luck, the gun wouldn't fall out and blow my toes off. Assuming it still worked. Despite my earlier display of confidence, I had some doubts. Fingers and toes crossed, I wouldn't have to find out.

When I dropped the second loaded magazine into the front pocket of my jeans, I declared my preparations complete. Nothing left to do but pour the coffee, the aroma of which had turned my living room into a Starbucks. Maybe, it would put Olinski into a better mood.

The coffee maker gurgled its last as Olinski tapped on the door. He strode in, clad in jeans and tennis shoes, followed by Havermayer, who had somehow managed to look like she'd stepped off the cover of *Vogue*.

What's she doing here?

I poured coffee for each of us. "I think I should have a way to record the meeting with Marcus."

Olinski stirred his coffee. "No. It's too risky. If he finds out, he might hurt you."

"I doubt that. He doesn't seem the type. And what if he incriminates himself? We'll have it on tape."

Havermayer broke in. "*He doesn't seem the type?* Two people are dead and one is missing. What makes you think you wouldn't end up like one of them?"

Detective Starchy at her best. Couldn't even blame

lack of sleep. "I can take care of myself, and I think it's worth the risk. Do you have enough evidence to charge him with either of those deaths?"

She glared at me, then shook her head.

"I didn't think so. This may be the only way to get it."

Olinski slammed his cup on the counter. "Fine, you can wear a wire."

I froze with a teaspoon full of sugar suspended in midair. "A wire? A recording device taped to my chest kind of thing?"

"Exactly."

I stirred the sugar into my coffee. "Do I have to? Don't you have some kind of pin with a camera in it I could wear?"

Olinski's smirk cut straight into my pride. "This is Riddleton, not the FBI. We don't have an electronics van like you see on TV. Besides, it would clash with your jacket."

Another knock on the door interrupted my snarky reply. Eric let himself in. What was he doing here? Olinski led him back out the door and returned a minute later. "He'll be right back. I sent him to get the wire and ledger sheet."

When Eric returned, he carried the contraption they would attach to my body and handed it to Havermayer, who signaled for me to follow her into the bedroom. Then, he passed me the ledger sheet I'd left with him earlier. My gut churned, and I broke into a sweat, which had nothing to do with the heavy jacket I wore. However, having my friend Eric here took a little of the edge off my anxiety.

Havermayer studied the disarray in my bedroom. She rolled her eyes, but, to her credit, offered no comment.

I removed my jacket and tossed it onto the pile of clothes on the bed. "Do I need to take my shirt off too?"

"It would be easier if you did." Her tone came across as more or less friendly. Perhaps, she'd softened toward me. Or maybe she ran out of starch.

I pulled off my T-shirt, deposited it next to my jacket, and smoothed my hair. Anything to take my mind off the fact I'd exposed myself to Ms Ironing Board. Not a situation I'd ever considered possible.

Havermayer uncoiled a long black wire with a microphone on the end and plugged it into a black box. Then, she taped the microphone to my chest in the space between my breasts. Both the gadget and her fingers seemed covered in ice. She draped the wire over my left shoulder and clipped the box to the back of my jeans where my jacket would hide it.

"Say something."

For the first time in my life, I had no words. My brain had dried up along with my mouth. "Like what?"

"It doesn't matter. Just say—"

"I got it. You're good," Olinski called from the living room.

Havermayer turned to me. "Okay, you can get dressed."

I threw on my T-shirt and reached for my jacket. When I picked it up, the Luger fell out onto the floor.

"What's that?" Havermayer pointed to the gun.

Heat rose into my cheeks. "I thought I'd bring it along for protection."

"You don't need protection, you have us. Nothing to worry about."

Except she wasn't the one who had to stroll into the

lion's den. I laid the gun on the nightstand and followed her back into the living room without its reassuring weight in my pocket. A trust exercise.

Olinski studied me when I reappeared. "You okay? You're doing great."

My definition of great and his differed without question.

I clenched my jaw against the cold sweat and willed my knees to continue to support my weight. No, not great. "What happens now?"

Eric glanced at his watch. "It's close to three, we should go. Marcus will get suspicious." He squeezed my shoulder. "Everything's going to be fine. Get him talking, we'll do the rest."

Olinski nodded. "We'll follow you to the Cunningham house and park on the street so nobody sees us. You'll be on your own when you turn into the driveway. But we'll be listening."

"What if I get in trouble?"

"Pick a rescue word. When you say it, we'll come in."

All the words in my writer's brain disappeared for the second time. No wonder I couldn't finish my book. Actually, I liked that word. "Book. How about book?"

Havermayer drew her brows together. "Can you work it into the conversation?"

"I'm a writer. I can work that word into any conversation."

Olinski and Eric chuckled, while Havermayer pursed her lips. Some of the tension drained away, and my heart rate slowed. I'd get through this if it was the last thing I ever did. With luck, I wouldn't have to worry about that.

Olinski met my gaze. "All right. Remember, your

goal is to keep him talking. Get as much information as you can, but don't be too pushy or he might get suspicious."

Eric rested his hand on my shoulder. "Just relax. We've got your back."

I nodded, as unconvinced as Havermayer was about my rescue word.

Olinski opened the door. "Let's go catch us some bad guys."

As they trooped out, I ducked into the bedroom and stuffed the Luger into the back of my pants, next to the box.

I sat behind the wheel of my Sentra, gun digging into my spine. Clouds hid the moon. The weather experts called for severe thunderstorms, but that wouldn't work for me. The noise and lightning flashes would distract me when I needed total concentration. Unfortunately, I didn't get a vote on the matter.

Not much traffic on the road to the house. Too late for the partygoers, too soon for Saturday workers. Periodically, I checked the rearview mirror, comforted by Olinski's headlights a discreet distance behind. I stopped at the driveway, and Olinski waved out the driver's side window as he eased into position behind me. I turned in.

The leafy branches over the road made my hair stand on end, scalp itchy, as though I'd wandered into a plasma light ball. I coasted off the dirt drive onto the circular cement driveway. The house had a dark, unnatural facade, except for a light in the center, upstairs window. The guest room next to Tim's office. No cars occupied the driveway. A perfect scene for a horror movie, and I bought in by trembling like a teenaged girl.

"I hope you guys are still there. I'm getting out of the car."

Deep breath in, slow breath out.

I opened the car door. Still no movement from the house. I straightened my shoulders and approached the front door, deafened by the leaves that crunched under my feet. I could do this. I *would* do this.

The tiny light from the doorbell glimmered in the darkness. With a steady hand, I pressed it.

Edna Babbitt opened the door.

My heart raced. *Why is she here?* I'd expected to meet Marcus. I had to let Olinski know. "Edna Babbitt. I'm surprised to see you."

She smoothed her hair back. No need, since the bun held it in an iron grip. "Wish I could say the same about you. Stupid cow."

The last of my fear disappeared into anger. "I'm willing to bet I'm smarter than you think."

"I doubt it."

"Where's Marcus?"

Edna smiled. A grotesque contrast to her hostile demeanor. "Upstairs, waiting for you. Did you bring the paper?"

I patted my jacket. "Right here, but I'll only give it to him."

She stepped aside to let me in. I squeezed by her into the living room, which no longer comforted me. The freak show overshadowed Aletha's presence.

I waved toward the stairs, and sweat dripped down my back. The electronics had better repel water. Not to mention the Luger. "Let's go. You first."

She sidled up the steps, careful not to expose her back to me.

I wanted to reach for the gun but didn't dare blow my cover, yet. "So, how are you involved in all this?"

"Who says I am?"

"You're here, aren't you?"

Edna reached the top of the steps and turned down the hall toward Tim's office. Light now gleamed under that door, as well as the guest room. My ears searched for signs of life in the silent house. They found nothing, as though we traveled through a tomb. Perhaps we did. Mine.

A sliver of darkness flitted through the light under the guest-room door as we passed. Someone was in there.

Edna pushed the door to Tim's office open but didn't enter. Curtained windows covered the far wall, and a couch and coffee table filled the left side of the room. The open door obscured the right. Nobody in sight. Was it a trick?

Edna lifted her hand, palm up, through the doorway. "After you. Marcus is waiting." Her tone carried a sinister undercurrent.

I forced my feet forward. When I'd cleared the doorway, she pulled the door shut behind me, and locked it.

CHAPTER TWENTY-EIGHT

Marcus Jones lay on the floor, unconscious and hand-cuffed to the leg of a desk. Drugged?

I bent to check on him. "Marcus?"

He moaned, and his eyelids fluttered. Feet pounded on the stairs. His free hand lashed out and seized my left ankle. I clawed at his fingers, but his grip imitated that of the squirrel in *Ice Age* clutching the acorn.

Rain drummed on the roof as the door lock slid open. I straightened and turned, and found myself face to face with Russell, along with the black hole in the end of the barrel of his gun. It grew larger and larger. This was my first time staring at a loaded weapon. TV bore no resemblance to reality.

My belly clenched, and angry tears pricked behind my eyelids.

It couldn't be him.

He broke the silence. "Hello, Jen."

How could he seem so calm? My mouth dried out, as if I'd swallowed the Sahara Desert. Would he shoot me? Sweat soaked the back of my neck. Havermayer had better have used waterproof tape. The collar of my jacket chafed.

The downpour muffled all sound.

Russell studied me from head to toe. "Nice look. Biker Babe, huh? I never would've guessed."

He looked like he'd stepped out of an ad for the latest James Bond movie, with his gray suit, white shirt, and skinny black tie. I didn't trust myself to speak. My chest tightened, air squeezed through my narrowed windpipe. What would he do with me?

"You came to find me. I knew I could count on you." A hollow cackle erupted from him.

Could Olinski hear what Russell said over the rain? If not, help might never come. I eyed the gun, the barrel now cannon-sized. Could I grab it? Not if I wanted to live. Mine had settled deeper into the back of my jeans. Stupid place for it.

"Step away from Mr Jones and turn around. Put your hands behind your head, and don't move."

I faced away from him with fingers entwined on the back of my skull, lips pressed together. "You don't have to do this, Russell."

His breath hot on my ear, he said, "So how did you manage your little Houdini escape the other night?"

My boyfriend tried to kill me. I shuddered.

Russell continued, "Tim wasn't so lucky. But then, he was dead before he hit the water."

I clenched my fists and gnashed my teeth. How had he hidden this arrogant side so well? Love really is blind. "Why did you kill him?"

"I heard you ask him about my necklace. I had to get it back, and he refused to tell me where it was. But you know what the funniest thing is? Tim was right. I *was* trying to kill him on the boat that day, not Aletha. To force her to pick a new beneficiary. Me. That's the reason I went to work in the bookstore to begin with. To seduce her, but she wasn't interested. She loved that idiot husband of hers, God only knows why. But we needed that money to keep Albert out of jail. The loser would probably take me with him." He shook his head and clenched his jaw. "Come on. Tell me how you got away." He backed up a step.

How did I not recognize him on the video? That bushy beard made all the difference. I turned around, hands still on my head. "First, tell me how my pen ended up at the crime scene."

He chuckled low in his throat. "I thought that was a nice touch, didn't you? The sail slug, too."

He murdered Aletha and Tim and Craig for money. My belly churned. "Not really, no."

"A writer with no imagination. Pathetic. Now, tell me how you escaped in Savannah."

"How did you find me at the lake that day?"

He lifted one eyebrow. "You mean that Saturday at the Cleavers'?"

"Yes."

Russell shrugged. "Easy. I followed you. Now enough stalling. Answer my question."

"You didn't know enough about me. Lucky for you. Now you're only wanted for two murders, instead of three."

"I'm not finished, yet." He gripped the back of my neck with icy fingers. The pain forced my arms down. I eased my hand toward the Luger tucked into my jeans, but Russell seized my wrist and pulled my arm up my back.

I fought nausea as he reached under my jacket to remove the weapon. "Little girls shouldn't play with guns. I'll take it for safekeeping. I wouldn't want you to hurt yourself."

"Don't worry. I wouldn't take the pleasure away from you."

"That wasn't a nice thing to say." Wind rattled the windows. He spun me around and forced me into the chair beside the desk. It tipped back but didn't fall. By the time I regained my balance, he had me pinned. With a thin rope he plucked from his jacket pocket, he tied my hands together behind the chair and my feet to the legs. "But I'm not offended."

I wiggled my wrists to see how much space he'd left me to work with. Not much. He must've learned his lesson. My ankles jerked, still sore from the last time he'd tied them. I bit my tongue and sneered at him. "That would require having feelings. You know they're going to throw the book at you when they catch you."

That's the safe word. Come on, Olinski. Now's a good time to make an entrance.

Russell's face darkened. He raised the Luger high and brought it down hard on the side of my head. Agony oozed from my left temple. Pain pulsed a steady drumbeat, which accompanied the room's spin. Sticky moisture covered my cheeks, a fog enveloped my brain. Outside, the storm raged like a philanderer's wife.

My eyelids stuck together. Blood? Rapid blinks didn't clear away the furry coating. I tried to focus on a new shape by the window. No details, but any American child would recognize Santa Claus. Albert Sikazian stood next to the curtains.

He held a drink in his right hand and surveyed the storm, his only movement a raise of his glass to his lips.

I tried to speak, but my throat had filled with cotton. I worked some saliva around my mouth, swallowed, and tried again. The croak I issued coincided with Russell's reappearance in my line of sight.

He grabbed Sikazian by the shoulder and spun him around. The whiskey spilled. "You idiot! You're not supposed to be drinking."

"Let go of me." Sikazian wiped his wet hand on his trouser leg. "And watch what you're doing."

"Stupid sot. And you thought you were too good to claim me as your son. You're a pig. I'm the big man now." Russell slapped the glass out of his hand, which spattered the contents over the curtains and carpet. He pulled the Luger out of his pocket and checked the magazine. "Take this and watch her until we're ready to go. If she tries to escape, shoot her."

He pressed the gun into Sikazian's hand and strode out of the room. Sikazian turned the weapon over in his fist, frowned, and laid it on the windowsill. He picked a bourbon bottle off the floor and returned to his storm watch.

Sikazian's Russell's father? This was about more than money. Russell wanted his due. I tried my voice again. "Albert."

No response. The tempest roared on. I tried once more, with the most volume I could muster.

He turned in my direction.

"Albert, where are we going?"

"To Hell." He raised the bottle to his lips and took a long pull. Beads of sweat trickled down his forehead, and the liquor swirled in the bottle as it came away from his mouth.

Would he help us escape? I had to find a way to use

his torment to my advantage. Maybe, a poke at his pride. "Why do you let him treat you that way? He's like a character in a book, or something."

Any time now, guys. I couldn't just say book, book, book. They were supposed to be listening for it. Perhaps they couldn't hear me. Or the squall interfered with the transmission. On my own, again. Just like Savannah. I handled it then. I could do it again if necessary. It would be nice if I didn't have to, though.

Sikazian continued to look out the window, bottle poised in midair. "Who?"

"Russell. Your son. Illegitimate, I assume?" The picnic video flashed into my mind. A mother's adoring gaze. "And Edna Babbitt is his mother."

"Then you know why he treats me so badly. He deserved to have a real father, not just a check once a month. Edna's husband died in a car crash on his way home from a six-month deployment in the Pacific."

So much for pride. Perhaps I could do something with his self-pity. "It's not your fault his father died."

"I am his father."

Blood had dripped into my eye. I tried to wipe it away with my shoulder but couldn't reach. My bonds held me fast to the chair. "It was pretty stupid for Edna to have an affair while her husband was at sea."

He took another swig from the bottle and faced me. "Edna's husband was a horrible man. And it was not an affair, more like a moment of weakness. Babbitt was supposed to come home the next day." He rubbed his eyes with his free hand. "I had a fight with my wife. Edna sympathized. We did not plan it. It just happened."

I picked up the story. "Then, Babbitt was killed in the crash on his way home. A few weeks later, she learned she was pregnant, and the baby couldn't have been his because she hadn't seen him in a while."

Another large swallow went down. "Both families rejected her. She had nowhere to turn."

"It must've been awful for her."

"Yes, she became hard, bitter. She was not always that way, you know. Actually, she was quite beautiful. I helped make her so unhappy." Tears spilled into his beard.

How long did we have until Russell came back? In the absence of Olinski and company, I needed Sikazian to help me move Marcus. "Albert, you have to help us get out of here."

"My wife never would have understood. I had two beautiful little girls. My career was on the move. I had everything to lose."

Come on, Albert, we can stroll down memory lane later. We have to go now. "Edna knew that, didn't she?"

"She started blackmailing me right after she told me the news. I guess it never occurred to her I might do the right thing without prompting." He shrugged. "It does not matter, now."

Marcus moaned and tried to sit up.

I broke Sikazian out of his trance. "Albert, do you have the key to his handcuffs?"

Sikazian looked at Marcus for the first time, as if he'd forgotten he existed. "No."

"Untie me, please, so I can help him."

He hesitated.

"Don't be a party to any more murders. You have two daughters yourself. What about Marcus's kids, Larissa and Latoya?" The girls had to be the children Angus had seen in the car, and Russell the hidden driver.

Marcus must've been at the house already, guarded by Sikazian.

Sikazian sobbed and set the bourbon bottle on the floor. He clutched the windowsill for balance. "I never meant for things to turn out the way they did."

Marcus moaned again.

I struggled with my bonds. The rope seared my skin. "What do you mean?"

"It was all over before I left California ten years ago. We agreed I had fulfilled my financial obligation to Russell, but he was not satisfied. They turned up here three years ago. Edna blackmailed me into giving her a job and money, and he wanted me to acknowledge him, make him part of my family. And he wanted money, too, of course. I had two daughters in college. There was no money, so I embezzled as much as I could from the company. Five hundred thousand dollars. Russell said it would be enough to give him a good start in life. He would not ask for any more. Idiot that I am, I believed him."

My struggles had created a bit of space between my wrists. I worked the rope. "What choice did you have?"

Sikazian picked up the bottle again. "I knew I would have five years to pay the company back. Then, the Green woman died and I posed as her father so I could take over the agency to house the homeless she had started with the money from the contest. It was the solution to all our problems. My problems."

"Until, they changed the date of the audit."

He glanced at me. "Until they changed the date of the audit. The next payment was not going to be in time."

305

"So, it was you who pretended to be Kingsley Franklin?"

Sikazian nodded and took a swig of whiskey.

"Did you leave the note on the car setting up the meeting in Savannah?"

"No, that was Russell." He wiped perspiration off his forehead. "It was all Russell. Edna had to go pick him up."

"Why didn't he drive himself home?"

"He never told me, but I suspect he knew the police would be looking for him, and he wanted to divorce himself from whatever they might find in his car."

The blood in the trunk. Clearly not his. Which meant the blood most likely belonged to Tim. My next question stuck in my craw. "Whose idea was it to kill Aletha Cunningham?"

"Edna presented it to me, but I think Russell came up with it. Either way, they had already made the decision. They only told me enough to keep me in too deep to stop them."

I swallowed hard. Aletha had died because Santa Claus had a one-night stand thirty years ago. I kept an eye on the door, lest Edna or Russell reappear. We still had to find the girls. "Albert, untie me."

He put the bottle down and stared out the window.

"Albert, please. You don't want to do this. You're not a murderer. Untie my hands!"

His shoulders drooped, face contorted. He loosened the ropes. I suspected he'd imbibed with gusto for a long time, in an effort to forget what he'd done. His booze breath flooded my nasal passages.

I called to Marcus, "Can you hear me?"

He groaned.

"Marcus, wake up. We have to get out of here."

"I hear you," he said, a bit louder than the thunder crashes.

A quick tug freed my hands. I untied my feet and rubbed my ankles to restore circulation. I propelled myself upright, shoved the chair out of the way, and turned to Sikazian. "Help me pick up this desk so he can pull his arm out."

Sikazian cleared his throat, his voice plaintive. "I never meant to hurt anyone."

Maybe, but your family sure did. "I know. Sometimes things just happen that way." I used my legs for a lift, but the desk wouldn't budge. I braced for another attempt to get my corner into the air by sheer force of will. It worked, barely. "Marcus, pull your arm out. Hurry. I can't hold it."

Marcus moved in slow motion, but managed to slide the handcuff until it dangled from his wrist. I let the desk down with a thump. I inhaled and jerked my head toward the door. Russell might investigate the noise. As I bent to lift Marcus to his feet, a tremendous flash of lightning split the sky. The lights flickered out. I froze.

Marcus wobbled. I supported him with an arm around his waist. Together, we lurched toward the window. He stumbled, and I shuffled my feet. I kicked over the bourbon bottle. My sinuses burned as the ninety-proof soaked into the carpet.

I secured the Luger in my free hand. Marcus crept forward. I guided him toward the door. "Come on, Marcus, put one foot in front of the other for me, okay? You can do it."

Halfway there, Russell came in with two candles in

short, brass holders. I raised my gun, but it slipped in my fingers. He put one candle on the file cabinet and yanked out his pistol. "Where do you think you're going?" He turned to Sikazian, who remained statue-like by the desk. "What the hell are you doing? Were you gonna let them walk out the door? Don't you know what'll happen to you if they go to the police?"

Sikazian stepped into the middle of the room. "I don't care. I deserve whatever I get, and so do you."

Russell strode toward him. "I care what happens to me, old man. I've got big plans."

I pulled Marcus toward the door, but my shoulder jabbed into the corner of the file cabinet.

Russell swung toward me. "Hey!"

Sikazian jumped him from behind. They fell to the floor. I dragged Marcus into the hallway. When I looked back again, the candle had rolled across the carpet and ignited a tiny flame under the curtains. Sikazian had Russell pinned. He looked back at me and said, "Go, hurry. I'll be all right."

Marcus staggered to the guest room next door. I stepped through the doorway. Marcus leaned over the bed and cajoled the kids out of the corner they'd huddled in. He picked up Latoya, who threw her arms around his neck in a death grip, and reached for Larissa. She allowed him to pull her to her feet.

The storm sounds receded. Marcus tried to hand Latoya to me, but she wouldn't let go. "It's all right, honey," he said, "I won't let nothing happen to you. I'll be right here."

The lights came back on as she released her grip and wrapped her arms around me, instead. I tucked the gun into my pocket and teetered under the unfamiliar weight.

Parenting. The world's oldest fitness program. I moved toward the door while Marcus picked up Larissa. We might make it.

"Isn't this sweet? One big happy family."

Russell blocked the doorway.

CHAPTER TWENTY-NINE

My heart slammed into my throat. This wasn't going to end without a fight. I handed Latoya back to Marcus, who set both children down at his feet, guided them into a corner, and stood guard in front of them.

I faced our obstacle. "Let us go, Russell."

He snickered. "You know I can't do that." His face had twisted into a maniacal mask, with always-perfect hair splayed over his forehead and blood-spattered shirt-tail hanging out.

What did I ever see in this lunatic? "I don't have to tell anyone what I know."

"You're a writer, or so you think. You'll tell everyone."

I ignored the jibe and played for time to figure out how to get the gun away from him. "I'm not writing about this. It's too strange, even for fiction. I couldn't sell this *book* if I tried." *Olinski has to hear me.*

Russell smirked.

"If I don't arrive home tonight, Russell, everyone's going to learn how you killed Aletha to get money to cover your embezzlement scheme. Did you kill Ida Green, too? And Craig Marshall?"

His brows shot up. "Not Ida. That was an accident.

310

It was convenient she didn't have any relatives. Craig figured out what we were doing. I had no choice." He narrowed his eyes. "What do you mean everyone will know?"

A crack in the armor? I edged closer to the door. "I wrote a detailed letter and mailed it to myself. If I disappear, the police will find it, along with a note giving them permission to open my mail." A very forgivable fib.

"You're bluffing."

A waterfall poured out of my underarms. I took my jacket off. "Are you willing to bet your life on that?" He had to accept the story.

Russell raised his gun to eye level. "Stop."

"I'm hot." I ignored him with manufactured bravado.

"Yes, you are." He flashed his crooked smile.

I swallowed back a wave of nausea. He could've brought me to my knees with one touch, two days ago. Before he'd tried to kill me.

A mental image of Aletha brought me up short. He'd murdered my friend. I held my jacket in front of me, a leather fig leaf slick in my palms. "Shut up, Russell."

His grin disappeared.

A hot ball of ice filled my chest. "Do what you want with me. Let Marcus and the kids go."

Russell stepped forward. I held my ground. I couldn't let him see my fear. The animal he'd become would feed on it.

He reached out and brushed my jaw with the back of his hand. "We could've made a pretty good team."

I grabbed for the gun.

Russell caught my arm in midair, and the bones in my wrist crunched together. My knees buckled.

He pushed the muzzle of the weapon under my chin. "I thought you were smarter than that."

Adrenaline bolstered my courage. "Nope. If I was, I would've been smart enough not to fall for you."

"We had fun."

His grin brought coffee up into my esophagus. I swallowed hard. "You used me."

Russell pushed me into Marcus, who steadied me. The girls whimpered in the corner behind him.

"Let them go, Russell. This is between you and me."

"He knows too much."

Marcus responded, his voice wavering. "I won't tell nobody about Billy, I swear. Nobody gotta know where you got the stuff. I thought we were friends. Remember all the times the three of us hung out together?"

"Well, friend, you were at the house that afternoon."

"You never told me what you and Billy were going to do Friday night. I didn't find out 'til I talked to Billy on Saturday afternoon. I tried to stop you, but it was too late. I was in the driveway when the bomb went off, and I hightailed it outta there. I ain't said nothing to nobody, though. And I won't."

Russell shrugged. "Well, I still can't let you out of here." Latoya whimpered and clung to her sister.

Marcus took a step toward Russell. "Kill me if you have to, just let my kids go. They served their purpose. You used them to get me here. They don't have nothing to do with this."

"Touching. Papa bear sacrificing himself for his cubs. Forget it." Russell waved the pistol at me. "Give it up."

Larissa screamed and pointed in Russell's direction. Orange light from the flames danced on the wall behind him. I rammed into him and wrapped my jacket around his arms as we fell.

"Run, Marcus!" We hit the floor with Russell on top of me. The air rushed out of my lungs.

His gun bounced across the carpet. He pulled away and scrabbled for it. I remained pinned by his legs. Marcus pushed the girls out the door in the direction of the stairs and reached to pull Russell off me. Russell lashed out, and Marcus stumbled down the hall.

As I turned over, the Luger dug into my side. I struggled to get it out of my pocket. Russell jumped from a half-crouch. I shot up my feet to hit him square in the bread basket. He fell back with a groan. I pulled the gun from my pocket and lurched upright. He lay on his side, knees tucked into his belly.

I pointed my great-grandfather's souvenir at Russell's head. He turned over on his back and propped himself on his elbows.

"It's over, Russell."

His gaze flicked back and forth between mine and the muzzle of the gun.

I backed around him, a safe distance away.

He watched my progress. A debate raged in his eyes. Then, he clambered to his feet and stepped toward me. "You'll never pull the trigger. You don't have the nerve."

With each step he took forward, I took a step back toward the stairs. I wiped my palms on my jeans, one at a time, the gun switched from one hand to the other. "Don't come any closer. I'll shoot you."

"Sure you will. Give me the gun before you hurt yourself. You couldn't shoot me."

"Don't kid yourself." The linen closet door hit me in the back.

Russell advanced, though at a slower pace. "Come on, Jen, give me the gun. You don't have it in you." Smoke curled around his head like devil's horns.

"You don't know what I have in me. Don't make me do it."

He stopped five feet away. Close enough to jump. "Last chance. Give me the gun, or I'll take it away from you."

My hands shook. I held the Luger at eye level and trained it on his face.

He lunged like a fencer.

I closed my eyes and squeezed the trigger.

Nothing happened.

Russell's cackle died in the roar of the flames, which devoured the walls behind him.

Now, I hated him as much as I'd imagined I loved him before.

I stared at the gun. The thumb safety had done its job.

Russell lunged again.

I flipped off the safety and fired. My hand jerked up. Pain shot through my ears, and the scene morphed into a slow-motion silent movie. My nostrils stank of burned powder. Bile coated the back of my throat.

I'd missed.

He snagged my arm.

I pulled away and tripped down the steps to where the staircase turned.

He jumped, pushed me against the banister. A loud crack reverberated behind me. I jerked my knee up and connected with his ribcage.

Russell grunted and pushed off.

I scooted toward the wall.

He clutched my shirt and lifted me toward the railing. I kicked his left leg.

He toppled into the banister. It gave way. His scream penetrated my deafened ears. My chest heaved, lungs desperate for air. I leaned down and peeked over the edge of the staircase. Russell lay sprawled on the floor, head twisted. His empty eyes stared up at me. My stomach spewed bile on the landing.

I'd killed Russell.

When I reached the ground floor, the fire illuminated the night through the glass doors. The lights flickered off, again. I surveyed the area, but could see nothing. Had Marcus and the girls made it outside to safety?

I pushed myself toward the front door. Thick, black smoke flowed across the ceiling. An orange strobe light danced behind me. The roof collapsed with a roar and generated a wave of hot air, which threw me face first into the door. I pulled it open, the knob searing the palm of my hand, and fell across the threshold. I coughed and sucked cool air into my smoke-filled lungs, hovering on the brink of consciousness.

Eric caught me under the arms and dragged me onto the grass. My head swayed and bounced with each step. It didn't matter. Aletha's beautiful house had collapsed. Russell posed no more threat to anyone. We'd survived.

CHAPTER THIRTY

Overhead lights zipped by, like the broken center lines on a highway, as the paramedics wheeled my gurney into a cubicle surrounded by curtains. I inched onto the ER bed, and nurses hustled to hook me up to oxygen and monitors.

"Try to breathe through your nose," one of them said. "That's where the oxygen is."

Another nurse gathered information from the paramedic about my condition.

I closed my eyes against the blur of activity. The adrenaline wore off, and one by one my muscles relaxed. I focused on the challenge of drawing cool oxygen into my lungs, and fought the urge to breathe through my mouth. I drifted off.

When I awoke, Brittany held my hand. Eric sat in a chair on the other side of the bed. I struggled to sit up, but everything hurt, and I collapsed back onto the pillow. "How long have I been out?"

Brittany squeezed my hand. "About an hour or so. The doctor tried to wake you, but you kept dozing off. You even slept through a chest X-ray. Well, sort of. You opened your eyes once or twice."

"Guess I crashed." I summoned the energy for a smile and turned to Eric. "Hey, buddy. About time you showed up."

His face reddened. "Your feed kept cutting out. We could only get about half of what was going on, none of which included your safe word. Sorry. We came running when we saw the fire." He rested his hand on my shoulder. "Blink sent me over to get your statement, but the doctor said not to wake you."

Blink. It was still funny, but laughter required too much energy. "What else did the doctor say?"

Brittany sat back in her chair. "You're going to be okay, but she wants to keep you until tomorrow to make sure your lungs clear and your oxygen level comes back to normal."

My response died in a cough.

Eric held a straw to my mouth, and cool water soothed my throat. "Thank you."

He pulled out a notebook. "Do you feel up to answering a few questions?"

I nodded, which tightened my neck muscles. A picture of Russell's broken body exploded into my mind. "I killed Russell."

Eric leaned toward me. "I know, but you had no choice. He would've killed you given the chance."

A tear dripped from the corner of my eye. "Maybe, but—"

"No buts. We heard that part. It was self-defense."

More tears. Slow, heavy drops, which pooled in my ears. "Did you get what you needed?"

Brittany squeezed my hand, again.

A grin stretched across Eric's face. "You were great. We got enough to wrap it up thanks to you."

At least something good came out of it.

Can I live with it?

A dark-haired woman in navy-blue scrubs opened one of the curtains. "Look who's awake. How do you feel?"

"Like I went twelve rounds with Muhammad Ali."

Nancy Miller, as indicated by the badge around her neck, smiled. "I'll bet. We're going to take you to your room, so you can get some rest."

The way I did in Savannah? "I doubt it, but I'm willing to give it a shot."

The floor nurse settled me into my room and I'd just begun to doze when someone tapped on the open door. I groaned and turned over.

Marcus stood in the doorway holding Latoya in one arm and his other hand resting on Larissa's shoulder.

"Hi, come on in."

Larissa ran to my bedside, then hesitated. I patted the blanket and she climbed up.

Marcus sat Latoya down beside her. "I know you're supposed to be resting, but the girls wanted to thank you for rescuing them. We won't stay but a minute."

I scooted up and raised the head of the bed. "I'm glad you stopped by. How are you?"

"We're fine. I'm a little groggy still, but the girls are good. How are you doing?"

"I'm okay. I got a couple of good lungsful of smoke, so they're going to keep an eye on me for a while."

"That's good. Well, you need to get your rest, so we'll take off now."

Latoya grabbed his arm. "But, Daddy, we ain't gotta chance to say thank you, yet!"

He looked at me and I nodded.

"All right, girls, but make it quick. Miss Jen's gotta rest."

"Thank you for saving us, Miss Jen," the girls chorused.

"And especially our daddy," Larissa added.

I blinked back tears. "You're welcome."

Marcus led them out and I rolled back over on my side, this time wearing a smile. He'd been there when Aletha died and lied about it, but he tried to stop it as soon as he learned what Russell and Billy had done. I could live with that.

I managed to get several hours of often-interrupted sleep, and woke up around four in the afternoon, starving. My breath came easier and my limbs, while still heavy, engaged with only a little prompting. Positive signs. The heart monitor displayed a normal, regular beat. Also a positive sign.

Brittany slept, curled in a chair by the window, which looked out onto a brick wall. Why bother with a window you couldn't see out of?

A uniformed Eric, followed by Leonard, came into the room, and she stirred.

Eric perched on the edge of the bed. "How are you feeling?"

Leonard hovered like a store security guard who suspected us of shoplifting.

"Much better, thanks." I meant it. "Aren't you guys supposed to be working? You know, making Riddleton's streets safe for democracy, or something."

Eric patted my knee, hidden under the blanket. "We stopped by to see if you were feeling up to giving your statement."

Brittany stood and stretched. "I think I'll go down to the cafeteria for some coffee. Anyone else want any?"

Every hand rose, so Eric sent Leonard along to help carry the cups back. A polite thing to do, but I suspected his true motive involved privacy. When the room cleared, I said, "I'm not sure what I can add to what you already know. You were right there with me, so to speak."

"True, but you can add context to what we heard. Maybe fill in some of the blanks."

I did my best to flesh out the complicated saga, which had begun so long ago. Eric scribbled in his notebook and asked questions once or twice. He confirmed Tim's blood had soaked the trunk of Russell's car. The autopsy had showed Tim had died right away, from a blow to the back of the head, then his body was dumped in the river.

Brittany and Leonard returned with the coffee, and Eric closed his notebook and tucked it into his shirt pocket. "We caught Edna Babbitt at the end of the driveway when she tried to run. We're holding her as an accessory to kidnapping Marcus and his daughters. She held them at her house until it was time for the meeting last night. Marcus is going to testify in exchange for probation for his part in it all."

"All he did was make the mistake of befriending Russell and introducing him to his other friend, Billy. He had no idea what Russell had planned. He even tried to stop it when he found out, but he was too late."

Eric shrugged. "I know, but it's up to the DA. I'm a peon, remember?"

Not for long, I'd wager. "What about Sikazian?"

"He died in the fire."

Too drunk to save himself. Albert had made some

320

mistakes, but he didn't deserve to die. I raised my cup in a silent toast.

My dinner tray arrived around five thirty, and Eric and Leonard returned to patrol. Brittany kept me company while I ate, then I sent her home to get some sleep. She promised she'd pick me up in the morning.

For the first time since that middle-of-the-night call, I found myself alone with my own thoughts, the hollow place in my chest filled with peace and satisfaction. I'd been tied up, threatened, almost drowned, and near suffocated by smoke from the fire. And more frightened than ever before in my life, but I'd made it through. I'd found Aletha's killer. Maybe, she'd rest easier now.

I wasn't convinced I would, though. Russell's vacant eyes would haunt my dreams. I suspected I'd have a lot of sessions with Dr Margolis in my immediate future. But I would make it. I might even turn the story into a novel one day. The Davenport twins, however, would handle the situation with more efficiency than I had.

Sunday morning, Brittany strolled in as I picked up the phone to let her know I'd been discharged. "You ready to go home?"

Home. I hadn't considered Riddleton home since my father died. Right now, though, there was nowhere else I'd rather be. Another lesson learned within the last few days. "Did you bring me some clothes?"

She handed me a bag and I escaped into the bathroom to change.

"I started a Fund Me page for you this morning. For your hospital bills." Brittany spoke through the door while I forced leaden legs into jeans.

"Thank you. I hadn't even thought about it, yet." I

eased my T-shirt over my head and bit my lip to stifle a groan.

When I emerged, Olinski stood by the bed with a large cardboard box. He winked at Brittany, then pulled a black and tan German shepherd puppy out of the carton and handed it to me.

My heart skipped a beat. I held the wriggly thing up for a closer look. A little girl. "What's this?"

Brittany laughed. "It's a puppy, doofus."

"No kidding." I rubbed her soft fur against my face, and she licked my nose. I inhaled deeply. Puppy breath. Perfume for all ages.

How can I take care of a puppy? I had enough trouble with my own upkeep. She snuffled my hair, which tickled my ear. I'd manage somehow. "Where did you get her?"

Olinski set the box on the floor. "You remember the dog that found you on the waterfront?"

"Of course."

"This is one of her pups. Her owner wanted you to have her. She said you needed a dog to keep you out of trouble. I picked her up this morning."

I buried my nose in puppy fuzz. Clean and furry. "She's wonderful. I'm going to name her Savannah." I scratched her ears, and the puppy rewarded me with another kiss. "You mean you drove all the way to Georgia?"

Brittany patted Savannah on the head and got her fingers licked for the trouble. "Detective Edwards met him halfway. They set the whole thing up. I didn't know anything about it until a little while ago."

I turned to Olinski. Was he my friend again? "I guess I owe you a thank you."

He doffed an imaginary cap. "Think nothing of it."

"Okay, that's all the chivalry I can stand." I looked at Brittany. "Can we go home now?"

Brittany glanced at Olinski. "I have something to tell you first."

I halted the puppy's ear scratch, and she poked my chin with her cold, wet nose. "What?"

"I called your mother to tell her what happened."

My mouth fell open, but before I could express my consternation, the door opened and my mother strode in, as if summoned by the mention of her. She hugged me, careful to avoid the puppy. "How are you? You missed a great party."

"I'm sorry. I was a mess, but I still should've called."

"No, you should've left it alone like I told you to. Someday, you'll learn to listen to me." She reached for Savannah. "Does she bite?"

"She's eight weeks old, Mom." Savannah pushed her head under my mother's hand.

Mom obliged. "So, are you coming home with me, or am I going home with you?"

My mouth fell open. "What do you mean?"

"I'm going to take care of you until you're feeling better."

"What about Gary?"

She leaned in for puppy kisses on her cheek. "He's a big boy. He can look after himself for a few days."

My mother would take care of me? Maybe, there was hope for us, yet.

I held Savannah up and kissed her between her soft brown eyes. "I think my place might be best, given the furball here. But we'll have to stop on the way and pick up a few things for her."

I handed the puppy to Brittany, and she put her back

in the box. Olinski took the rest of my belongings, and Nurse Nancy came into the room with a wheelchair. She glanced at the carton and smiled. A conspiracy of the highest order.

I shuffled toward the door.

"Oh, no you don't." Nancy patted the back of the chair. "You know the rules."

My argument fell on deaf ears, and as she rolled me into the hall, Brittany said, "Oh yeah, I forgot. Ruth called. She said those chapters you sent her need a lot of work, and she wants three more by Friday. Otherwise, you're kaput."

Now, where have I heard that before?

EPILOGUE

I sat at my favorite table in the corner by the window of the bookstore, a ring of shiny new keys looped around my right forefinger. Aletha's attorney had the locks changed since he couldn't be sure he'd retrieved all the old ones. It seemed fitting in a way. Shiny new keys for a shiny new responsibility. With luck, I'd work as well as they did.

I looked out at the street, as I'd done so many times before, but peace didn't come. Aletha wouldn't be showing up with my umpteenth cup of coffee this time. Russell had murdered her and Tim for money, all the while pretending to care about me. Ravenous Readers would never be the same haven it once was, but perhaps I could build a new life here. In honor of Aletha and all she stood for.

My mother stayed for a week. I sent her on her way this morning before Riddleton PD had another homicide to investigate. To tell the truth, though, she did do everything for me until I recovered from my fiery adventure. Physically, anyway. I could've lived without her vacuuming every day, however. By the time she left, the living-room carpet was begging for mercy.

And she adored Savannah, who'd declared herself mistress of the manor the first time she waddled through the doorway. I marveled at Mom's efficiency and wondered where that person had hidden while I was growing up. It didn't matter. The past had no place in my new future.

The prospect of juggling the bookstore and writing my second novel had sent my brain to the Arctic, frozen in time, unable to function. Brittany couldn't help; my best friend had her own responsibilities to worry about. But, for the first time in my life, I had new friends willing to jump in until I finished my book. Why, I couldn't begin to guess. But as my mother recommended when I told her about it, I wouldn't look a gift horse in the mouth.

At nine on the nose, Lacey and Charlie came through the door loaded down with coffee and pastries and joined me at my table for our first official Ravenous Readers staff meeting.

A rush of warmth sped from my ears to my toes. Something good might come from Aletha's death after all. Together we'd bring her dream to reality. She deserved that much.

"Hey, guys! Ready to get started?"

ACKNOWLEDGMENTS

I would like to acknowledge and thank everyone who helped me bring this dream to reality, including but not limited to:

My agent, Dawn Dowdle, for her faith in me and all her hard work making this happen.

My editor, Cara Chimirri, and the rest of the Avon team for their enthusiasm for, and dedication to, this project.

Cate Hogan, for helping me turn a story worth telling into a story worth reading.

Ann Dudzinski, Julie Golden, Liz Goldsmith, JJ Grafton, Arya Matthews, and Suzanne Oldham for suffering through draft after draft without a hint of complaint.

And, last but definitely not least, my furry best friend, Sadie, for patiently being there through it all.